# THE
# DIAMOND
# SETTER

## Moshe Sakal

TRANSLATED FROM THE HEBREW BY
### Jessica Cohen

OTHER PRESS

NEW YORK

Copyright © Moshe Sakal 2014

Originally published in Hebrew as הצורף
in 2014 by Keter Books, Jerusalem

English translation copyright © Jessica Cohen 2017

This translation was supported in part by a grant from the
Yehoshua Rabinovich Tel Aviv Foundation for the Arts

Production editor: Yvonne E. Cárdenas
Text designer: Julie Fry
This book was set in Weiss and Bliss by
Alpha Design & Composition of Pittsfield, NH

1 3 5 7 9 10 8 6 4 2

Library of Congress Cataloging-in-Publication Data

Names: Sakal, Moshik, author. | Cohen, Jessica (translator)
Title: The diamond setter / Moshe Sakal ; translated from the Hebrew by Jessica Cohen.
Other titles: Tsoref. English
Description: New York : Other Press, [2018]
Identifiers: LCCN 2017027132 (print) | LCCN 2017027985 (e-book) |
ISBN 9781590518922 (e-book) | ISBN 9781590518915 (paperback)
Classification: LCC PJ5055.4.A375 (ebook) | LCC PJ5055.4.A375 T7613 2018 (print) |
DDC 892.43/6—dc23
LC record available at https://lccn.loc.gov/2017027132

*For my grandfather*

**MOSHE SAKAL**

*1918–1998*

# CAST OF CHARACTERS
## (IN ORDER OF APPEARANCE)

**MENASHE SALOMON:** a jeweler

**TOM:** Menashe's apprentice and the narrator

**ACHLAMA JAVAHERI:** Menashe's customer

**HONI KADOSH:** a soldier

**AMIRAM KADOSH (A.K.A. "KADOSH"):** Honi's father, Menashe's landlord

**SHAYU KADOSH:** Amiram's father, Honi's grandfather

**AYELET KADOSH:** Honi's sister

**ADELA SALOMON:** Menashe's mother

**RAFAEL SALOMON:** Menashe's father

**MONA:** Rafael's mother

**AUNT GRACIA:** Mona's sister, Rafael's aunt

**HASSIBA KADOSH:** Gracia and Mona's sister, Shayu's mother

**MOUSSA KADOSH:** Hassiba's husband, Shayu's father

**FAREED:** a Syrian-Palestinian illegal alien

**LEILA:** Fareed's grandmother

**ABED:** Fareed's grandfather

**SHAKER:** Abed and Leila's son, Fareed's father

**SAMI JABALI:** Leila's father

**SUAD JABALI:** Leila's mother

**SHLOMO/SALIM, JULIETTE:** Menashe's siblings

ONE DAY IN THE SUMMER OF 2011, a Syrian citizen sneaked across the border into Israel, not far from the town of Majdal Shams. In his pocket was a piece of a blue diamond that had once belonged—so I was told—to European royalty, as well as to the Ottoman sultan Abdul Hamid II. After entering Israel, the young man took a bus to Tel Aviv. He had not told anyone in Syria of his plans, and almost no one in Israel knew where he'd come from.

Who was this man and what was the purpose of his trip? All we know is that he was twenty years old, the scion of two families divided by national conflict yet bound by passion and secrecy, from back in the days when the Middle East was steeped not only in blood but also in love.

This is his marvelous story—and the story of many others who live in this land.

# CHAPTER ONE

# MENASHE

*1*

ON A SUMMER AFTERNOON IN TEL AVIV, Achlama Javaheri walked down Allenby Street on her way to a jewelry shop on Plonit Alley. When she stopped at the corner of Yehuda Ha'Levi Street, she noticed a large advertisement: ZIPPORAH UZAN FROM KIRIYAT GAT ANSWERED THE PHONE AND WON 100,000 SHEKELS! The picture showed a woman holding a huge check that said: "100,000 New Israeli Shekels." Farther ahead, on the corner of Balfour Street, Achlama saw another poster, with a red caption that she murmured out loud: YOSSI LEVI FROM KIRIYAT HAIM WON A NEW CAR! On the corner of King George Street was a third sign, even bigger than the first two: KEREN GOLDBERG FROM REHOVOT WON AN APARTMENT!

"Madness," Achlama thought. "It used to be, people who won the lottery would put a paper bag over their head with holes cut out for the eyes so no one would recognize them. Now someone wins the lottery and they plaster his picture all over town, and next thing you know he's got crooks and scoundrels and the evil eye after him." She paused, then concluded, "The evil eye is the worst."

Achlama had reached Plonit Alley by now, and she stopped outside the jeweler's storefront. Before knocking on the door, she put her nose up against the window and squinted. When she heard a buzz, she pushed the door open and walked in.

"Ah, the brand-new widow," came the jeweler's deep voice, "good day to you."

Achlama blushed and returned the salutation. She had come to the shop because she had discovered something shocking, which she felt an urgent need to share with Menashe.

She glanced at me and said hello. I looked down and readjusted the safety glasses on my nose.

My uncle's protective glasses were so large that they covered almost his entire face. The torch he held in one hand spewed fire onto a gold ring that was nearing its melting point. With the other hand he gripped a tiny piece of gold between a pair of tweezers, preparing to weld it onto the ring.

Achlama watched him tensely. The ring glowed red and a tiny crater bubbled up on its surface. The jeweler quickly attached the piece of gold to the crater and welded it to the ring, then dipped the ring in a cup of clear liquid, where it sizzled briskly. He lifted it out with the tweezers and placed it delicately on his workbench.

"What are you in the market for today?" he asked with a smile.

Achlama looked at the main display table. Under the glass were rows of gold chains with pendants set with garnet, turquoise, amethyst, and citrine. A small red-striped ceramic dish contained antique rings of yellow, red, and white gold, some of them diamond studded. Gold earrings set with turquoise stones were arranged in a nearby case. And in the last case, adjacent to the jeweler's bench, strings of white and gray pearls with gold and silver clasps were laid out in circles inside each other.

"I'm just looking today," said Achlama. She glanced at the turquoise earrings.

"The eye covets what the heart desires," said the jeweler.

Achlama sighed. "Really, Menashe, I'm just looking."

"You are welcome to look as much as you'd like," the jeweler said, "just remember that everything is for sale." He accentuated and drew out "everything."

Menashe opened a few small wooden boxes of gemstones and chose one stone from each box. He compared them all, then carefully arranged them on his workspace with the tweezers. He pierced nine small holes in a rectangular gold board and began setting the stones on the board in three rows.

"And he made the breastplate of cunning work, like the work of the ephod," the jeweler intoned, quoting from the bar mitzvah Torah portion he had recited forty-nine years earlier. "Of gold, of blue, and purple, and scarlet, and fine twined linen. And they set in it four rows of stones: the first row was a sardius, a topaz, and a carbuncle: this was the first row. And the second row, an emerald, a sapphire, and a diamond. And the third row, a ligure, an agate, and an amethyst." When he got to the word amethyst—*achlama*—he pinned his blue eyes straight on his customer; she turned her head awkwardly and looked around.

There was a polishing machine tucked away in an alcove, where I sat listening quietly while I polished rings—an apprentice's job.

The air-conditioning soon dried up Achlama's sweat, and her breath steadied. She approached the jeweler's bench, carefully avoiding the thorny cacti growing in planters along the perimeter of his workspace. She took a deep breath and was about to say something, but then she looked at me.

"You can speak openly," Menashe told her. "That's my nephew, Tom. He's helping me out in the shop."

"Yes, we've met. A nice young man. Very handsome." She still wasn't sure.

"Say what you have to say, Achlama," the jeweler urged her. "Besides, you should know that whatever you leave out, he'll just make up anyway."

"Why, is he a wizard?" She smiled nervously.

"No, he's a writer. Sees through walls. What you don't tell him, he'll find out on his own. Or worse—he'll invent it. If he decides your life is worth writing a story about, God help you."

"All right." Achlama took another deep breath, hesitated briefly, and forged ahead. "You know, Menashe, that my husband left me many years ago. After he left, I heard lots of stories about what he was doing for money—gambling, all kinds of dirty business, and worse. He brought shame on our family. We weren't living together anymore, but you know that with us Persians you never get divorced. We stayed married on paper, so people wouldn't talk. His poor parents, he *killed* them . . . When he went into prison for the second time, his father had a heart attack. His poor widowed mother used to visit him every week with food and newspapers. I never visited. I sent the kids with their grandma so they could see their father. I didn't want to see him ever again, after he walked out on me like that. He didn't pay any alimony, and I had to feed those children on my own and make sure they got a good education. And they never lacked for anything. They grew up like princes."

Menashe nodded. Achlama had been coming to his shop for years, and he'd heard it all: the years of struggling, how she brought up the kids and cleaned houses for money. And recently, the husband's death and her inheritance: a large sum of money, an apartment, and a vacant lot in Jaffa.

"I have something to show you, Menashe," Achlama said. She took a small box out of her pocket and handed it to him.

"What is this?" Menashe asked.

He thought she was giving him a piece of jewelry to repair. But when he opened the box, he was astonished to behold a precious stone: the family's blue diamond, which he thought he would never set eyes on again.

## 2

A few months ago I came back to Tel Aviv after five years in New York, where I'd studied history in college by day and worked as a security guard at the Israeli consulate by night. I spent my long shifts in the dark consulate offices on Second Avenue and Forty-second Street sitting opposite a flickering television screen with my textbooks, seminar papers, and flashing cell phone. I didn't carry a weapon, but if necessary I could alert the guards at the building's main entrance.

Every year on the High Holy Days, my uncle Menashe arrived for ten days. And every year I gave him the bed in my studio apartment and slept on the couch. On his first day in New York, he always asked me to take him to Ground Zero, where he would pose for the camera, standing erect with a fedora on his head. Only after the ritual photo shoot did Menashe feel that his annual visit to the city could really begin. In the afternoons he went to meet his friends at the Cactus Society. He'd been an avid member for years and loved to learn about new species, buy seeds (which he smuggled into Israel in his suitcase), and take photographs to hang in the gallery of pictures on his living room wall.

He also took advantage of his visit to stop by the jewelry shops on Fifth Avenue ("a little industrial espionage"). When he went into one of these stores in his starched suit, dapper yellow fedora, open-necked silk shirt, red-gold pendant around his neck, and white gold band inset with Persian turquoise on his finger, the proprietors recognized immediately that this was a customer who knew a thing or two about jewelry. And they treated him accordingly — with suspicion and respect.

Menashe had a principle: He never bought anything from another jeweler. He feigned indifference to the items he saw in the fancy Fifth Avenue displays, but sitting on the airplane on his way back to Israel, he conjured up new ideas for his own jewelry.

Menashe always found a backhanded way to ask me about my maternal aunt Rachel, his ex-wife. When I was ten, Rachel found God and moved to Jerusalem. She took Maya, their only daughter, with her. That was in 1991, the year when, I later learned, Menashe's shop was robbed and he lost the blue diamond that Achlama was now attempting to return.

I am the only person who is still in Menashe's life from his old family. Maya was married off to a Hassid and moved to London a few years ago, and she has almost no contact with her father. I see Rachel occasionally when I visit my family in Jerusalem. But I don't tell Menashe about her; there's hardly anything to tell.

A few years ago, Menashe left his native Tel Aviv and built a house in the rural town of Gan Yavne. Every morning he drives to the shop on Plonit Alley in his old Mazda. As a child, I sometimes heard stories about various women in his life after he and Rachel separated, but as far as I know he never had a significant relationship again.

After I came back from New York, I started editing Hebrew translations of English books for publishers. The pay was insulting—at most I made thirty-five hundred shekels a month, and that was only if I worked extremely fast. One day Menashe called and said he had a proposal for me. We arranged to meet at his usual café on the beach right at the edge of Jaffa, where you can look out over the Mediterranean all the way to the horizon: Tel Aviv sprawls out on the right, the rocks of Jaffa on the left, and straight ahead lies Andromeda's Rock, a plain-looking rock that juts out of the water with an Israeli flag billowing on its peak.

"Look at the sea," Menashe said as he sipped a beer. "This city is bent on destroying itself. It just keeps destroying, then building, then destroying again. But the sea is the one thing that can never be destroyed. It will be here long after we're gone, long after the city slowly sinks into the sand."

I listened quietly and thought about my beloved Tel Aviv, this ragged city I had returned to after years of absence.

Down on the beach, fishermen spread out a large net and slowly waded into the water until they were almost submerged. Each held a corner of the net, making sure its edges stayed just above the water so that any fish they trapped would not be able to jump back in.

As Menashe's beer glass emptied, he grew dreamy and contemplative. He leaned his head on his hand, and the big turquoise ring protruded from his finger. After a long silence, he asked how I was settling back in. I said it wasn't as difficult as I'd expected, but added cautiously that I didn't think the process was over yet.

"What's for sure," he said, "is that since you came home, I've lost my excuse to go to New York. My friends from the Cactus Society know I'm not coming this year, and they're grumbling about me being a cheapskate. I told them they're all invited to Israel. I'll take them on a night tour of the cactus garden in Holon." He plunged into silence again. An Arab boy riding a scrawny horse passed by on the beach.

"Was there something in particular you wanted to talk about?" I asked.

"I'll get to that soon," Menashe said, and took an olive from a little dish on the table. He nibbled the flesh and then sucked on the pit for a long time. "I've been thinking about you a lot," he said finally. "You know that you're like a son to me. Of what little family I had, you're really the only one who still cares about me. Rachel doesn't care if I'm dead or alive. If you could only have seen how she used to look at me when we first met! She was so in love with me. I was in love, too. But we were young, and we didn't know that being in love wasn't enough. And then Maya was born, and the rest you know." He sighed, then abruptly changed his tone. "Listen, I want you to come and work in the shop with me for a while."

"Me?"

"Yes, you. Why not?"

"What do I know about jewelry? I've never done anything with my hands."

"Then I'll teach you. What a jeweler needs, first of all, is to be sensitive. Everything else can be taught. You're still young, but you've seen a thing or two in your life. You polish the words you write, and I can teach you how to polish gold. Show me your fingers."

I held out my hands.

Menashe took my soft hand in his rough one. Every evening he scrubs his hands with a special cleaner that removes the black stains from his skin. But some of them don't come off. "Yes," he said, "you have delicate fingers."

"I used to play the piano," I reminded him.

"You don't play anymore?"

"Menashe, I haven't played since I was thirteen. My teacher committed suicide, don't you remember? For the record, though, I should point out that he killed himself after I'd stopped taking lessons. Anyway, why don't you find someone experienced, or a jewelry student from Shenkar?"

"You know I don't trust anyone. Only family. And there's something else. I'm in my sixties, I'm no spring chicken. I've been working in this shop for forty-five years, since I was seventeen. That's nothing to sneeze at either. If, God forbid, something happened to me, who would take care of the shop? Who would even care? All the work I put into it is worth nothing if there's no one who knows what to do with it all. I want to be sure that my shop is in good hands."

I didn't say anything.

"It may look like a relic to you now," Menashe went on, "but in the '70s, when I used to get to work at eight in the morning, there'd be a line of people outside, like it was the welfare office or a doctor's clinic. Back then, jewelry meant security—people thought it was safer to have jewels than to hide dollars under the floor tiles. People don't buy as much jewelry nowadays, and no one hides anything under the floor tiles anymore. Now people sit at their computers moving their fingers this way and that, and that's where their money is: nowhere. But I can tell you that there are still people who love jewelry. I have a core of regular customers, I work almost exclusively with regulars. One good customer is worth more than a hundred occasional browsers. These are families who've been coming here for decades, and they know Menashe will never cheat them. I'm their family diamond setter, that's what they tell me." Menashe's gaze broke away from the sea and he looked at me. "Besides, let me tell you, this job will give you lots of ideas for your writing."

I smiled. Everyone thinks their life is interesting enough to be immortalized in a book. But what could be so fascinating about an old shop run by an aging jeweler, where the only customers were lunching ladies who stopped by for new earrings or gold chains or strings of pearls to drape over their generous cleavage?

A few days later, I started my apprenticeship.

## 3

Menashe has worked at the little shop on Plonit Alley for decades. Every day he sits in his chair under the harsh fluorescent lights, king of his castle. His eyes are protected by large safety glasses, like a coal miner's. Here in this tiny kingdom he polishes and welds gold, insets diamonds, and fuses granite with opal. He monitors customers while carefully holding a fire-breathing torch to weld two pieces of gold together.

There are three topics that Menashe knows everything about: gold, diamonds, and cacti. He learned about gold and diamonds at home, from his father, Rafael. Cacti, on the other hand, are his own private obsession. On his workbench in the shop, for twenty-five years, he's kept a faded copy of Avraham Steinman's *Guide to Cacti for Balconies and Gardens*, his bible when it comes to succulents. Menashe's potted cacti act as a barrier between the customers and his workspace.

Menashe has countless stories about jewelry and endless quotes about diamonds and gold. "Man comes from earth and to earth he returns," he likes to say, "but diamonds, once they're out in the air, nothing can get them back in. Even when you think a diamond has completely vanished, it always turns up in the end—but it always happens in a place and time of its choosing."

I knew from my first day in the shop that Menashe's favorite topic of discussion was the blue diamond, which was known as "Sabakh." "When I was a boy," he told me, "my parents were always talking about Sabakh, and I realized that it was deeply connected to our family. When I was a little older, my father told me that Sabakh had come from very far away. From India. It wasn't called Sabakh back then, it had a different name, and it was much bigger. This diamond went through amazing adventures—miracles—before it ended up in our hands. And quite a few tragedies, too. But I only learned about all that much later."

"What was its name before it was called Sabakh?" I asked.

"Its first name was the 'Tavernier Blue.' It traveled all the way from India to Europe, and then to Istanbul, which was still called Constantinople back then, and finally ended up with my family, but only a small piece of it. And it was cursed."

"What do you mean, cursed?"

"Well, I never had any proof that it meant to harm us, and I certainly wouldn't claim that all my family's troubles were that little diamond's fault. But I'll get to that. My father, Rafael, told me that the first time anyone heard about Sabakh was in northern India, where it was inset in Shiva's third eye. But one day someone stole it out of the statue, and ever since then it's been taking revenge on anyone who tries to keep it."

"Your father didn't believe that, did he?"

"You have to understand something: My father loved diamonds. He used to sit reading books about diamonds for days on end. He knew all the stories about Jean-Baptiste Tavernier by heart. This man, Tavernier, was a big adventurer and a famous gem merchant in the seventeenth century. Every night at bedtime, Father told me about diamonds like the Koh-i-Noor, the Daria-i-Noor, and the great Sancy. But more than anything, he liked to talk about our diamond, our little piece of the Tavernier Blue, which became Sabakh. He didn't tell me these stories just for amusement. He wanted me to understand Sabakh and care about it. He told me again and again that it was our family treasure, the only thing in the world we could count on. So for him, the diamond was blessed, not cursed. He said Sabakh had always protected our family in Damascus, and that it would keep protecting us in Tel Aviv and anywhere else we went, as long as we took care of it."

Menashe paused and looked at the photograph of his parents on the wall. "You know, Tom, diamonds are just like people: Some come into the world easily, and some worry you to death by the time they're born. Do you have any idea how diamonds are born? It happens a hundred miles or more below Earth's surface. There's carbon down there, which forms into diamonds over billions of years because of the immense pressure and the high temperatures—over one thousand degrees Celsius. The diamonds sit there for years, until one day there is a volcanic eruption, and then special pipes called kimberlite carry them up to the surface."

He gave me a look I'd seen before, and I knew he was about to tell one of his anecdotes.

"There are some diamonds," Menashe explained, "that completely change the fate of the people who wear them. Our blue diamond, the Tavernier Blue, belonged to Marie Antoinette before she was guillotined. During the French Revolution it was stolen and somehow ended up in the hands of King George IV. He even wore it for his coronation! George IV was a notorious hedonist. He lost his mind when he was a young man, he was a political failure, his people hated him—even though they also admired him—and he had a miserable marriage. Eventually the diamond was polished and sold to an English banker named Henry Thomas Hope. I'm almost positive that was his name. Anyway, they say that Hope lost everything and his whole family died of starvation. After that, the diamond was sold to Sultan Abdul Hamid II in 1908 or 1909, perhaps even earlier.

"The sultan had thirteen wives and more than two hundred concubines. He gave the Tavernier Blue to one of the wives, I think her name was Subya. Not a bad gift, eh? Well, it turned out to be a big mistake. Subya was involved in a plot against the sultan—she conspired against her own husband. The Ottoman Empire was in bad shape in those days. Long story short, the sultan's advisers told him the diamond was cursed and would bring him bad luck, so he took it back from Subya and went to a soothsayer for her counsel. She told him that if he split ten carats off the diamond, the curse would be lifted. And that is exactly what he did: He had his jeweler take off a ten-carat piece, which he named 'Sabakh.' A few years later, when the Ottoman Empire was in dire financial straits, the sultan had no choice but to sell the large diamond, but he was adamant that he would not sell Sabakh, even though he was still afraid of the curse.

"One night the sultan dreamed that he traveled to Damascus and met a Jewish girl who sang exquisitely. Her voice was more beautiful than any he had ever heard, and in his dream he recognized that she was singing in Arabic with a Damascene accent. When he awoke, he ordered his emissaries to go to Damascus, find the girl from his dream, and bring her to him. They went to the Jewish quarter, where they searched and searched, and finally they found—believe it or not—my paternal great-aunt, Gracia, the most famous chanteuse in town. They brought her to the sultan's palace, where they held a grand banquet and invited her to sing for the sultan. He fell in love with her at first sight, apparently, and after dinner he stayed alone with her. The next day, he gave her Sabakh."

"He just gave her that diamond as a gift?"

"Yes. Well, it was actually more of a deposit. He asked her to keep it for him. He didn't tell her he was afraid to keep it himself, of course. Years later, when the sultan died, he left the diamond to Aunt Gracia in his will. And ever since then, it's been in our family. Until the robbery, when someone stole it from me."

"Wasn't Aunt Gracia afraid of the diamond's curse?"

"I don't think so. My father certainly didn't believe in cursed diamonds. But he was a fatalist. He thought that whatever was supposed to happen would happen. All he knew for sure was that we had to keep the diamond until it decided it was time for a new owner. Father and Mother came to

Tel Aviv in 1949, and a few months later Father opened the shop where we sit now. But that, you already know. When I was fourteen I started coming here regularly, and when I was seventeen, Father decided it was time to retire.

"You're Ashkenazi, Tom, so you may not know this, but we Sephardim believe that a man truly lives only when he has children. At synagogue, when a father is called to the Torah, his sons stand up. The whole congregation looks at him and his sons, and they pay him respect according to the number of sons. He reads from the Torah, and the sons keep standing. He finishes reading, makes his contribution—also according to the number of sons—then goes back to his seat. He shakes the oldest son's hand, then the other sons' hands, and he sits down. He leans back in his seat, at ease, and his sons follow his lead.

"You've seen pictures of my father. Today he almost looks like a stranger to me: big gray hair, thin lips, fancy suit, thin gold wedding band. I never knew his eyes. I never dared look straight into them. I couldn't even have told you what color they were. I loved his fingers, and I was always surprised by how gentle they were. Sometimes, when he slept, I was brave enough to stand in the doorway and really look at him.

"He never talked about his business with me. Not the successes and not the failures. He only spoke to Shlomo, my brother. Shlomo was just four years older than me, but he was the eldest, and so he was involved in all the business. He had power of attorney, he knew where everything was, and of course he knew about every sum and asset the family owned, and any possessions that had disappeared.

"I remember as a boy hearing Father tell Mother in the kitchen: 'That's how it is, Adela, there's nothing more to discuss. I had that money, and now I don't. Someone else has it. And if he's a crook, I don't care—may he go in good health. *Ili faat, maat*—what's gone is dead.' If my mother tried to say anything or make him promise to ask her before he made a decision next time, he would just get up and shut himself in his room.

"He didn't get angry at people. He was a tradesman. He sold jewelry, but he didn't make it. He didn't know jewelry the way I do. He would come to the shop at eight thirty in the morning, always in his smart brown suit. At one o'clock he would go out for lunch with the newspaper tucked under his arm. He came back to work for a while in the afternoon and then he went home. At home, my mother put his slippers down in front of him. He put on his pajamas and a robe, tied the sash around his waist, and sat down to eat dinner quietly. Shlomo, my brother, always sat next to him and they ate together, without saying a word, each reading a section of the newspaper. I stayed in the kitchen with my mother, and she would hover and serve them their food.

"On one of those days in the kitchen, my mother said to me quietly, 'Father lost some money again.' She put aside the zucchini and eggplants, washed her hands, and started kneading dough. She scattered flour on the countertop. 'That's how it is,' she said, 'he just doesn't care. If someone took it, they must have needed it, and that's that.' She said these last words in Hebrew, not Arabic. I suppose she needed to consider every sentence and choose the exact right words in her new language, the way you select cucumbers at the market—one by one, based on size and color and firmness, not the way she picked out fava beans from a sack and knew instinctively, without thinking, which ones to cook and which to throw out. Then she went back to Arabic.

"'I keep telling him, but he won't listen,' she said. 'Anytime someone comes to ask him for something, he just says yes. He doesn't stop to think. He won't tell them he needs to sleep on it. Whatever they say, he agrees. Whatever you tell him, he thinks it's reasonable. I keep trying to get through to him, but he won't listen. I tell him: "Rafael, you're losing everything! Why let all that money go? What about our children? What will you give them when they leave home? And a dowry for your daughter? She's just a girl now, but we have to think about these things. What will we live on when the money runs out?"

"'You'll see, Menashe,' she told me, 'the day he runs out of money, they'll all disappear. He won't have anyone left. When he walks down the street now, people come up and grab him and ask him to go to lunch. And he goes. He can talk with anyone, he's an interesting man, a wonderful storyteller. In Syria they were crazy about him. Not like here, where he sits at home, quiet like a fish. He can find a common language with anyone, he knows at least three languages. In Syria he used to make up such interesting stories. Then he'd sit at home and write them down. But I worried: It's no good, a grown man leaving all his friends from work to sit at home writing stories all day. I told him, "You need to get out, find a job." So he said, "I'll be a teacher." And he went to teach French at the Alliance Française in Damascus. He taught all morning, then sat at home writing. Just like that—teaching and writing, writing and teaching. I stopped saying anything, because what could I say? He's stubborn.'

"Then my mother told me about when they left Syria. 'One day,' she said, 'your father got up, left his job at the Alliance, and went to work at the Bourse. He did well in business, because to be a good trader, people have to like you. In Syria your father was always well dressed, clean shaven, with a thick head of hair, and his shoes were always shined. He had a firm handshake, and when he shook someone's hand he looked them straight in the eye. People trusted him. Everywhere he went, they said, "Come in, Mr. Salomon, come in." He did business during the day. A little, not a lot. He liked eating lunch in restaurants, and in the evening he would come home for dinner. He has a good appetite now, too, but not like then. The food was better there. We had a good life.

"'After they declared the State of Israel, in Tel Aviv, a friend of your father's helped us. He got us laissez-passer papers and found a mover to take all our furniture. First we went to Beirut, and we spent a few months there. Then they smuggled us into Israel. We walked a lot, maybe seven hours, before we arrived. Do you know how we crossed the border? In a taxi!' My mother giggled. 'And in Israel, we took another taxi to Haifa. And from there to Sha'ar Ha'Aliya, where they sent all the new immigrants. Every family got a couple of beds, and your father had to stand in line for food, morning, noon, and evening. It was very difficult. Afterward, we used our money to buy this apartment. But while it was being fixed up, we lived with your father's sister, Juliette, and her family. They had a house that used to belong to Arabs. They didn't pay for it. And we all lived there.'

"My mother told me it was very crowded in my aunt's house. They already had my brother, Shlomo, and Mother was pregnant with me. The apartment on Dizengoff Street wasn't livable yet. It wasn't even hooked up to the gas. Father, who had been such a bubbly man in Syria, a seasoned trader with connections high up, hardly knew anyone in the new country. I think if my mother hadn't insisted—'We're moving to the apartment on Dizengoff, gas or no gas!' she announced—they would have stayed at his sister's for a long time.

"So they moved into the apartment. It smelled like fresh paint. There were three spacious rooms, but Mother wasn't satisfied. She knew very well that some people were still living in transit camps, in the *ma'abarot*, making do with tents or rusty shacks where the rain leaked in. She also knew that there were refugees who had lost their whole families in Europe, and they had nothing. She knew all that. Still, she wasn't satisfied.

"'Where is the house we had in al-Sham?' she would say to Father—she always called Damascus by its Arabic name, al-Sham, which means 'the northern country.' 'Where is our garden and the rosewater and the divan and the apple trees? Where are our wonderful feasts...? We're so close to al-Sham, but it's a different world here. The food is rationed, and I have to dust the house endlessly, all day long.'

"My father didn't answer. He sat in the kitchen listening to his music on the radio: Umm Kulthum, whose songs were as long as exile. When he was in the kitchen, no one else was allowed in. One of our neighbors, a Romanian woman, peeked in one day and said Father was suffering from melancholy. She showed Mother a book with pictures of melancholics: wide-eyed, well dressed but with a distant look, sitting at a table with their heads on their hands. And that is just how Father used to sit in the kitchen in our little apartment on Dizengoff Street: his head resting on his hand, his big eyes staring at the wall, days on end.

"But then Shayu came. Shayu was Father's cousin, who had left Damascus and immigrated to Palestine in the '30s. He said to Father, 'I'm giving you a shop in my building off King George Street. Go there and do some work. You can't be shut up at home all day. You have to get out, get to know the city, meet new people, make connections.'

"So Father did what Shayu told him. He came to this little shop—it's all of 130 square feet—and became a tradesman. What did he trade? A little silver, some promissory notes, some land. Anything that came his way. But he always lost, and by the time I started here, at seventeen, Father had nothing left. No money, no stocks, no investments. The only asset our family had was Sabakh. Father had kept the diamond all those years in a secret hiding place in his bedroom, which only he and my mother and Shlomo knew about. Once a year, on the anniversary of their arrival in Israel, he took out the diamond and showed it to us all.

"To this day I remember those occasions. Mother used to cook a festive meal. When Aunt Gracia—who, you remember, had been given the diamond by the Turkish sultan—was still alive, the ritual was held in her home on Ha'Kovshim Street. She would wear the silk scarf she wore on the day she sang for the sultan. After she died, we'd stay at home, shutter all the windows, and light a candle in the middle of the living room. And there, around that candle, we would all gather to look at Sabakh.

"A few weeks before the Gulf War, when they were saying rockets were going to fall on Tel Aviv, Shlomo came to the shop and gave me the diamond to keep in the safe. Our father had sent him. And then, just when the war started, a thief broke in and took the blue diamond. But that's another story. It'll be excellent material for your book. I'll tell you someday."

## 4

In the evening, Plonit Alley was desolate. A man rode past on his bicycle. A couple strolled hand in hand. A tall red-headed woman stopped to examine the window display, and Menashe quickly arranged the necklaces, bracelets, rings, and gemstones in their trays and put everything into the safe. He didn't want to open the door—not for this woman or for any other customer. He was in a foul mood. He dimmed the lights and stayed in the shadows until the window-shopper looked up in surprise and walked away.

He was scheduled to meet his lawyer, Amir, an old high school friend, to discuss a letter Menashe had received a week earlier from his landlord:

*Mr. Menashe Salomon*
*Plonit Alley*
*Tel Aviv*

*Dear Mr. Salomon,*
*We hereby notify you that on November 10, 2011, renovation works will begin in the building, in preparation for its conver-*

*sion into a hotel. You are therefore requested to remove your*
*possessions and vacate the premises on or before that date.*

*Please note: any articles remaining on the premises on*
*November 10, 2011, will be immediately removed.*

*Thank you for your cooperation, and best wishes for the*
*new year.*

*Amiram Kadosh*

Menashe folded the letter and put it in his pocket. He left the shop and walked down the alley to King George Street, then up to Allenby Street and on toward the Carmel Market. As he made his way through the stalls, he stepped on vegetable scraps, crushed flowers, and chicken bones covered with cartilage and blood. There was a fishy odor, combined with a stench of blood and various other market smells. He walked all the way to the big parking lot on Ha'Kovshim Street and turned right toward the beach, then headed south on the promenade, following the shoreline to the point where Tel Aviv meets Jaffa, or, as his father used to call it, Arous 'al Bahr—Bride of the Sea.

From this angle, Menashe could look out at the Jaffa Port and see the Bride of the Sea facing the waves as she had for thousands of years. Jaffa's minarets pierced the sky, and its courtyards were sheltered by palm trees. The village of Menashiyya had once stood here, but it had been destroyed and gradually replaced with lawns and parking lots. A few of the old buildings still remained as a vestige.

Menashe kept walking along the shore until he came to the café where his lawyer was waiting. It was the same café where he and I had met on the day he asked me to come and work with him. He sat down opposite Amir and his eyes sought—and found—Andromeda's Rock with its billowing flag.

"This is not going to be an easy case," Amir said. "Did they tell you anything?"

"Kadosh came by the shop a while ago," Menashe replied. "Asked how I was, how's business, the usual chatter. Just before he left, he said casually, 'You know, we're starting renovations soon.' I said, 'Good, it's about time. The building needs work.' And he said, 'Yes, but it's going to be a very thorough renovation.' I said, 'Wonderful.' And then he said, 'You'll get a letter soon. But you should know there's going to be a hotel here. A boutique hotel.' That's what he said. Then he walked out. Then last week I got this letter."

"How long did your father have the shop?"

"From 1950 until he retired, in '66."

"And since when have you been there?"

"Since I was seventeen."

"More than forty years..."

"Yes."

"How much rent do you pay?"

"Kadosh is the son of Shayu, my father's cousin. Father paid Shayu a token sum every month, just to keep up appearances. Twenty years ago Kadosh and I agreed on a moderate fee, and I pay him every month. It's linked to the dollar exchange rate, so right now it's at three thousand shekels."

"That's not very much. Do you keep the receipts?"

"Of course."

"Do you have a lease?"

"No."

"Did your father have a lease?"

"What are you talking about? It was a family matter. Shayu didn't worry about leases. He loved my father, and Father wasn't worried. Honestly, he lived a good long life without any worries."

"Have you told your mother about this?"

"Poor Mother, she doesn't know anything."

"Maybe she kept the paperwork?"

"I asked her once, a few years ago, because Kadosh was hinting that he might sell the building. He dropped the idea, though. Anyway, my mother said she didn't have anything. Father didn't keep that kind of paperwork. There's nothing."

"In that case, it's going to be very difficult to ensure a spot for you in the building after the renovations," the lawyer explained. "I'm not sure we can even get compensation."

"I don't want compensation," Menashe said. "I don't care about that. I want to stay in my shop—boutique hotel or not."

"Excuse me for interfering, Menashe, but people do sometimes relocate their businesses. Couldn't you look at this as an opportunity for change?"

Menashe did not answer, but his eyes said it all.

# CHAPTER TWO

# FAREED

*1*

HE CROSSED THE BORDER UNDER COVER of the commotion that erupted between demonstrators and Israeli army forces on a beautiful day, perhaps the most beautiful of his life. This was the day when he would see the landscapes and houses he had heard of like distant rumors, in the place his grandparents called Palestine. And it was all thanks to Sabakh, the blue diamond. In his pocket was a box, and in the box—the diamond.

Fareed carried one small bag. It contained a few pairs of underwear and socks, two shirts, some pita, three peeled cucumbers, a map, a book, and a sweater. He wore shorts, brown shoes, and a baseball cap.

He had not told anyone he was leaving. Not his parents and not his sister, Noor. He just left his house and walked to the border. To his astonishment, it was remarkably easy. After he crossed the border and found himself in Palestine,

Fareed got on a bus with some Israeli activists and a few tourists. He spoke in English, and the journey went smoothly. He listened to music on his earbuds and looked at the scenery. He had no escape plan, no contingency plan. One thing simply led to another: all the people who surged toward the border, the riots that erupted, the gas the soldiers used to disperse the protesters, and the whole tumult that allowed him to cross the border and casually get on a bus headed to central Israel.

A few hours later, he stepped off the bus on the outskirts of Tel Aviv.

He found a money changer and bought five hundred dollars' worth of shekels. He took out his map and asked some passersby a few questions in English. They pointed to his location on the map. It wasn't far from the sea, but not the sea he was looking for. Not the sea of Yafa.

Fareed got on another bus and looked out the window as he traveled: streets, cars, three- and four-story houses, marble-coated skyscrapers. Now they seemed to be in the heart of the city. He closed his eyes, suddenly exhausted in a way he had not felt all day. Reminding himself that he really was in Tel Aviv, a sense of terror crushed his chest. What was he doing here?

He found himself outside a large shopping center with yellow and white trim, which was bisected by a road with a footbridge crossing overhead. Orchards and tin shacks used to cover this exact spot. The landowner, an Arab from Yafa named Hinawi, went from shack to shack collecting rent. When the tenants couldn't afford to pay, he would stop for a cup of coffee and continue on his way. Years later, he was murdered, and in 1948 the Hinawi family left Yafa for Egypt. They were declared "absentees" by the State of Israel and their lands were reassigned to new owners. Fareed had read all this in a book, where he had also learned about the destruction of the slum neighborhood called Nordia, and how Dizengoff Center was built on its ruins.

He debated going inside and began to wonder whether his parents were worried about him. Had they known he was here, infiltrating the heart of this city, what would they say? But it would never occur to them that he'd crossed the border. He was too delicate, they thought, too cowardly. Fareed put his hand in his pocket and felt the box with Sabakh. The diamond had been through so many tribulations—this short voyage would not be its downfall.

At the entrance to Dizengoff Center he had to pass a standard security check. "No," he answered the guard's question, in English, "I don't have a weapon."

He rode the escalator to the top floor, went into a restroom and locked himself in a stall. He took out the box, unwrapped the cloth, opened the lid, and examined the diamond.

"It's your first time in Palestine, Sabakh," Fareed whispered. He turned the stone from side to side to better plumb its refractions. "What do you have to say about that?" He held it up to his eyes. But the diamond didn't answer.

He left the mall, but no one could tell him which bus to take to Yafa, because of the reforms: the national transportation system had implemented efficiency measures, which included replacing the old bus routes with new ones. Ever since the reforms, he was told, no one could get anywhere. The buses were empty, or worse—full of people who thought they were going where they needed to go but soon realized they were not. Instead of reaching the marble-clad apartment buildings of Ramat Aviv, for example, they found themselves deposited in the southern neighborhoods or on the outskirts of Jaffa. Arab passengers wanting to get to their homes in Yafa, conversely, ended up wandering among the detached houses of Ramat Chen, where, more than six decades ago, the orchards of Salameh village had flourished. It was all smoke and mirrors.

Still, through trial and error, Fareed managed to find the right bus. He said hello to the driver, who did not answer. He paid and the driver handed him his change with one hand and turned the wheel with the other. And they were on their way to Yafa.

The streets of Tel Aviv passed wearily before Fareed's eyes. It was afternoon, and he realized he hadn't told Rami exactly when he was arriving. The bus turned onto a congested street, and Fareed read the Arabic on the sign: YAFA ROAD. The driver cursed and rubbed his eyes. They sat without moving for a long time.

Finally the bus started inching forward, and Clock Tower Square revealed itself. Fareed had heard so much about the square from his grandparents. During the First World War, they had told him, Yafa was bombed, and swarms of locusts descended upon the city and its fields. In the town center stood the clock tower, surrounded by a square. It had been built at the beginning of the twentieth century to honor Sultan Abdul Hamid II—the same sultan who was so closely bound with the Sabakh diamond. Not far from the square had been Yafa's markets, among them Souk al-Malbasa, the clothing market, and Souk al-Attarin, the spice market. Fareed wondered how much of all that still existed.

All the riots they'd told him about, when Arabs and Jews had fought over this territory in the 1940s, had happened here at Clock Tower Square. As soon as he stepped off the bus he saw a police building on his right. Two police officers, a man and a woman, were standing outside next to a patrol car. Fareed kept to the other side of the road and started looking for Yefet Street. He found it fairly quickly and walked up toward the Ajami neighborhood.

Just that morning, before crossing the border, Fareed had shut himself in his room in Damascus, double-locked the door, and memorized the route from Clock Tower Square to Rami's apartment. Now all he had to do was follow the route and hope no one stopped him and asked to see his papers, and, of course, that Rami was home.

To his left was Abulafia Bakery, with a long line of customers waiting at the window. Fareed stood in line and ordered a *sambusak* filled with hard-boiled egg. He took the warm turnover wrapped in paper and continued on his way. The street twisted and turned, lined on either side with long buildings. Then came shops: groceries, a cell phone store, two restaurants. He wanted to stop everywhere and look, to roam all over Yafa, but he wasn't brave enough. He finished eating, tossed the paper in a trash can, and picked up his pace.

According to the map, Rami's apartment was not far. Fareed turned right on Sha'arei Nikanor Street. There was a shop on the corner selling charcoal and hookahs, and just after that a Jewish-Arab youth club across the street from a day care center. Farther down the road was a house, and then another house that Fareed stood and stared at for several minutes through the gate. It had a pomegranate tree in the garden, and two stone lions worn by time and rain perched on either side of the front steps. He tore himself away and kept walking down the narrow street. Every so often he saw graffiti on the walls: *waqaha*, one of them read, in Arabic, and then explained in what Fareed assumed was Hebrew: *chutzpah*. Similar translations were provided for other words: *khatar*—danger, and *huriyya*—freedom.

When he passed the third house on the left, his heart started pounding. But he didn't dare stop, only gave the house a sideways glance. The road curved downhill, and the old houses gave way to new marble buildings two or three stories high. Then, straight ahead, between two buildings, he saw the sea. The Yafa sea.

At the end of the street stood a restaurant with tables scattered around the courtyard. A group of people sat drinking beer, smoking, and eating out of dishes piled with *maqluba*. Fareed turned the corner, and after passing a very old building, he finally recognized Rami's house from the picture: a two-story building with a grand but crumbling entrance; only the windows attested to the residence's glorious past. Three steps led up to the front door. A ginger cat lay sprawled across the second step, serenely licking her nipples. Fareed walked in and went up to the second floor. He stopped outside the door and steadied his breath. He knocked twice, and when there was no answer, a third time. The door finally opened.

"Fareed!" Rami pulled Fareed in and hugged him. "They didn't stop you at the border? Have you had something to eat? You look tired! How did you get here?"

"It was a long journey, but I'm fine." Fareed was happy to speak Arabic after using English all day.

Rami was tall and thin, wearing a white tank top that exposed much of his smooth chest. One of his eyebrows was pierced, and his cheeks were covered with black stubble. He poured Fareed a glass of water and they sat down in the living room, which had colorful, ornate floor tiles.

They'd met online. When Fareed had started taking an interest in Yafa, after hearing his grandmother Laila's stories, he'd studied the neighborhood of Ajami in maps and read online about various businesses in the neighborhood. He was especially intrigued when he came across Shami Bar, whose name alluded to his hometown of al-Sham. He played a few songs from the bar's Facebook page and read posts left by Arab residents of Yafa. One of them, Ramadan (Rami) Saleh, a nursing student who tended bar at Shami, had an interesting profile, and Fareed wrote to him.

They corresponded every day for weeks, and got to know each other so well that Fareed imagined that the distance between their near-yet-far cities was shrinking. In time, he felt as though his body was in Damascus but his head, his dreams, his passion—all these were in Yafa. When he came up with the idea of taking a trip to Yafa to explore his roots, he wrote to Rami, who tried desperately to dissuade him.

"Are you crazy?" Rami wrote. "They'll shoot you at the border. They have no qualms. You think they don't have enough Palestinians in Israel? They don't want another one. And anyway, nothing scares the Israeli army more than an unarmed Arab. If you went at them with a submachine gun, that would be one thing. But to just walk over, and with the way you look—with your curly hair and your pale skin? No way, forget it. Very bad idea. You won't make it here alive."

"I knew that's what you'd say, Ramadan," Fareed wrote back, "but I don't care. The uprising here is starting to spill over toward the border. I read that there's going to be a pro-Palestinian protest at the border again, like the big one they had on Nakba Day a couple of months ago, and people will try to get across the border. I want to be there. Will you meet me?"

"Don't be ridiculous, of course I want to meet you! You can stay with me. I just think it's a really bad idea."

A week later, Fareed wrote to Rami about a few technicalities and said nothing further on the matter. He didn't tell him about Sabakh or about his larger plan. In fact, he himself wasn't exactly sure how things would turn out. But he waited impatiently for the date, and for the first time in his life he felt he had the courage to do something.

"So," Rami said, now that Fareed was here in his apartment, "do you think you'll stay with me the whole time, or do you have other plans?"

"I don't know yet. But I figure I'll draw less attention in Yafa than I would in Tel Aviv."

"That's for sure. What about your parents? Won't they be worried?"

"I'll tell them I decided to go visit my friends in New York. They're used to me being impulsive. It won't be a problem. I might ask Noor to reassure them first. I trust her."

"Whatever you do, don't tell anyone you're here," Rami warned.

"Obviously not. So what are you up to today?"

"I'm working a shift this evening. Do you want to come with me?"

"To Shami Bar? Of course!" Fareed said. "But I want to take a shower first."

"Sure. There's time before we have to leave. The shower's back there."

After Fareed had showered, he threw off his towel and lay down on the living room couch for a nap. Before he shut his eyes, he took Sabakh out of his pocket and placed it under the pillow.

He woke up with a start, disoriented. It was dark outside. He went to the window and looked out. He could just about glimpse the sea in the distance, between two buildings. There was a full moon, and not a single star in the sky. Fareed assumed Rami was sleeping in the other room. He lay down again, pulled the box out from under the pillow, and took out Sabakh. The blue diamond's color was dulled in the darkness, drawing him to delve into its deep, dark refractions. Something about Sabakh seemed different since their arrival in Yafa: Its silence was now secretive. Fareed stared curiously at the stone and thought of the lines: *Hold fast thy secret and to none unfold, Lost is a secret when that secret's told.*

In one of Scheherazade's tales, which he'd read as a young boy, three sisters quoted those lines to a porter who came to their home. Then they gave him wine to drink, which addled his mind. The porter felt as if he were in a dream and started kissing the three ladies. The lady of the house undressed and bathed in the pool. When she stepped out, she sat naked in the porter's lap, pointed to her privates, and asked, "My love, what is the name of this?" The porter tried to give this thing hidden between her legs a name: womb, vulva, pudenda, clitoris. Each time, she slapped him. Finally, she told him the name: "Basil of the bridges." Then the second sister took off her clothes, bathed in the pool, threw herself at the porter, and asked him to name the thing between her legs. Again he tried in vain to say the right name. The woman slapped him and said it was called "the husked sesame." And the third sister, after bathing nude in the pool and jumping into the porter's lap, revealed to him the name of the thing between her legs: "the Inn of Abu Mansur." Finally the porter stood up, took off his own clothes, and started swimming in the pool, naked. When he stepped out, he threw himself onto the ladies' laps and asked them to name the part between his legs. The three laughed and said, "Your pecker!" The porter said no and took a kiss from each of them. They said, "member," and he said no and took a hug from each.

*"But morning overtook Scheherazade, and she lapsed into silence,"* said Rami. He was standing near Fareed; his hair was wet and he smelled of cologne.

"Oh, you're awake?" Fareed rubbed his eyes. For a minute he was worried about Sabakh, but when he reached under the pillow he found it there, safe and well.

"Yes. And you were talking about Scheherazade in your sleep. Come on, we have to go."

The street they took to the bar was narrow, and there were guys sitting on the curb on either side. Some of them smoked, some held bottles of beer. They greeted Rami, a few in Hebrew and others in Arabic, and curiously eyed the stranger. Rami introduced Fareed to two of his friends, Khaled and Faadi. They asked where he was from, and he said New York.

"Welcome to Yafa," said Faadi. "No trouble when you came in?"

Fareed wondered if they'd been following him. "Why would there be trouble?"

"You know, with airport security."

"Oh," Fareed lied. "No, they were okay."

"It's because of your face," Khaled said. "You don't look Arab. So, how long are you staying in Palestine?"

"Two weeks," Fareed answered. "Maybe more, I'm not sure yet."

"Are you planning to travel?" Faadi asked.

"Like where?"

"You know, tourist places—Jerusalem, Akko, Nazareth."

"I haven't figured that out yet."

"You might want to stay away from the problem areas up north," Faadi cautioned. "Did you hear what happened at the Syrian border today? Riots again. They say a few guys managed to get into Israel."

"Cute guys?" Khaled quipped. "I hope they come to the bar!"

Rami glanced at Fareed out of the corner of his eye. Fareed looked calm on the surface, but he bit his lip and looked down at the ground.

"Do they think they're going to import the Arab Spring over here?" Faadi wondered.

Khaled laughed. "More like the Zionist Autumn... Remember what Barak said, back when he was prime minister? He said Israel was a villa in the jungle."

"Why are you making light of it?" Rami asked. "There are demonstrations in Tel Aviv now, too. Israelis want their jungle. Everyone's talking about regime change—it's no joke." When he noticed Fareed's puzzled look, he explained. "It all started with cottage cheese. A whole lot of people called for a boycott on cottage cheese because it was so expensive. Then this woman in her twenties couldn't find an apartment to rent because everything was too expensive and there was so much demand, so she put up an event on Facebook and invited people to come live with her in a tent on Rothschild Boulevard, across from the national theater. That's how it began, and now there are loads of tents up and down the boulevard, which is Tel Aviv's most upmarket neighborhood."

"That Daphni woman with her blond hair, how come no one would rent her an apartment? It's not like she's an Arab!" Khaled commented bitterly.

"Stop with that, we have a tourist here," Rami reminded him.

Fareed was still confused. "Wait, I don't understand. Are there really people living in tents on the street?"

"Oh yeah," Rami replied. "Tons of them. Maybe a thousand. But people are already saying they're just spoiled kids, that they'll pack up and go back to sleep at Mommy and Daddy's in a few days."

"Do you really believe anything can change here?" Faadi asked Rami. "I mean real, profound change?"

"I'd like to think it can. Maybe for once, people here will learn something from the countries around them."

"Dream on," Khaled retorted. "The day some gorgeous Syrians or Saudis come visit us in Yafa, we can talk about the influence of Arab states on this villa in the jungle. I wouldn't hold my breath, though."

"Oh, I thought you were into Jews," Faadi teased, "and preferably blond ones."

"I'm not too picky when it comes to cute guys," Khaled responded. "But my mother would like to see me with a nice Muslim boy. She'd compromise on a nice Arab Christian, but definitely not a Jew. My grandmother couldn't care less what anyone's religion is—she's a Communist. But she has one condition: He can't be from Yafa. She says men in Yafa are ugly and not nice. She's a snob, she lives in Nazareth. Won't set foot in Yafa, no matter what."

Fareed was astonished. "You mean your grandmother knows you're...?"

"Of course!" Khaled said. "You wouldn't believe how she adored my first boyfriend. She cried more than I did when we broke up. We used to sleep at her place when our parents wouldn't let us stay with them. After a while my parents calmed down and accepted him, but even then my boyfriend used to visit her for advice or to grumble about me."

"Don't think everyone here is like that," Faadi clarified. "Most gay Palestinians in Israel are closeted. It's a very conservative society. Even our leaders, the ones in the Knesset, say things like, 'Arab society is not yet mature enough to contend with this issue.' What *is* it mature enough to deal with, then? Bunch of clowns, those guys. What's for sure is that the Shami Bar, here in Yafa, is an oasis. It doesn't represent anything going on in this country, certainly not the discrimination and racism against Arabs. So don't get the wrong idea..."

"What Faadi is trying to say," Khaled intervened, "is that you have to watch out for pinkwashing. Do you know what that is? He doesn't want you to go back to New York and tell all your friends how peachy everything is in the only democracy in the Middle East. Bottom line is we're second-class citizens here, and it doesn't make any difference that we're allowed to fall in love with men and that Israeli society accepts us, supposedly. That goes out the window the second we turn up at the airport and try to get on a flight — that's when they forget that I have an Israeli passport just like any Jew who was born here, and they go through my luggage like I'm a terrorist or an illegal alien."

"Okay, come on, enough politics. We're here for the cute guys," said Faadi.

"Yeah, and I have to start my shift," Rami added. "I'm here to work, not to have a good time."

A few young men and women, wearing short summer clothes, sat at the bar. A heart-shaped string of tiny light-bulbs twinkled on the wall. There were two DJs at the stand. One was short, thin, and muscular, with a pencil mustache, wearing starched shorts and an unbuttoned shirt. He was swaying his hips to the rhythm. The other DJ had a big head of hair and held a cigarette between his fingers. They played the Lebanese pop singer Nancy Ajram. A few people danced on the tiny square between the bar and the door.

Rami went behind the bar and got to work. He changed a keg of Taybeh beer, then started pouring drinks. Fareed sat down and stared at the customers. Rami gave him a beer, and Fareed leaned his elbows on the bar with his body half turned toward the dance floor. A few minutes later they were joined by a young blond man, who sat down next to Khaled, hugged him, and kissed him on the neck.

"This is Avi," Rami said in English. "Avi—Fareed."

"Shalom," Avi said and held out his hand. Fareed shook his hand and smiled, though he felt embarrassed. Rami started talking about the social justice protests, and everyone agreed to go to the demonstration planned for the following week. Only Maha—a pretty redhead who had joined them, wearing a black tank top and a necklace with a pendant in the colors of the Palestinian flag—objected. She thought they shouldn't get involved with the protests because they weren't advancing the Palestinian cause. But the others argued that if the protests led to real economic and social change, they would have a profound effect on the political situation in the long term. After a fervent debate, Maha pulled Avi to the dance floor. Rami went back to work, and Fareed sipped his beer and looked around awkwardly. This was not how he had imagined his time in Yafa. Eventually he was persuaded to dance, but a few minutes later he said goodbye to Rami and went outside.

## 2

Fareed was born in Damascus in 1991. When he was five, he moved to New York so that his father, Shaker, could attend medical school. After completing his studies and a residency in ophthalmology, Shaker was offered a job in the city, but the family returned to Damascus because Shaker's father,

Abed, was ailing. At fourteen, Fareed had to readjust to life in Damascus, where everything was so different. To ease the transition, Shaker enrolled his son in an American school.

Fareed knew little about his family, and if truth be told, he didn't ask much. He knew that his paternal grandparents had come from Palestine, which was a place not far from Damascus but unnamed on the map. He knew they'd left their homeland and relocated to Damascus, and that was all. After Abed died, there was only one person left from the old world whom Fareed felt close to: his grandmother Laila. But she rarely talked about her childhood. He remembered hearing about a tower with two clocks, about the sea, about summer trips to Lebanon, and fragmented stories about the necklace she always wore, a delicate gold chain with three intertwined lines.

When Fareed turned seventeen, he decided he would go to college in the United States. But at eighteen he thought it was too soon to leave, and he deferred for one year. He sat at home and read books. He uploaded songs he liked to a website, and a year later he started a blog. On the "About Me" page he wrote:

19 years old.
Favorite music: Radiohead, Mashrou' Leila
Favorite authors: Albert Camus, Paul Auster
Movies: Almódovar, Cinema Paradiso,
    anything by Adel Imam
Favorite quote: "Never seek to tell thy love /
    Love that never told can be / For the gentle wind
    does move / Silently invisibly" (William Blake)

That evening in Yafa, Fareed stood in the middle of Rami's apartment with his hands in his pockets. He had to get ready for the demonstration and still wasn't sure what to wear. When Rami told him about the rally, which was being billed as the "March of the Million," Fareed was apprehensive. It was bad enough that he had infiltrated Israel and reached Yafa by the skin of his teeth, but now he was supposed to risk taking part in a political event? And he hadn't even done any of the things he'd planned yet. For two days he'd just walked from one end of Yafa to the other, stared at the sea, and read a book.

Rami reassured him: It's not a political demonstration. But how could such a thing exist, a nonpolitical demonstration? That's what Fareed kept asking. Would there be signs? Yes. Police? Yes. A march? Yes. Slogans? Yes, lots of slogans. So how was that not political?

Rami insisted the march was apolitical—it had nothing to do with the Israeli-Palestinian conflict—and eventually Fareed believed him. He had to. In the past two days Rami had become his guide. Almost everything he said, even the most outlandish claim, turned out to be true. Right down to the smallest detail.

But what if Fareed got stopped at the protest?

He wouldn't, Rami promised. If he blended in with the crowd and didn't stand out, nothing would happen. If he threw himself on the road afterward and yelled slogans against the police, they might arrest him. But there was nothing to worry about at the demonstration itself. On the contrary, Rami explained, the police were on their side, since the protesters were trying to improve the working class's conditions, after all. They could hold up any signs they wanted, call out slogans until they were hoarse, even in Arabic.

An hour later they left Yafa and started the walk to Tel Aviv. They were joined by Khaled, Avi, Maha (who had been talked into coming), Faadi, and some other people Fareed didn't know. He told everyone he was from New York, that he'd been born in the U.S. but spoke Arabic because his parents were Syrian. They crossed Clock Tower Square and walked along the promenade.

It was the first time Fareed had seen the Tel Aviv beach. There were breakwaters and restaurants along the beach with chairs spilling out all the way to the water. There were tall streetlamps, a broad strip of sidewalk with cyclists careening past, and shaded benches facing the water. On the other side, the street was lined with hotels, a cinema, and parking lots. And now there was also a huge mass of people making their way into the city center.

They walked for about half an hour. The streets around the rally site were cordoned off. Police cars were everywhere, but unlike at other demonstrations Fareed had seen, the officers did not look tense. It was hard to tell if they were even armed. There was an air of indifference. Groups of kids in matching shirts identifying their youth movements poured in from every direction, alongside clusters of young men beating drums, couples walking hand in hand, and individuals carrying signs. They all had a determined look in their eyes.

Rami was right. In fact, the event was so removed from the usual preoccupation with national and ethnic conflicts that no one paid any attention to a group of Arabs from Yafa calling out slogans. People barely glanced at their signs, and no one stopped to read the Arabic on their shirts.

The police looked content. The protesters were not throwing eggs or flour or stink bombs at them. Instead, they showered them with love. When Fareed asked what the demonstrators were shouting, Rami said they were inviting the cops to join them, since they were being exploited, too. As the Yafa group neared the end of the street and crowded into Rabin Square, Fareed started wondering what the objective of this love rally was, because if everyone loved everyone else, why go out demonstrating? Residents cheered from balconies all around and threw flowers onto the crowds. The noise surged into a deafening thunder, then ebbed, then rose again. People climbed up lampposts and sang songs in praise of the revolution. Hordes of protesters swarmed into the square from every direction. There were signs in English, Israeli flags, rainbow pride flags, and not a hint of violence.

Fareed started to feel it—a love that depends on nothing, a love that does not seek fulfillment but simply exists, breezy and light. It erupted inside him and rattled his body. He was carried along on the waves of sound that thundered across the square, on the bodies of these people who trod so lightly, who were not really protesting or breaking anything, but simply pouring into this space, colossal and numerous, demanding to be acknowledged, to be recognized, noticed, to be allowed to move forward, demanding their right to convene in the square, to flow into this urban center in rivers and streams, to hug the police and to just be.

And there, in the heart of this enormous, all-embracing love, amid the hundreds of thousands who had come to the square, borne by the masses, Fareed realized he had made a grave mistake crossing the border. It was in this apolitical demonstration, where no one was dispersed or shot and no one jailed, no one dragged by their arms and legs into a police van, that Fareed became acutely aware of his foreignness. And he sensed, even if he did not know exactly how it would happen, that he would meet a terrible fate in this country, the country his grandfather Abed and his grandmother Laila had longingly called "Palestine."

Later that night, he lay in the dark on Rami's sofa bed and his fingers played with Sabakh, the blue diamond that worked in mysterious ways. From the moment a diamond surfaces, Laila used to tell him, nothing in the world can push it back underground. Fareed suddenly had the idea that he should just be done with the diamond once and for all, turn himself in to the Israeli police and ask them to send him back to Syria. But how would he get rid of Sabakh? He could go outside and bury it in the courtyard, he could walk to the beach and throw it in the water. He might just flush it down the toilet or poke it through the drain in the sink. If this diamond was so clever, if it had been through such incredible tribulations since the day it was mined in India, across France and England and Turkey and Damascus and now Yafa—then it would find its way back.

But how would Fareed find *his* way home? A different person, he told himself, someone unlike him, would be able to stand his ground. If he was going to end up at the Israeli police anyway, perhaps he should just turn himself in now.

But he wasn't brave enough. Besides, he was afraid the diamond might take revenge on him. Greater and more important people had suffered at the hands of Sabakh. Fareed wasn't certain that he really believed in the diamond's power; Laila's strange stories had always struck him as dubious. But at the same time he could not shake the impression that it was after his grandmother had taken possession of the diamond that she had been forced to leave her home and live in exile.

Was that Sabakh's plan? Was that the reason Laila had invited her beloved grandson to her home and told him her life's story?

He soon fell sound asleep.

## 3

Fareed covered all of Yafa by foot. As it turned out, it was not that big, certainly not for an infiltrator with lots of free time. Where did he go? Anywhere he could glimpse the sea, or at least know that if he turned around and ran he would soon see it. There was only one place—the house on Sha'arei Nikanor Street where his grandparents had lived—where he did not have the courage to go.

Still, he had returned. The right of return be damned—he himself had returned. It was the return of one individual, but nevertheless a return.

Before his own private return, he had read about refugees turning up at their old homes out of the blue. Some found ruins—not a single wall preserved, only a heap of stones buried under overgrowth. Sometimes all that remained of an entire village were four arbitrary walls. The skeleton of a mosque, for example. Those who returned searched for their homes among the weeds and stones, but all they found was a well. The well was stopped up by a large rock, and they had to suffice with that.

There were others, too, who came all the way to Palestine to evict the people occupying their homes and found old acquaintances, residents of the city who, in 1948, had rented apartments from the Israeli Custodian of Absentee Property. These "absentees" were the owners, but for decades the state had rented out their homes, sometimes to Arabs, who took up residence and treated the homes as their own. But they did not touch the furniture or the pictures.

And there were those who crowded onto the deck of *Al Awda*—The Return—at the port of Limassol, Cyprus, in 1988, intending to return to Palestine. But a limpet mine blew open a hole in the ferryboat and prevented the voyage.

Some returned as characters in fictional accounts, like the book Fareed read, a story full of wrath and prophecies of doom. It was about a couple who returns to Haifa to look for their son, whom they left behind in the chaos when they fled the city in 1948. They find in their home a Holocaust survivor with her adopted son—none other than the fruit of their loins, who has been raised as a Jew and served in the Israeli army. Before leaving, the parents acknowledge that the only possible resolution will be through war.

There were also serendipitous returns, like the Palestinian who was imprisoned by the Israeli army during the first Intifada. After his arrest, he asked the warden, "Where am I?" The warden told him the name of the village where the prison was located, and, miraculously, it was the village the prisoner had left twenty years earlier, in 1967. From that moment on, his imprisonment seemed less onerous. He put his nose up to the window bars and breathed in the aroma of the soil of his village. He squinted, trying to make out the houses. He was happy.

All these things Fareed saw in films and read in books.

Fareed belonged yet did not belong to Yafa. He was bound in some way to this place, although he did not seek a well, nor did he find one. He had not come to evict invaders from his house, because none of the houses were his, except for one. The house on Sha'arei Nikanor Street used to belong to Abed and Laila. But how could he prove that? He didn't even have a key.

He did have Sabakh, and that was enough.

Laila had told him everything: what happened in Yafa and what happened afterward. She had done so calmly, neither defiant nor apologetic. This was simply how the events had transpired, and who were we to judge?

CHAPTER THREE

# AUNT GRACIA

*1*

AUNT GRACIA'S APARTMENT FACED THE MEDITERRANEAN, with windows open to the four winds. On one side was the sea, and on the other were the narrow streets climbing up from the beach to Allenby Street, which snaked away from the shoreline until it was swallowed up among Tel Aviv's buildings. Far beyond them lay the northern land, under lock and key. Aunt Gracia could look out of the southern windows to Jaffa, and since coming to Israel in 1949, that was where her feet took her on the rare occasions when she left home.

For years, Aunt Gracia was unaware of the many goings-on just beyond her doorstep in Tel Aviv, not to mention events unfolding in the rest of the country. Her window faced elsewhere, her eyes were drawn far away, and hardly anyone maintained contact with her apart from her close relatives. And Sami.

She did not respond to things that occurred beyond her immediate surroundings. Perhaps she did not even know about the huge fire atop the Eiffel Tower, the new constitution and women's suffrage in Egypt, the Winter Olympics in Italy, or the independence granted to Morocco and then Tunisia. She did not know about Martin Luther King Jr. in America, or the Islamic Republic in Pakistan, or the homecoming of four Israeli prisoners of war from Syria. She did not know that the city of Ashdod had been founded, or about the polio vaccine, the first World Judo Championship in Tokyo, or the first Eurovision Song Contest. She was, however, informed of the newly founded city of Dimona in the south of Israel.

Gamal Abdel Nasser was elected president of Egypt, the Italian SS *Andrea Doria* sank at sea, Egypt nationalized the Suez Canal and barred Israeli vessels, the Israeli army launched a retaliation campaign, President Eisenhower declared "In God We Trust" America's national motto, in Israel the term "manifestly illegal order" was coined in response to the massacre at Kafr Qasim, and the Cuban Revolution broke out. Of all these things, Aunt Gracia was blissfully ignorant.

She was certainly told of the Suez Crisis. And that Egypt was bombed to try to force it to reopen the canal. But she had nothing to say about either of these events.

Once a week, after lunch, little Menashe used to kiss his mother Adela goodbye and walk south on Dizengoff Street until he came to the market. He knew that when he emerged from the stalls, not far from the sea and from Jaffa, his greataunt Gracia would be waiting at home, at almost any time of day. She always invited him into the living room, served tea, peeled a cucumber for him, then swiftly chopped and deep-fried potatoes, her gold bands jangling on her wrists as she worked. Then she sat down opposite him. Sometimes she spoke tersely, other times she talked a lot, but her words were flat, with no high or low cadences. And all Menashe really wanted was to hear her sing. But she refused.

"You see, Menashe," she said once after a long silence, as she stroked his soft brown hair, "I sang when I lived *there*. *There* they wanted me to sing, they listened to me quietly, they applauded, gave me money, courted me. But here..." She looked out the window and followed the Tel Aviv street all the way to the sea and beyond. "Here they've forgotten me. Not forgotten—worse: No one even knows that there used to be a singer in Damascus named Gracia, that even the Ottoman sultan sent emissaries to bring her all the way to Istanbul to sing for him. Have I ever told you about when I went to the sultan's palace, Menashe?"

She had, many times, but he wanted to hear the story again. He thought perhaps if Aunt Gracia got carried away with her recollections, she might forget the vow of silence she had taken when she came to Israel and sing for him. And then, when that happened, for one elusive moment, he would feel like a sultan. Sultan Menashe. So he nodded and gazed at her silently. His brown eyes wandered over his aunt's face, with its subtle makeup, and the brown hair piled on her head and held down with countless invisible pins, and her green eyes, which always seemed to be facing the wrong way, looking inward.

Aunt Gracia told him about Sultan Abdul Hamid II's palace in Istanbul, named Yıldız, which means "star" in Turkish, and about the sultan himself. "The sultan tended to the palace and the gardens all around. He had gardens like the French king's in Versailles! With flowers from seeds sent from Europe. There were fountains, and exotic herb bushes, and a little zoo where all the animals lived in peace and no one was allowed to kill them." Gracia knew that Menashe would appreciate this part of the story, being so concerned for the welfare of animals. After all, he had seen them slaughtered with his own eyes.

"The sultan's palace was like a small city," she continued. "It had a theater, and a big library, and many, many rooms. There was one room with pictures of all the cities in the sultan's empire. They say he built the palace furniture himself, because he was very talented—at handicrafts and music and literature. He translated European operas. But history did not forget the other things he did. They called him the Red Sultan, because he had blood on his hands."

Menashe looked down and thought about a different pair of hands, the ones belonging to Grandpa Menashe, the *shochet*, which he had seen not long ago. But he didn't dare interrupt his aunt's story. He stared at her gold chain and longed to run his fingers over the pendant inset with a red stone. She noticed.

"Do you know how much the sultan loved jewelry, Menashe?" she asked with a smile. "He wore a gold ring inset with agate that was made in Mecca, and he always kept a gold pocket watch. When he was a guest at weddings, his servants would throw pieces of gold at the bride and groom. That was the custom. He asked his jewelers to set precious stones in the desks he built, and every time he had a daughter, they gave her a tortoise as a gift because they believed it was a talisman for long life. The sultan's jeweler would take the tortoise's shell and coat it with gold, and they would use the shell to pour water on the newborn and bathe her every night in a tub made of pure silver. That was the custom."

"You mean the jeweler killed the tortoise?"

"Yes." She regretted telling him that. But Menashe's thoughts were already elsewhere. He kept watching her quietly as she told him more about the sultan, afraid to interrupt. He fingered the tablecloth, which was embroidered with delicate gold thread.

"Did you know that the sultan had an aunt whom he loved very much? Every time she came to visit him in the palace, he waited in the living room with all his servants, and when she entered she held out her hand and said, 'My boy!' And the sultan kissed her hand and said, 'At your service, my aunt!'"

Menashe grinned. He liked the stories about the sultan. But he wanted his aunt to sing for him. He kept listening patiently.

"I always tell you everything that happened, Menashe, because you are a very sweet boy. And it's thanks to you that I remember things that happened long ago, in another world, in another life. Do you think we can hold on to everything that happens to us? You'll grow up and discover that your body changes, and you change on the inside, too, and all the things that happened to you—there is no proof that they really did happen. Even memory does not always last. You turn your face up to the sky, inhale and exhale, close your eyes, and some little thing comes back to you for a quick second. But do not believe that moment will truly return. Everything you do in life happens for the first time and the last time. There is nothing afterward, and there won't be anything left. If you understand that, you will be able to genuinely enjoy the things you do. You will be able to hold on to them as tightly as possible before they escape you forever. Do you understand, Menashe?"

He wanted her to sing, and the more he listened the farther away her singing seemed. It was important to him to hear Aunt Gracia's songs, which belonged to a different time and place. He felt close to those melodies, although he couldn't even imagine them because they always got stuck in his mind on the first note. But they were a part of him, even before he was himself.

"I was a young girl," Aunt Gracia said. "I used to sing even as a little girl, and the whole family was very proud of me. Do you know who is responsible for my singing? My sister."

Aunt Gracia's sister, Menashe's paternal grandmother, was named Mona. Menashe had never met her. She died in Damascus long before he was born. He knew that his grandfather had died first, on the eve of his parents' wedding, and that Mona had died later. He pictured them like dominoes: One teeters and falls, knocking the other one over. First him, then her.

"Your grandmother was blind. When we were little girls she went everywhere with me. I respected her a lot, because she was the older sister and she always knew everything, even without eyesight. Mona knew me better than anyone else, even better than our parents. Every night before going to sleep we would lie in bed and talk. I would tell her everything I'd seen that day, and she would tell me about things she imagined. I tried to picture the things she described—events that happened in different worlds—and I almost envied her for being able to think up all those things, for having time to imagine and lots of space in her mind, because she wasn't confined to thinking about one thing or seeing only one thing. You know, Menashe, every time you turn to look at one thing, you miss all the other things one might see. And those things, Grandma Mona saw. At night we would lie next to each other holding hands as she talked, with our eyes shut, until we fell sleep. Together we watched the sights that came to her mind during the day. And you see, I wanted to give her something in return for all the wonderful things she showed me. But I had nothing to give. Everything I saw, everything I knew suddenly seemed so boring. So do you know what I did?"

"You sang?"

"*Shater!* Smart boy! Yes, I sang high notes and low notes, I invented stories through songs, stories that you tell with words and music. They were my gift to Mona. I was fifteen or sixteen. One day our uncle, my mother's brother, was standing outside the room and he heard me singing. The next day he took me to a café where he knew the owners, and I stood up in front of all the customers and they told me to sing, so I did. When I sang, everyone stopped talking and looked at me with wide eyes. Afterward they all applauded, and then my uncle took me home. But the next day my father found out what had happened, and he went to my uncle's house and they had a big fight."

"So your dad didn't know you went to sing?"

"You see, my uncle wanted to help us. Because in those days we had no money at all. When he took me out that evening, my father thought I was going to have dinner at his house. After the big fight, I stayed home for a few days without knowing what was going on. A week later, Mother came into our bedroom. I sat by the window looking out at the apple trees, and she stood behind me and said, 'Do you like to sing, Gracia?' I said, 'Yes, I love to sing.' And she said, 'Then I will allow you to go with your uncle in the evenings and sing. But you must come home straightaway with him afterward.' I didn't understand why she said that, but I turned to her, and she kissed me and hugged me tightly. Her cheek was against mine, and it suddenly felt damp, and I said, 'Dear Mother, why are you crying?' But she didn't answer, she just kept hugging me, and the sobs came up and up from her chest, and I wondered if she was ill or if something had happened to Father. In the end she pulled away, looked into my eyes and said, 'You are a smart girl, Gracia. And you have a great talent. But promise me you will not talk to any men there, no matter what they tell you, and that you'll come home with your uncle every night. Promise?' I said, 'I promise to do anything you ask, dear Mother, just so long as you're not sad.' She smiled, stroked my hair, turned and left the room. And so, from that day on, I went to the café with my uncle every evening. After a while they invited us to other places as well. Mona told me she heard there was talk all over town about the Jewish girl with the wonderful voice and the beautiful songs. More and more people came to my shows, and the money went to my family. Our

Friday night dinners started being very grand, with lots of meat and fine dishes on the table. Even Mona helped my mother cook."

"But Grandma was blind."

"Yes, but she could do lots of things, like trim the green beans, sort the okra..."

"Without seeing?"

"She could feel. She shelled the fava beans and made meatballs, she kneaded the *kubeh* and stuffed it with meat, and she knew how to shape *atayef* and fill the crepes with cheese. But I wasn't allowed to help. They said I had to rest, because I went out singing in the evenings. And so I would lie in bed with my eyes closed and smell all the aromas from the kitchen, and I really was very tired. But I loved to sing."

Aunt Gracia stopped talking. She reached out and took an apple from a bowl on the table, peeled it quickly, and cut a piece for Menashe. He grabbed it and munched silently. The apple peel lay on the table in a long green coil.

"And just as my mother warned," Aunt Gracia continued, "there were men who wanted to talk to me. I was pretty, but not as pretty as Mona. She was beautiful, but she didn't know how beautiful she was, of course. I used to describe her face to her, and she would feel it and then feel my face, but how can you explain what a beautiful face is to someone who has never seen any face? She wanted to find love. Every night she told me how she longed to find someone who would know how to touch her and listen to her, and that she would take care of him and know him better than a woman with a thousand eyes could. I promised to find her someone. You think I'm joking? I knew that one day the man who would fall in love with my sister would arrive. And he really did."

Menashe smiled. He knew that Aunt Gracia was going to tell him about Grandpa Salim, who really did arrive one day and fall in love. At first he fell in love with Aunt Gracia herself, but she explained that it could never happen. She didn't have time for a lover, she only wanted to sing. She told him about her sister, and when his curiosity was aroused, she told him Mona was blind. He was a little taken aback, but when they met it was "love at first sight," Aunt Gracia said with a giggle. How exactly did Mona see her beloved if she was blind? And how could she fall in love with him "at first sight"? Menashe could only imagine. He wanted to keep thinking about his grandparents, whose story fed his dreams for many long nights, because he knew that on the night they met, a seed was planted that would one day, years later, lead to his own emergence into the world. But that was after his grandfather teetered like a domino and fell, followed two years later by Grandma Mona, whose eyes closed forever and she never saw another thing—neither with her real eyes nor in her mind's eye. But before that happened, long before, Aunt Gracia repaid Mona for all her wonderful stories about faraway places, because Gracia herself traveled all the way to the sultan's palace in Istanbul and brought back the blue diamond.

As Menashe's thoughts spiraled on, he pricked up his little nose and the smell of the sea came in through the window. Although he was only seven, Menashe could already distinguish one smell from another, and he thought about how not long ago the sun had stayed in the sky until evening, and the winds at night had died down, and the rain had stopped. Father had started coming home when it was still light, and Mother complained of the heat, and Aunt Gracia lay sprawled on the couch in her little apartment, surrounded by jewelry and clothes from Damascus, with the crystal lamp in the middle of the ceiling and the crystal dishes on the table, and the gifts she had received in those cafés in Damascus.

Summer was here.

Aunt Gracia lay on the couch wearing only a thin robe. Menashe looked at her and remembered the legend his teacher, Ms. Sylvia, had told the class one day when they went on a tour of Jaffa.

They walked around the ancient town and stopped at Napoleon's cannons. The teacher told them about the great emperor who had set off to conquer Europe and the Middle East, and her eyes were ablaze. She talked excitedly about the cannons, which had pounded and pounded at the walls of the fortified city until they broke through. Then Ms. Sylvia led the children to the bottom of the hill, where, standing on the shore, she pointed to a rock out at sea and said, "Here before you is Andromeda's Rock."

And this is the legend she told them:

"Once upon a time in Jaffa, there was a beautiful princess named Andromeda. Andromeda's mother, Queen Cassiopeia, boasted of her daughter but also envied her. She went around telling everyone about Princess Andromeda, claiming she was the most beautiful woman in the world, more beautiful than even the nymphs in the sea. The nymphs heard this and asked Poseidon, King of the Sea, to avenge their insult. Poseidon loved Andromeda, but he loved the nymphs more. So he sent a terrifying monster to destroy the city. Andromeda's father, King Cepheus, could not sleep. He was worried about his city and felt guilty because he knew that all this was happening because of the queen's pride and his daughter's beauty. He waved his hands and cried out, 'Cursed is the day when Cassiopeia birthed the beautiful Andromeda!' He went to see an oracle, who was a clever man who knew everything. The oracle told him he had to sacrifice Andromeda to Medusa, a terrifying sea monster with writhing snakes instead of hair, which would bite anyone who came near. The most terrible thing about Medusa was her eyes. Anyone she looked at immediately turned to stone. But there was no choice: They snatched poor Andromeda, chained her to the rock you see here, and she waited for the Medusa to come and devour her. But then a miracle happened. Right here in the sky above us, the hero Perseus flew past. He did not have wings, but he had flying sandals. He held a shield and a large sword, and he chopped off Medusa's head, freed Andromeda, and flew away with her to a desert island, where they lived happily ever after."

That was Ms. Sylvia's story.

Aunt Gracia was worn out by the heat and lay on the couch like Andromeda passed out on the rock. Menashe looked at her with trepidation. She looked like half princess and half monster. He could see her bosom through her dress, and she had barely any makeup on. Her brown hair was adorned with thin golden ribbons, and her skin glistened gold with perspiration. Her thighs were stacked on each other, and she was massaging musk ointment on her thighs, calves, and feet. She couldn't reach her toes, so she asked Menashe to do those.

"My boy!" she called.

"At your service, my aunt!" replied Sultan Menashe.

He got down on his knees, almost bowing at Aunt Gracia's feet. The scent of musk pierced his nostrils and made him dizzy. His little fingers invaded the gaps between Gracia's toes, all of them at once, and precisely at that second her head lolled back and one soft sigh escaped her lips. Her eyes were closed. He considered reaching out his little tongue to tickle her between the toes. Her hand would be covering her eyes because the sun was hanging over the sea, and the air would be tinged with purple and orange, and it would be difficult to breathe, but in between his aunt's peals of laughter Menashe would identify a different sound, a sound he had heard once before when he came to visit.

The apartment door was unlocked that day, and he walked in. There was no one in the living room. Menashe went to the kitchen and poured himself a glass of water. He thought Aunt Gracia must have gone to the market. But then he heard laughter coming from her bedroom, and a few words in Arabic, spoken in an unfamiliar male voice and in Gracia's. But it was not her usual voice—it sounded as though she were speaking very quickly and then very slowly. Then there was silence.

Menashe drank his water and looked out the window. He could see a road behind a row of squat houses. The road curved back and forth going south—away from al-Sham, where his entire family had come from. He was the only one born here on this land. On the other side of the street was the sea. It looked as though someone had covered the water with yellow marbles, and behind all the marbles the sun looked out at Tel Aviv and Jaffa with its one eye. Jaffa was piled up in a heap—or at least that was how it looked to Menashe. He knew that in Jaffa there was a square with a clock tower, and the signature of Sultan Abdul Hamid II inside the ticking clock, and a market, and another market, and friends of his father, Rafael, some of whom still lived there. People sat in cafés drinking the anise tea they called *yansoon*, smoking hookahs, playing backgammon. And he knew that time passed much more slowly there.

These were Menashe's thoughts, and he forgot that the door to Aunt Gracia's room was shut and that only moments before he had heard her voice coming from there. Suddenly he heard a shout. To his left, the glimmering yellow marbles on the sea twittered, and Menashe thought he could hear the muezzin calling from the mosque in Jaffa. Jaffa was far away, yet still he imagined he could hear the clock in the tower ticking faster and faster. Or perhaps it was his heart. The door opened. From the corner of his eye, Menashe saw a tall, broad-shouldered man with a black mustache standing in the doorway, wearing nothing but a pair of large white underwear.

"There's a boy here," the man said in Arabic.

Menashe looked at him and felt his face turn red. He looked down at the floor, not before glimpsing the strange man's huge chest, his skin glistening with sweat, and his large purple nipples that protruded as if someone had pinched them and tried to pull them out. Menashe saw one more thing: a mark of some sort on the hollow of the man's neck. Only after he walked past Menashe, very close, did Menashe realize what it was: teeth marks. Something in the way the bite was imprinted on the skin reminded Menashe of the unfamiliar sound he had heard in Aunt Gracia's laughter when the door was shut.

"What boy?" Aunt Gracia's voice rang out from the room. She moved the man aside with her bare arm, revealing her body behind him. The man walked to the bathroom, and a few seconds later they could clearly hear a stream hitting the water. The man whistled a happy tune, and Aunt Gracia, who had been out of breath just moments ago, stood there quietly. Her hair was pulled back as usual, with all the pins hiding in it. She wore a robe that Menashe recognized—a red robe with yellow dots, which was a little too small for her but she liked it because it reminded her of those distant days in al-Sham.

Aunt Gracia stood facing Menashe without saying anything, but then she opened her arms and said, "Come to me, my sultan." Menashe hurried over to be enfolded in her embrace. Aunt Gracia's body had a sharp smell, which he inhaled through his nostrils. At first a warm sensation enveloped him, but after a few seconds he felt dizzy and almost fell over. Aunt Gracia put her hands under his armpits and led him to the couch. But he did not want to sit down. He stood there, cradled in her body. The man with the mustache came back and stood in the kitchen. He drank several glasses of water, one after the other.

"Sami, come and meet my sultan," Aunt Gracia said in Arabic.

The man she called Sami put his empty glass down on the wooden kitchen table. "How many sultans do you know?" He grinned. "I thought there was only one."

"This is the Crown Sultan. Sultan Menashe the First."

Sami walked over slowly. He bowed his head at the boy, reached out a large hand, and pinched Menashe's cheek. Then, with the very same hand, he patted Gracia's cheek lovingly. His shirt was on the couch and he started dressing. The sweat on his skin had dried almost completely. Gracia wanted to help button his shirt, but he gently brushed her away. He surveyed her and Menashe and said, in Hebrew, "You look alike."

"Are you leaving?" Gracia asked in Arabic.

"You have a visitor," Sami replied in Hebrew. "And not just anyone—a sultan!"

"The sultan came without informing me," said Aunt Gracia, insisting on using her language. Menashe could not tell whether she was angry or joking. Maybe both. "He forgot to send his eunuchs with a note, and so I could not welcome him as one welcomes a real sultan."

"Well, now you can host him properly." Sami stood behind Aunt Gracia, lifted her hair, and kissed the back of her neck.

"You'll come tomorrow?" she asked.

He did not answer, and she closed her eyes and sighed. Then he patted Menashe's cheek twice, put on his shoes, and left.

Aunt Gracia kissed Menashe's forehead. "Sit on the couch and rest, sweetheart. You look tired. I'll be back in a minute."

She walked away, and Menashe lay down with his eyes closed and listened to the shower water. For a moment the window was flooded with orange light, as if all the yellow marbles had exploded above the sea. He opened his eyes a crack and looked out, but he couldn't see anything. He must have dozed off, because he suddenly felt Aunt Gracia's hand on his shoulder.

She was wearing a different robe now, and her skin exuded the scent of musk. Menashe waited for her to lie down on the couch and ask him to rub her feet, but she did not say anything and did not lie down. She went into the kitchen to make lemonade. She brought Menashe a glass and then turned away and leaned on the windowsill, looking far out, at the sky that was now a dark purple.

## 2

"What's wrong, Menashe?" asked Aunt Gracia, rousing Menashe from his thoughts. "Menashe, what's wrong?" she repeated.

"Nothing."

"You look sad."

"I'm fine," he tried to say, but he felt a sting in his eyes.

"How are Mom and Dad?"

"Fine."

"And Salim?"

"Shlomo? He always wants to go to the beach, but after school Dad takes him to the shop to help out."

"And little Mona?"

"She's always shouting."

"What's the matter, my sultan?" Aunt Gracia asked again after a pause. "Are you angry because I didn't tell you I had a boyfriend?"

"No."

"But look, I'm not angry at you for coming to see me without telling me. I'm glad you came and met Sami. Isn't he nice?"

Menashe didn't answer.

"He's a good man, Menashe, a really good man. And he loves me."

The boy's eyes were hazy with thoughts. He was preoccupied with other matters. "I don't want Rosh Hashanah to come," he said.

"But why not? I thought you liked that holiday!"

Menashe knew that shortly before Rosh Hashanah his mother would take him to the tailor to get a new suit made. There would be white drapes hung on the windows at home, and white bedspreads and white tablecloths. When they sat down for the festive meal, Father would dip a piece of bread in sugar, take a bite, and pass it around to each of the guests. There would be a plate on the table for the ritual blessings, and on the plate would be a sheep's head, beet leaves, pomegranate, *lubia*, dates, and green pumpkin jam boiled in sugar.

They would not nap during the day on the holiday. Father and Salim would be at synagogue, where they would read all one hundred and fifty verses in the Book of Psalms twice, because that makes three hundred, which in gematria has the numerical value of the letters k-p-r, the Hebrew root for "atonement."

"I don't like Rosh Hashanah," Menashe declared.

"But why?"


Shortly before Rosh Hashanah the year before, while Adela was preparing the home with white tablecloths, white bedspreads, and white drapes on the windows, Rafael came into Shlomo and Menashe's room one evening and said, "Come with me, boys." The three left the house and went out to the street. Shlomo and Menashe walked behind Rafael without a word, heading south on Dizengoff Street.

Rafael stopped outside the building where Adela's parents lived. The door on the top floor was half open. Sounds of conversation came from the apartment, but the living room was empty. Outside one of the rooms in the small apartment was a large crowd. Rafael headed over there, followed by his two sons.

Rafael pushed his way into the room, and Shlomo paved his own path, stood next to his father, and put one hand on his shoulder. Menashe stayed in the doorway. He found himself surrounded by grown men, most of whom he knew—they were the relatives he always saw at synagogue and at festivities held in the event hall in Ha'Tikva neighborhood. There was a smell in the room that he had trouble identifying, and he also noted peculiar sounds, some of which were castigations and some a sort of foot stomping, as well as a panicked, animal hum, furniture shifting, muffled curses, and a desperate attempt to instill order. There was a momentary silence that was swallowed up in the crowd's rustle.

Menashe pushed his way into the room. He did not see his grandfather standing in the middle, wearing his white robe, his black hair neatly parted and smoothed down, his mouth open and teeth visible, his large fingers clutching a glistening knife. Menashe did not see the sheep that lay there flailing.

An hour earlier, the sheep had been hurried onto the steps so that it could prance up to the top floor, which it did—with neither revulsion nor joy, but simply by necessity, only to be pushed into this room and stood in the center, then to lie with its limbs spread out and pant from the heat and the suffocation, then to fight with all its strength—which it knew instinctively was its last remaining strength—and then surrender desperately and submissively to the knife that had severed the heads of so many creatures in both Damascus and Tel Aviv.

The sheep fell silent and the commotion escalated. At that moment, Menashe managed to make his way through the crowd and cling to his father's trousers. He watched his grandfather, who lowered his gaze until his eyes met his little grandson's, and he smiled at the boy. Menashe looked down, not before catching sight of the patches of boiling blood pooling on his grandfather's white cloak.

Then there was a crowd gathered around Menashe. Father and Shlomo shook his shoulders and asked, "Are you all right?! Are you all right?!" But he was not all right. His eyes stung and his mouth was parched and he hunched over and tried to stop himself but he could not, and then he vomited.

When he recovered, he was in the living room. His grandmother sat beside him holding out a cup of tea and a biscuit. He buried his head in her lap and remembered the sheep in the next room and was overcome by nausea again. Men kept coming in and out of the room. Now he understood why his mother did not go to her parents' apartment: Adela came from a family of *shochets*, which was precisely why she had not eaten meat from a very young age. Adela was at home now. Aunt Gracia had not come either, and Menashe was in the care of his grandmother.

For many days afterward, throughout the High Holy Days, Menashe lay in bed curled up with his knees against his stomach, his fingers spread over his knees. His stomach ached. His forehead touched the cool wall, and he remembered those moments when the sheep had swelled up, the way the wool had gradually pulled away from the skin as though any minute the creature would explode and its innards would spill out onto the men crowded into the room, or perhaps a miracle would occur and its body would lift up off the floor, take flight, and float out the window like a balloon.

In the months that followed, Menashe spoke often about what had happened in his grandparents' apartment. Rafael listened silently and promised not to take him there again. But then Menashe's memory made twists and turns and played tricks on him, and the next time he spoke with his father about the events, Rafael looked at him in astonishment and said, "But that was on Passover eve, not Rosh Hashanah eve!" And Menashe retreated into his silence.

His father told him the ancient legend of the Valley of Diamonds: "Once, in a faraway land near the Black Sea, there was a valley with a large cave full of wonderful diamonds. All the people in the world knew of this cave, and they all wanted to reach it, but there was a problem: Anyone who tried to enter was immediately attacked by the terrifying vultures who guarded the cave's entrance. One day a king commanded his servants, 'Go to the valley and bring me back the diamonds, otherwise I shall behead you!' The frightened servants went to consult a wise man, and the wise man told them, 'Take some fine sheep, slaughter them, and toss the pieces of sheep flesh into the cave.' And that is what the servants did: They killed some fine sheep, cut them up into pieces, and when they got to the cave in the Valley of Diamonds, they threw the meat in. The vultures smelled the meat and quickly went inside and ate the sheep flesh, which had diamonds stuck to it. Then the royal servants completed their mission as the wise man had advised: They went to the vultures' nests and found pieces of diamond in between the eggs. They brought the diamonds to their king, and the great king rewarded them handsomely, and they lived happily ever after."

Menashe looked at his father wide-eyed. He pictured everything: the cave and the diamonds and the vultures and the pieces of flesh and even the vultures' nests with eggs resting inside. But hard as he tried, he could not understand how his family could have thought to drag a sheep all the way to the apartment on Dizengoff Street and kill it in that little room. He refused to go back to his grandparents' apartment for a long time, and only after Rafael promised that all they would do there was eat french fries and hummus and have *ma'amul* cookies for dessert, did he agree to go.

# CHAPTER FOUR

# HONI

*1*

A WEEK BEFORE MENASHE'S MEETING with the lawyer, a soldier walked into his shop. He wasn't especially tall, he had black hair, round glasses, and a cell phone in his hand. Menashe took off his safety glasses and exclaimed ceremoniously, "Well hello, Honi *Ka*-dosh! To what do I owe the pleasure of your visit?"

Honi Kadosh stood there and said nothing. He gave me a sideways glance, leaned against the wall, shifted from one foot to the other, and finally took an envelope out of his bag and handed it to the jeweler. Menashe opened the envelope, unfolded the letter, and studied it. His face turned red.

"It is clear to me," Menashe said after considering for a moment, "that your father did not send you here by chance. He knew exactly what he was doing. After all, he could have sent a courier. Amiram Kadosh can afford a courier, can't he?

So he wants to throw me out of my shop and open a boutique hotel. And it's just me standing in your way. That's the thorn in your side, my measly little 130 square feet?"

Honi lowered his head and did not answer, but a moment later he looked up with a furious, distant look in his eyes.

"I know exactly what's going on with this letter," Menashe continued. "Your father probably told you, 'I want you to take this letter to Menashe Salomon, show him who's boss.' Your father does not forget and he does not forgive. As long as his father Shayu, of blessed memory, was alive, everything was fine. But then Kadosh decides he wants to settle the score with me, as the family representative. I pay him rent every month, but that's not good enough for him. Three thousand shekels a month! All he had to do was wait for me to die so he could get his hands on my shop. But no, he's impatient—he wants to get ahead of nature!"

Honi looked down again, and Menashe went on:

"This business I built, all the customers I've been gathering with tweezers for forty-five years—none of that interests him. So he writes a nice letter and sends his son. And why does he do that? Because he wants you to learn that you can't be sentimental in business. I'm willing to bet that's what he told you: 'You can't be sentimental in business.' Oh, yes, I know Kadosh like the back of my hand. Well then, Hanan, you go tell your father that Menashe Solomon does not give up without a fight, and that I will use any means available to me. And tell him one more thing, tell him that if your grandfather Shayu, my father's cousin, were alive today, he would be ashamed of his son."

Menashe was the third shopkeeper Honi Kadosh had visited that day in the building on Plonit Alley. The first was Gruzovski, an optician who had rented space from Shayu since he came from Poland in the 1950s. When Honi walked in, he found the optician sitting at his table screwing a lens into a brown frame. Honi said hello and Gruzovski glanced at him and went back to his work.

"Mr. Gruzovski, my father sent me to see you," Honi said. When there was no response, he added, "He wants to know if you got the letter."

The optician put his screwdriver down, picked up the glasses frame and examined it from all sides. Then he gripped it, twisted it this way and that, and bent it a little more until he was satisfied.

Honi tried again. "So...did you get the letter?" He began to wonder if the optician was deaf.

When Gruzovski finished his work, he eyed the dark-skinned young man in his shop. He motioned for Honi to come closer. Honi approached and put his face near the optician's. When the two men's faces were very close, the optician narrowed his lips, and before Honi realized what was happening, a glob of thick spit flew out of Gruzovski's mouth. He pulled back in disgust. He was about to walk out but thought better of it. He felt humiliated. What would he tell his father—that the old optician had spat on him and chased him out of the shop? He swallowed his pride and asked again, in a slightly trembling voice, "Did you get the letter or not?"

When he realized he would not get an answer, he turned to leave. As he reached for the door handle, he finally heard

Gruzovski screech, "You tell your father that I will drop down and die before I leave this shop! You tell him that, in exactly those words. Let him come and drag me out—he won't be able to. I will burn this shop down and die in it before he gets it from me! You tell him that."

Honi slammed the door behind him and went to drink some fresh-squeezed orange juice at a nearby kiosk, to calm his nerves. Then he went back to the building and tramped over to Mr. Laniado's newspaper store.

Laniado was an old Syrian Jew from Aleppo—a Halabi—who had rented the shop twenty years earlier when he retired from his previous job. "Shop" was a generous description of his domain: Laniado's nook was a narrow passageway that at one point had connected the street to the building's courtyard. In this slim cavity, no wider than four feet and no longer than six, the elderly Laniado sat hunched over on a bench with his walking stick on the floor and both hands on the stick just above head height. He sat there all day long, dozing off in between bouts of shouting. What did he shout about? About all the swindlers who parked their cars on the sidewalk right outside his shop and left them there while they ran errands. Any driver who did this lived to regret it the moment he stilled his engine, when the old Halabi jumped out of his alcove and waved his stick at the car, yelling, "Swindler! Swindler!"

Honi remembered the newspaper seller as a child, and he had seemed like an old man even then. He remembered being afraid of Laniado's furious attacks and the cane he shook at the "swindlers." To be on the safe side, Honi did not go into the shop but stood just outside, taking half a step forward and placing one foot in the alcove, which had a permanent musty odor of old newspapers.

Mr. Laniado sat on the bench as usual, his head drooping slightly forward between his shoulders, his hands perched on the cane's carved wood handle. Upon sensing the uninvited guest, the Halabi opened his eyes. He quickly shut one of them and kept monitoring Honi with one red eye.

"How are you, Mr. Laniado?" Honi asked with a wary smile.

The Halabi shook his head. "Praise God, it could be much worse."

"Listen, my father sent me to see you. First of all, he wants to wish you *Shana Tovah*. And second, he wants to know if you got the letter he sent a few days ago."

"Letter?" One thin tooth was visible between Laniado's lips. "What letter?"

"This letter." Honi took a copy from his bag and gave it to the Halabi.

Laniado took the letter with a trembling hand, held it close to his eyes, and began reading. "This is a very nice letter. Very nice indeed," he summed up with a grin and handed the paper back to Honi.

"Did you read what this says, Mr. Laniado?"

The old man nodded, still grinning, his tooth peeking out between his lips.

"So you understand that you need to leave the shop very soon?"

"I understand. I completely understand," Laniado answered.

"And you understand that they're building a hotel here, and there won't be any shops anymore? Do you understand that, Mr. Laniado?"

"Yes," said the Halabi. "Now you understand this: I'm an old man. No one buys papers here anymore. Ever since your grandfather Shayu died, I've just been waiting for your father to do something with this building. No shops? Fine. So instead of sitting around here, I'll sit around at home. That's that."

Honi nodded. He wished the old man a happy new year, backed out of the shop, and slipped away in relief. Now all he had left was the jeweler.

## 2

After work I said goodbye to Menashe and left the shop. I walked up King George Street and turned toward the Great Synagogue. I stopped at Phantom, the café at 108 Allenby Street, and ordered a slice of poppy seed cake. I walked into the back to a secluded area behind shelves of platters piled high with baked goods. There were a few tables there, with copies of the free daily newspaper, and an oval Formica counter with some round barstools. I sat down at the counter and looked at my face in the mirror on the wall. The waitress came over with my cake. I glanced at the pictures from the social justice protests on the front page of the paper: tents pitched on Rothschild Boulevard, people sleeping on the small grassy areas between the paths, others playing guitar or taking part in debates, and scenes from the massive demonstration, with politicians confronted by social activists.

There were a handful of customers in the café. In one corner, an enormous man sat at a table with his wife. His stamp collection was spread out on the table, and his huge stomach spilled so far out that he could barely lean forward. He reached out and picked up a rectangular stamp, held it up to his glasses and widened his eyes as he examined it. His wife wore slippers, and her pink socks were visible under her pant cuffs. Gray roots showed in her red dyed hair, and she had one hand on a shopping trolley.

The couple told the two men at the next table that they had recently sold their apartment on Allenby and bought a new five-bedroom with a big balcony in Ness Tziona, which they would be moving into soon. They said there was a train to Tel Aviv not far from their new place, and although they wouldn't be able to come to Phantom every day anymore, they would try to visit at least twice a week. "For the life of me I can't understand those kids sleeping in tents on Roth- schild," the woman said. "You'd think someone was forcing them to live in Tel Aviv!"

The man looked up, observed his wife, and went back to his stamps.

While I ate my cake, I took out my notebook and started going over my notes. A minute later I caught sight of a familiar face in the doorway: Honi Kadosh. He stood between the cakes and the *bourekas*, scanning the other customers, and I heard him order a cheese-and-spinach *boureka*. He recognized me only when he sat down two seats away at the counter. In the fluorescent lights, I could see his corporal ranks and the blue ribbons indicating he was doing his military service at the army radio station, Galei Zahal. There was a glimmering pin on his shirt pocket with the station's logo.

Honi put his iPhone on the counter and pressed a button, and all the apps glowed on the screen. Now the device—and not just I—knew of his presence here at Phantom, a pastry shop that had somehow managed to stand still for the past five decades and survive against all odds in modish Tel Aviv.

"I didn't know you hung out here," I said.

"Cool place, eh?" He seemed slightly embarrassed.

"Yeah. It always feels like a '50s movie."

"I know, it's amazing. You're not drinking?"

"I'm waiting for my mint tea."

"Hot tea, in August?!"

"I love drinking tea, winter or summer."

"Me, I need caffeine, and lots of it."

"Tired?"

"Unbelievably. I've barely slept for a week."

"How come? Guard duty?"

"No, I don't do a lot of guard duty. Once a month, if that."

"So, Honi...Is that your real name?"

"No, it's a nickname my sister gave me, and it stuck. My real name is Hanan, which just sounds too old."

"I guess your sister thought you were like Honi Ha'Meagel, that guy from the legend who drew the circle?"

"She used to make fun of me when I was little, because I was always afraid there would be a drought. And one day our teacher told us the legend of Honi the Circle Maker, and how there was a terrible drought, and he drew a circle around himself in the dust and swore to God that he wouldn't move until it rained."

"If I remember correctly, it worked, didn't it?"

"It worked a little too well—it started raining cats and dogs! So then Honi started praying for the rain to stop. He drove God nuts. It kind of reminds me of King Midas, you know? He wished for everything he touched to turn to gold, and when his wish came true he ended up being the poorest person on earth, of course. A blessing that becomes a curse."

Honi sat silently for a while, and I asked, "So what's up?"

"I'm working on a special program. I've been lying awake at night thinking about it."

"I'm surprised you have time to put together a program. Isn't everything crazy with all the protests?"

"It's crazy for the soldiers who do the news. But I'm not in news, I'm in documentary, and things are never crazy in our department. Except on Holocaust Day and Remembrance Day, of course."

We both snickered.

"I produce *Up Close and Personal*—do you know the show? We're not that busy right now, so I asked my boss if I could do a special on the social justice protests. Something more in-depth than a two-minute news item."

"Wait, whose side are you on here—the protesters' or the landlords'?"

"Very funny, Tom."

"Well, your father owns a building in a prime location that must be worth millions."

"True, but I don't own any property myself. Kadosh owns the apartment I share with my sister. Our mom died last year, and I bet he'll marry some girl soon and they'll make me a little brother, and the new kid will inherit everything. But I don't care. I'm getting out of here as soon as I'm done with the army."

"Where are you going?"

"Maybe Berlin. My mother was Polish, so I have a European passport."

"Does your dad know about this plan?"

"Obviously not."

"So what exactly is going to be in your program?"

"I thought it would be good to do something on the rental market over the past century, you know. Interview landlords and tenants, figure out how they interact, what kind of relationship they have, then wrap up with the tent protests."

"Do you take part in the protests?" I wondered.

"I'm not allowed to. I'm a soldier."

"So? You could go in civilian clothes."

"Some kind soul would probably snitch on me and they'd kick me off the radio. What about you?"

"I go every Saturday evening."

"No, I mean, what are you writing?"

"How did you know I'm a writer?"

"I read an article of yours on a blog once," Honi said. "Something about a woman poet, I think."

"Sylvia Plath. That was when I was reading her obsessively. But I don't write articles anymore, otherwise I'll never finish my novel."

"You're writing a novel?! What's it about?"

"Let's just say there'll be a few things in there that you might recognize. It's called *The Diamond Setter.*"

"As in, the diamond setter who makes jewelry on Plonit Alley...?"

"More or less. It's based on real events, but I wouldn't call it autobiographical."

Honi grinned. "Wait, don't tell me. Your jeweler has an apprentice..."

"How did you guess?"

"Gut feeling. So basically, you're writing about Menashe."

"I'm writing about a jewelry shop that's been around since 1950. One day the jeweler's landlord turns up and threatens to throw him out so he can build a boutique hotel."

"Funny."

"I'm not joking."

"Is that the whole novel?"

"Not exactly. There's a frame story. Or a depth story, really. It's about a famous blue diamond, and a Syrian who comes to Israel with part of the diamond in his pocket and ends up in Jaffa."

"Wait, are you writing about that guy who tried to get in on Nakba Day?"

"He didn't just try, he really did get in."

"Where is he now? Back in Syria?" Honi tried to remember the newspaper story.

"That's the whole question. I mean, in my book it's the question. In real life they sent him back to Syria."

"He was a teacher, right? A guy in his thirties?"

"Yes, but in my story he's different. Younger. And cute."

"What's he doing in Jaffa?"

"Searching for his roots. His grandparents were born there. And he doesn't come empty-handed."

"Right, he brings the blue diamond, you said that."

"Exactly. The diamond is real, by the way. The Ottoman sultan gave it to Gracia, Menashe's great-aunt. Do you know what she was in Damascus?"

"Refresh my memory . . . ?"

"She was what they call a chanteuse."

"Chanteuse—what's that? Like, a singer?"

"Something like that. More like a kind of Arabic geisha. I thought you were related, aren't you? I mean, your dad and Menashe?"

"Distant relatives. There's been some kind of family rift for decades. I've heard stories about the crazy Salomons ever since I can remember."

"So I guess you know that your grandfather, Shayu, was really close to his cousin Rafael, Menashe's father."

"Of course. But what made you want to write about all this?"

"What do you mean?"

"Well, I've interviewed a lot of authors for the radio. And if there's one thing I've learned, it's that a good story starts with some obsession of the writer's. I mean, it doesn't matter what you're writing about, as long as you have a passion for your topic, your plot, your characters."

"That's true."

"So where's your passion here, Tom? It can't be the diamond."

"Why not?"

"Because you're not really interested in that. Or in the shop and all those stories about jewelry. All that stuff Menashe tells you about the blue diamond—there's no way you take that seriously."

"It doesn't matter whether or not I take it seriously, Honi. Maybe it's all just superstition. It doesn't make much difference. What really interests me is all the events that one little gemstone caused. The way it affected the family, my characters. After all, even if the stories aren't true, you can't deny that they led to all sorts of things happening—in Syria and in Israel."

"What things?"

"Aha! That's exactly what I'm writing about. Intrigues, affairs, voyages, betrayals. Secrets and lies, as they say."

"What secrets?"

"Let's not get into that now."

Honi laughed. "Seriously? You're not going to tell me? You are publishing this novel, aren't you?"

"All in good time."

"Fine." He glanced at his phone. After a pause, he noticed the paper next to me on the counter. I passed it to him and he looked through the commentary pieces. "Useless," he said, and handed it back.

He struck me as precocious. There was something almost elderly in the way he pronounced judgment on the newspaper, and I was discomfited by the discrepancy between the assertion and his boyish face, with his thick lips and almond eyes and long eyelashes. I didn't say anything. Maybe I needed to get to know him better.

We paid and left the café together.

## 3

That evening, Honi went into the bathroom in his apartment, locked the door so his sister couldn't come in, and took a picture of himself in the mirror with his phone. He deleted the picture and took another one, with his shirt off. The flash obscured his face, but you could clearly see his arms and stomach, chest, small nipples, and a slightly blurred mark across his abdomen, a scar from appendix surgery when he was four. He uploaded the picture to Grindr, his latest addiction, where it showed up first in the series of pictures on the screen. That was because users' pictures were arranged by order of distance, from near to far, and Honi was closest to himself—at least geographically. Once the picture was uploaded, other men's images popped up all around it. He was Honi the Circle Maker.

Honi left the bathroom and sat down in the kitchen, where his sister Ayelet was making dinner: scrambled eggs with mushrooms, tomato salad with lots of basil and cilantro, and toast. The table was piled with little cups of fresh, quivering *malabi* pudding covered with a bright purple layer of pomegranate juice and garnished with crushed pistachios. Honi was tempted to grab a cup, but he knew they were for the Shack, and Ayelet would be angry if her brother ate into her inventory.

She asked him to make sure he paid the municipal and water bills and reminded him they had to call a plumber to check if there was a leak somewhere, because the last couple of water bills had been abnormally high. "It's probably because of your baths," she observed.

"Why do you say that?"

"You fill the tub twice a day. Does that seem reasonable to you? And in a drought year?"

"It's always a drought year in this country, remember? And anyway, I don't tell you how to bathe. I've always taken two baths a day and it had no effect on our bills. So why now?"

Ayelet was chopping onions. She wiped her eyes with her sleeve and didn't say anything.

After a couple of minutes, Honi got up and went to his room. He checked on his phone to see who was close, who was far, and who was even farther, until the pictures disappeared around a bend.

For months now, Honi's gaze had been fixed not on trees or people or sidewalks or the road, but on his phone, which offered up an entire world: countless opportunities, unrealized desires, disappointments foretold, and dreams that would never come true unless he suddenly discovered an extraordinary reserve of courage within himself. He did not believe for a second that could happen.

He was location-based. Anywhere he went, someone out there knew he was here and not there. That someone was not God or an invisible entity. That someone—like a voice from on high making anonymous pronouncements—was merely an algorithm programmed to do one thing: to know.

The algorithm knew everything about Honi, or at least the most important thing: the precise point in space where he was located at any given moment. It was always hovering above him and could always testify, when needed, that he was there and not somewhere else. The algorithm was his alibi for a little sin he had not yet committed, but it was also the guarantee that this little sin would one day come to be. When? Maybe today, maybe next week. Maybe never.

## 4

On the day Honi decided to produce a radio show about the social protest movement, he went to the head of the documentary department at the station to get permission. He was sure there would be an enthusiastic response, but to his great disappointment he met with firm refusal. The department head, a man of about sixty with gray hair and a faint mustache, claimed the topic was already being covered ad nauseam on the station's news programs and was "too overdone." He encouraged Honi to focus on his weekly interviews for *Up Close and Personal*, to keep training new soldiers, and to prepare for the intensive programming on Holocaust Day and Remembrance Day, which they'd need to start working on in a couple of months.

But Honi insisted. "We have to do a special on the protests! We can't just leave it for the news. It's not something you can cover in a two-minute segment. This movement is radically changing the country!"

Corporal Honi Kadosh's claims fell on deaf ears. But he didn't give up. He quietly lay in wait for his chance, which arrived a week later when the presenter of the weekly literature program announced she was going overseas for a few weeks. The department head told Honi, "All right. If the station commander authorizes it, you have my go-ahead for the special."

After a few more bureaucratic delays, all the necessary authorizations came through and Honi started outlining

the program. He narrowed down a list of suitable inter-
viewees, spoke to leading activists, hung around the tents
on Rothschild Boulevard, and consulted other producers at
the station, who referred him to some economists and other
academics.

When we met after work one day, in what had become
our regular café, Honi came straight from Rothschild Boulevard abuzz with new ideas. He had an audio recorder and
a microphone imprinted with the station logo. When we sat
down behind the *bourekas* and cake platters to devour our
pastries—walnut cake for me, spinach *boureka* for Honi—he
took a few printed pages out of his bag and handed them to
me. It was the opening segment he'd written for his show.
I scanned the first couple of pages and was surprised by
Honi's astuteness. I knew he was an intelligent young man,
but I never imagined he could be so articulate, or that he had
anything meaningful to say. "I'm wondering if you're allowed
to say all these things on army radio..."

Honi laughed. "No one's going to hear this show anyway." But his eyes were serious.


That night we went to Shami Bar. After the first drink, I
bought Honi another, and I let him buy the third round so he
wouldn't feel like a kid being taken out. It was one thirty a.m.
when we left. Honi asked if I wanted to drop by the radio station, which was only a few blocks away, and I agreed.

We walked down Yefet Street and turned left on Yehuda
Ha'Yamit. We kept walking until the Galei Zahal building
emerged on our left. Honi pressed a button outside the main

door, and two seconds later there was a buzz and he pushed it open. We were welcomed by bright fluorescent lights and a redheaded soldier seated at a desk with her rifle propped in front of her.

"What's up, Stav?" Honi asked her.

"It's all good," she said. "Time's flying tonight, actually. Who's this?" She gestured at me.

"This is Tom, he's working on the special with me."

"You're working on the special this late at night?"

"I'm working around the clock."

"Got it. So d'you want to take him in?"

"Just for a few minutes. I need to pick up something I left in the office."

She gave me a sideways glance. "And you need backup?"

"He's afraid to wait outside on his own in Jaffa at night," Honi said. He gently stroked my shoulder.

"Okay." She grinned. "Whatever you say."

"You're a cutie, Stav," Honi said.

"Look who's talking." She giggled.

We went in.

On the way upstairs I saw pictures of famous radio announcers hanging on the walls. The rooms I glimpsed as I walked behind Honi looked like ordinary army base rooms, not at all like a radio station. There were ugly Formica tables in advanced stages of decay, dirty floor tiles, messy surfaces, clothes strewn around, binders on the floor, pieces of paper, and cigarette butts everywhere. Honi grabbed his binder and said he wanted to show me something, so we went one floor down. We walked into a random office, which turned out to lead to another office, which was being renovated.

The room was dark and completely wrecked, and shadows flickered on the whitewashed walls. We could see the lights of Jaffa through the empty window frames.

We stood next to each other looking out. Honi held his arm out and took a picture of us with his phone. I let him post it on Instagram, but then he relented to my pleas and put the phone back in his pocket. And then, only then, he finally surrendered to my embrace and tilted his head up slightly until our eyes met. I kissed him.

## 5

After his mother died, Amiram Kadosh suggested to his son and daughter that they move into their grandparents' old apartment, on a little street that intersected with Rothschild Boulevard. He promised the place would be "like new," and they jumped at the rare find.

Amiram hired workers, who knocked down the walls in the old apartment, overhauled the ancient plumbing and electrical systems, installed electric blinds, pulled up the old floor tiles and replaced them with satiny ceramic ones, and built two bedrooms separated by a living room with a balcony. Ayelet got the big room because she was older. There was no debate.

Honi and Ayelet had been in the apartment for two years and nothing seemed to have changed: Honi was still a soldier, Ayelet was still studying jewelry making and running the Shack, a popular juice and grilled-cheese stand.

When Honi came home that night, he found his sister watching TV in the living room. He silently poured himself a glass of lemonade and sat down next to her.

She turned to look at him. "What's the problem, Honi?"

"Nothing."

"How was your day?"

"Fine."

"How much longer do you have left to serve? Is it six months?"

"Eight."

"Right. Almost done."

"Yeah."

"So what's the problem?"

He told her about the jeweler and the other tenants in the building on Plonit Alley, and about the letter their father had sent them all.

Ayelet seemed surprised. "He didn't tell me anything about that. Are you sure?"

"Yes, I saw the letter."

"Just like that? He just told them they have to move out by Rosh Hashanah?"

"Yep. Because none of them have a lease."

"Nothing at all?"

"You know what Grandpa was like. He didn't mess around with that stuff."

"True," Ayelet admitted. "But it's not like Kadosh." She, too, called their father by his last name, never "Dad." "So how did they respond?"

"The crazy old guy from the newspapers is happy to get out. The optician is threatening to burn down the store and kill himself. And Menashe..."

"What about him?"

"He's threatening a lawsuit."

"That'll cost him a ton of money."

"Unless he wins."

"It could take years. Does he have the money and the nerves for that kind of ordeal?"

"I don't know. Hey, did you ever hear about the robbery at his place? An armed robbery?"

"Yeah, Kadosh told me about it once. But they hardly took anything, did they?"

"They took a diamond."

"One diamond?"

"Not just any diamond. It's a famous diamond." And he told her what he knew about the robbery and the blue diamond.

"What made you think of that now?"

"Because the whole thing sounds fishy to me," Honi said.

"What does?"

"Everything. What he says about the diamond and the bad luck, and all the other stuff he tells everyone. It's like it's all in the past, it's all happened already, but I feel like there's something unresolved. It sounds to me like Dad's trying to take revenge on him now."

"On who?"

"On Menashe."

"But you just told me he's kicking the other tenants out, too. Maybe he has no choice, maybe the municipality is forcing him to do it, did you think about that? Why would you think it's revenge?"

"You know him," Honi argued. "He couldn't care less about most things in the world, so why is he acting like this now?"

"Well, why?"

"I don't know."

"Are you becoming a detective, Honi?"

"What do you mean?"

"You sit there at the jeweler's, you come home and sit here brooding about all the stuff he tells you, God knows what schemes you're up to. I know you, you're not just talking. I'm sure you have a plan."

"I don't have any plan."

"That's good to hear, because listen to me: You're getting too involved. Leave Kadosh alone, give him some credit. He's not a bad person, at the end of the day. And you know he's had a difficult year since Mom died."

Honi sat quietly for a moment. Ayelet turned back to the TV.

"Do you know anything about what happened all that time ago between the families in Damascus?" he asked.

"Kadosh told me," Ayelet answered without looking at him. "So I know."

"Don't you think there's a connection?"

"Between what and what?"

"Between what happened there and Kadosh's behavior now."

"I told you what I think, Honi. I think you're looking for mysteries where there are none. You're wasting your time."

Honi didn't answer. After a few minutes he got up, went to his room, and shut the door.

CHAPTER FIVE

# ME

1

I STARTED WRITING WHEN I WAS SEVENTEEN. As a young boy I
sang and danced and acted in plays. At twelve I successfully
auditioned for a part in *The Little Prince*, and for several weeks
I sat on the kitchen counter with my back to the window
every day and memorized my lines with my mother. Mom
stood there facing me with her feet slightly apart, one hand
on my knee and the other holding the book with pictures of
the prince. We read every single word together.

I had blond hair, and I loved the theater because it gave
me the chance to wear outlandish costumes. I loved the smell
of the auditorium before the audience came in, the heat given
off by the big spotlights, the red seats, and the carpeting
after the vacuum cleaner left delicate stripes in it. I loved the
pastrami-and-tomato sandwiches at the snack bar, the instant
coffee, the Tuv Taam candy bars my dad bought me during

long rehearsal days. I had braces, and every time I bit into the chocolaty mounds, most of the chocolate got stuck in the wires and was impossible to lick off.

At around the same age, my parents made me take piano lessons. My teacher, Uri, was a gifted and frighteningly meticulous young man of about thirty. He had straight brown hair, wore glasses with an old-fashioned frame that made him look older and slightly dour, and his long arms were covered with dense hair all the way to his wrists. Uri agreed to take me on because he said I had talent, and that if I practiced diligently for seven hours a day, I could one day become a professional pianist.

With the high point of his career already behind him, Uri knew he would never be an internationally known pianist. He handpicked his pupils, mostly musicology students, and I was his only twelve-year-old. Lessons were held at his home, in a room that looked out onto a small garden with ficus trees, where wagtails hopped around the grass in autumn. I practiced Bach, took short breaks to go to the bathroom, and came back for the second part of the lesson, which was devoted to theory. As I played, the metronome ticked on my left, and Uri's soft, deep voice accompanied me with a low hum on my right. Every so often he reached out and flipped through the music book. At some point in the lesson, usually toward the end, the apartment door would open and Uri would hold his head up slightly, raise his eyebrows and then furrow them, as though he were remembering something very distant and worrying.

But the door to his room was always shut and no one dared disturb us during the lessons. Uri would write down my homework in pencil, with clear handwriting, then walk me to the door and wish me a good evening. Every time I came back for the next lesson and sat down beside him on the piano bench, he would report that Hermine had asked that I put the toilet seat up before I used the bathroom. I promised I'd remember, but Hermine—his girlfriend, whom I never saw—was not pleased.

Uri was also not pleased. Not with my progress, and not with the number of hours I devoted to practice every day. He reminded me that I should appreciate the fact that he'd chosen me from among all my peers, that he'd turned down students older than me and no less talented. He promised again that if I only practiced enough, I could be a professional pianist and play overseas. The potential contained in the word "overseas" made me sit down and practice for three hours every day for a whole week.

A few years earlier, my parents had gone on a tour of "Classical Europe." My father was thirty and my mother twenty-seven. They deposited the three of us with my grandparents and set off for France, England, Holland, and Belgium.

On the first day, I cut my finger with a utility knife. Grandma, who had seen a thing or two in her life, let out a curse and quickly bandaged my finger. The cut was deep and quite long, and all the frustration, despair, and anger at my parents for going overseas were embodied in my screams of pain. Grandma complained about the noise. "You're the oldest son," she said. "You have to be a role model for your siblings. How will they learn an example from you?"

I gritted my teeth. The blood oozed out of my finger and pooled in the bandage, until it finally clotted. The bandaged cut kept pulsating like a little heart in the middle of my finger. I went back to my room, sat down on my bed, and held a shoe box pierced with holes. I carefully lifted the lid and peeked inside. I was hit by the smell of silkworms and gnawed mulberry leaves, and the faint odor of a couple of pupae that had already formed in the corners of the box.

I shut my eyes and tried to imagine "overseas" and the silent, wild expanses that were engulfing my parents at that very moment. I knew they were very far away, but it was hard for me to envision the vastness of the distance. Farther than their workplaces, farther than Grandma and Grandpa's house, farther even than Haifa or Metula. They had taken their passports and crossed the border, and were now wandering amid a frightening overseas territory that was the very opposite of everything I knew.

When it was finally time for them to come home, I drove to the airport with Grandma and Grandpa. A large, silent glass wall stood between the passengers returning from overseas and the welcomers. And there—beyond the glass pane that towered from floor to ceiling—I saw them and I stuck up my still-bandaged finger so that they would be alarmed when they saw me and feel sorry for their firstborn. They blew kisses and smiled guiltily.

In those faraway days of my late childhood, all of Uri's talk about overseas and his promises of the international concert halls where I would perform aroused in me mostly dim fear. Eventually the inevitable moment arrived. When it did, I was sitting at the piano, as always. To my left was the metronome, whose single arm was clasped like a stuck zipper.

Again Uri said that Hermine asked that I lift the seat before urinating. I told him I'd decided to stop taking piano lessons.

The room fell silent, and after a moment he lifted the piano lid and played a Chopin prelude.

When I got home, I sat down with my parents and told them what I'd done.

"But Uri says you have a gift!" Dad exclaimed.

"But we just bought you a piano with all your bar mitzvah money!" Mom said.

I looked at them and thought about Uri. I imagined Hermine yelling at him because his pupil wouldn't lift the toilet seat. Why had I done that? When I think about it today, I suppose it was my sheepish way of leaving tracks in that apartment. A territorial marking aimed at Hermine. I disobeyed her. I created tension between my piano teacher and his invisible, imperious lover. And perhaps there was another explanation, too: In those faraway days when I was saying farewell to my childhood and beginning life as a young male, my refusal to obey Hermine's will was also an act of resistance against that simple yet critical demand made of every man: that he put up the toilet seat.

In the end, nothing could change my mind. I held steadfast in my decision, and I never went to Uri's apartment again.


A month later, *The Little Prince* was performed in front of two hundred people. The audience cheered for the blond boy who traveled across the stage wearing white and silver, with a golden crown perched on his head. All the other actors were two or three years older than me. A lanky boy whose face was covered with acne played the part of the rose, and I held a watering can and watered him. The audience laughed and cheered for several minutes. That same day, in his room in Ramat Aviv, in the shade of the ficus trees, with birds chirping in the background, Uri put a gun to his temple and pulled the trigger. Blood spurted on the Chopin scores and on the metronome. The birds startled at the sound and fled the garden with a terrified flutter of wings.

# 2

All these years the same memory has always come back to me: Uri sits in his room at the piano with one of his students next to him. His ears are pricked up. When the door slams, he knows Hermine has come home.

He met Hermine shortly after she enlisted in the army. He was ten years older than her, and his career as a pianist was already over. At first they met every week, then twice a week, until one day she turned up at his apartment with a white rose between her teeth and a letter in her hand. Uri read the letter Hermine had written him and realized he was lost.

The ten years stood between them like an abyss. He was in love with her like an adolescent but resented her for the age difference. And more than resentment, he felt that those years were his fault, that they were his mark of disgrace. Over and over again he thought back to himself as a ten-year-old boy sitting at the piano, when she was just being born. He thought about his bar mitzvah, when she was a three-year-old toddler. About his first kiss, the first time he fell in love — all these had happened when she was a little girl.

But as their relationship deepened, Hermine told him about her adventures and the affairs she'd had with older men before she met him, and it gradually dawned on Uri that in fact she was far more experienced than he was. His own boyhood had been devoted entirely to music, and even later he was no Don Juan. From then on the tables were turned: Uri thought about her first kiss when he'd traveled to give his first concert in Vienna. About her desperate crush on her math teacher while Uri sat alone in his room practicing Satie's "Gymnopédies." About the twenty-six-year-old basketball player who was her first "official" boyfriend just as Uri was rehearsing with a Greek contralto he would accompany on Schubert's *Winterreise*.

And then the jealousy started. She put on her military uniform every morning and went to her office in the Tel Aviv base, where she was surrounded by male soldiers. Her officers were twenty-three or twenty-four years old. Sometimes she stayed on the base for night shifts. She went on excursions and field assignments up north and down south, and who knew how many burly officers surrounded her then? And worst of all: She began planning her post-army trip.

Hermine talked to Uri a lot about "overseas." In the evenings she waited tables and saved every shekel for her trip. She was planning to visit a high school friend who had already finished her army service and was working in Germany with a Ministry of Defense delegation. Uri could not leave his work for more than a couple of weeks, and they agreed that after Hermine visited her friend in Germany, they would meet in Madrid and travel together. Uri had dreamed for years of seeing Velázquez's portraits of dwarves at the Prado Museum, and Hermine had no particular preference for where they should meet — as long as it was in Europe.

Hermine was still officially living with her parents in Kfar Saba, but in reality she slept at Uri's place every night. She would come to his apartment after her army shift, always careful to be quiet and not disturb his lessons. She held a special grudge against her lover's youngest pupil, who never put the seat up when he peed.

Since I never saw her, I began to wonder if Hermine even existed at all. Perhaps she was a cover story for something, or perhaps a ghost, a figment of the piano teacher's imagination? But no, it was clear that Hermine was flesh-and-blood, one hundred percent woman. The evidence was that she was driving Uri insane. He became restless almost all the time. The musical pieces that had been his support and comfort lost their purpose. He played less well, taught less well, and his thoughts were mired in the space between him and Hermine, or rather between Hermine and the world.

Uri soon began developing an aversion to "overseas" — any overseas. He imagined that his beloved was about to conquer all these new grounds without him, and he almost forgot that he himself had visited the same destinations several times and had even performed in them, conquering a few hearts. All that was no longer relevant to Uri. He was filled with anxiety about the future. Once he tried to talk to Hermine and tell her honestly how jealous he was, how her past adventures drove him mad, but she brushed him off. After that, he said nothing. But the future, all the experiences and discoveries awaiting her—how could he live with them?

Her army discharge was approaching. The wagtails had departed for autumn lands a few months earlier, new birds had arrived, the trees were blossoming, their fruits blushed and fell to the ground, the metronome slammed its arm from side to side with a precision that was somehow desperate. Uri turned over another page in the calendar and found that Hermine's trip was imminent.

During the two weeks preceding their temporary separation, Uri's anxiety grew so great as to overshadow everything. But he maintained his composure in Hermine's presence. When they stood together at the airport, he looked at her cute suitcase, at the backpack strapped to her shoulders, and scratched his head. Then he leaned over and planted a long kiss deep in her neck.

An hour later, when he sat in his car and looked up at the sky, he saw a plane take off over the clouds. He thought it was her plane but wasn't sure. Only then did he understand that he hadn't dared talk with Hermine about the things she would or would not do while she was far away from him. He went home and got into bed. He waited for a long time until she phoned to say she'd landed safely in Berlin, her friend had picked her up at the airport, and they were now drinking tea in the friend's apartment. In the evening they were going out to a party.

Uri did not sleep all night, or the next night. Three days after she left, he sat down at dawn and wrote her a letter, and that afternoon he sent it to her friend's address in Berlin.

*My Love,*

*I'm trying to write this letter partly to formulate and understand myself what I feel and what I'm going through. After you left, I realized that it bothers me that we didn't have a face-to-face talk about your trip, in terms of the Topic, which is taboo between us. That conversation didn't happen, and in the end I gave up on the idea and convinced myself that maybe it was better that way. But now I think that it could have been better if we had talked. By the way, I have no idea now what I would say to you if we had the talk. It's a complicated subject, after all, and it's hard for me to imagine what the conversation would bring up.*

*Anyway, now you're there. And I'm telling you again how happy I am that you went and that you're having fun. I certainly know how exciting the city you're in can be—Berlin is such a fascinating place in so many ways. And when you think about it, it won't be that long before we meet—in fact, we'll be together in Spain in less than four weeks!*

*Yet still I'm writing to you because I feel there is some sort of situation here that I am part of, but it's a given, it was handed to me this way, and I have to deal with it and that's it. And while sometimes I'm completely at peace with this story, there are times when I really lose my mind. My imagination works overtime. And then I get upset and I invest unbelievable efforts to calm myself.*

*Is that despicable? Maybe. I would like to be able to be indifferent (and in many ways I really am), but I can't help the fact that sometimes it doesn't work out that way. And then I feel*

*bad about this difficulty I have, and then I can hate myself in
a really horrifying way, and eventually, even if I manage to
get through these hard feelings, I feel completely exhausted, after
clawing myself out...*

*Now I'm getting a bit startled by what I've written to you
here. But I think it's natural. There is something frightening
about opening up like this. But I feel close enough to you to
write these words.*

*I love you,*
*Uri*

Hermine wrote back immediately:

*Sweetheart,*

*First thing, I want you to know that nothing you feel could
be despicable to me, and I'm trying to take your feelings very
seriously.*

*I do try to be attentive to what you're going through, but
I realize now that I wasn't sensitive enough about this subject,
and that's okay, because we love each other and we're learning
how to communicate.*

*And if that is the case, then I apologize.*

*The truth is, I feel that we gave each other a lot of messages
even without having a direct conversation about "Will I or
won't I sleep with other men?" But maybe that's the convenient
way of looking at things for me. Either way, it's important for
me to let you know that I didn't consciously avoid talking about
the subject. I guess I just thought that kind of conversation*

was a little unnecessary. I will even say that I would prefer to talk to you about it directly, but I thought there were things better left unsaid. Because like you, I also don't know what that conversation would look like—and I'm also a little afraid to hurt you and to get hurt myself.

Anyway, I don't expect you to protect me from things that are hurtful or difficult for you—quite the opposite. There are things about our relationship that are so special and moving (and boundary pushing!) and it naturally also invites things that are difficult and sometimes unpleasant, for each of us. And so it's important that we talk. And just as I'm not asking you to suppress anything, I also hope I can learn to ask when I need to.

You have to remember that we have the space and time (at least until we die—after that, who knows?) to do anything we feel like, to expand and take off (in both senses...), because love is not dependent on anything and it's only really good when it's unexpected and uncompromising.

It's important for me that you also know that what you are describing is not alien to me, and of course I feel those things inside myself, but maybe in slightly different ways.

All I ask, and on this matter I think it's mainly your decision, is that you decide how you would like us to discuss the matter, what we're talking about and what we're not, about who and why, and that you be very clear with me, otherwise I don't know if I can take it.

Kisses, my love,
I love you very much, and I miss you,
This city is awaiting our shared visit.
Hermine

Uri read the letter over and over again. His thoughts stopped on "there were things better left unsaid" and wandered along a curvy line to the cosmic declaration concerning time and space. His eyes then roamed farther down and halted at the parentheses after "expand and take off (in both senses...)," as he murmured to himself over and over again her words about "love is only really good when it's unexpected and uncompromising."

In some respects Uri found Hermine's response very moving, and in others it provoked an anxiety he had never known before. He had read what Baudelaire had written about love in his journal: "Love greatly resembles an application of torture or a surgical operation. For even when two lovers love passionately and are full of mutual desire, one of the two will always be cooler or less self-abandoned than the other. He or she is the surgeon or the executioner; the other, the patient or victim. Do you hear these sighs—preludes to a shameful tragedy—these groans, these screams, these rattling gasps? Who has not uttered them, who has not inexorably wrung them forth? What worse sights than these could you encounter at an inquisition conducted by adept torturers? These eyes, rolled back like the sleepwalker's, these limbs whose muscles burst and stiffen as though subject to the action of a galvanic battery—such frightful, such curious phenomena are undoubtedly never obtained from even the most extreme cases of intoxication, of delirium, of opium-taking. The human face, which Ovid believed fashioned to reflect the stars, speaks here only of an insane ferocity, relaxing into a kind of death."

# 3

"How's the book coming along?" Menashe asked me about two weeks after he got the letter. Honi was in the shop with us, as he was almost every day before I left work with him. My uncle looked dejected, and perhaps he hoped a conversation with me would lift his spirits. He held a torch in one hand and a sawed ring with a tiny piece of gold on it in the other.

"Very well," I answered. "I'm writing about a piano teacher and his girlfriend at the moment."

"A piano teacher?" Menashe raised his eyebrows. "I had a customer once who was a piano teacher. A very impressive young man, but no self-confidence. It was something..." He was lost in thought for a moment. "But didn't you say you were writing about a jeweler?"

"That, too."

"I don't understand." He pressed a pedal with his foot, and the torch spat fire on the ring. "Who's your protagonist, then?"

"The jeweler is one of the protagonists. But there are lots of others."

"Why? Isn't the jeweler enough?"

"Yes and no. My jeweler is a slightly problematic character. He's an emotional cripple."

"Then you should write his character based on people you know in real life. Me, for example. Maybe I could be your inspiration? I want you to know that I have no problem with that. On the contrary."

"I do get inspiration from you, Menashe." I examined his expression carefully.

"Then maybe you should get more. I can teach you a lot: about jewelry and about human beings. Then you can sit down at home with all the things you learn from me, take what interests you, piece things together from here and there—the way I weld a piece of jewelry—and then you'll have a book."

"Yes..."

"I get what Menashe is trying to tell you," Honi interjected.

"Oh really, Honi?" I smiled. "You get it?"

"Yes. What he's really saying is this: Why is it, in literature nowadays, that everything has to be cut up and truncated, without one single straight plotline? Why do they always have to interrupt the chapters with laundry lists, bits of recipes, weather forecasts, horse races—"

"Well, look who we have here: Honi Kadosh, renowned literary critic!" I interrupted.

"I know what you're going to say in your defense," he went on. "That it's postmodern, it's the zeitgeist. I've heard all about that in my stories for the radio. You know what Picasso had to say about that?"

"I wasn't aware that Picasso lived in the postmodern era."

"Very funny. No, I mean something he said about cubism."

"What did he say, Hanan? Please enlighten me."

"He said, 'Before you make cubism, learn how to draw a horse.' Or in other words, what does a piano teacher have to do with a jewelry shop?!"

"Kiddos," Menashe intervened from behind his goggles, still blowing fire on a piece of jewelry, "I won't have any bickering in my shop. You two play nice."

Honi and I looked at each other and smiled sheepishly.

"The piano teacher has a lot to do with the jewelry shop," I answered. "In fact, he's closely related to the story I'm telling. But you'll have to be patient. Besides, Menashe, you need to take into account that the story is never exactly where you expect it to be."

Honi shrugged. The jeweler kept working quietly. After half an hour we said goodbye to Menashe and left the shop together, heading to Rothschild Boulevard.

# CHAPTER SIX

# ADELA

*1*

A FEW DAYS LATER, when Honi left his sister at the Shack and walked toward the jewelry shop, he noticed that scaffolding had been erected on the building next door, to support it when the bulldozers knocked down the walls. The street was quiet, for now, and the old building stood there indifferently, not knowing that very soon it would have to splutter and cough and put up a fight against massive forces of destruction. Would that be the fate of the jeweler's building, too?

At the end of the alley, before he turned onto King George Street, Honi ran straight into his father. Amiram Kadosh seemed happy to see his son. He even hugged Honi and mussed his hair. Honi pulled back a little but finally leaned his cheek in the hollow of his father's neck for a split second.

"Come on," Amiram said, pulling away and looking at Honi warmly. "I'll take you out for dinner."

They sat facing each other in a fish restaurant on the beach.

"What's new?" Amiram Kadosh asked.

"Nothing. Everything's fine."

"How's the army?"

"Okay."

"Hard?"

"No."

"How much longer do you have?"

"Less than eight months."

"It'll fly by. Have you thought about what you want to do afterward?"

"Maybe travel."

"Where?"

"Haven't decided."

"What about university?"

"I'm not in a hurry. I want to rest for a while."

"Are you tired?"

"No."

"Then why do you need to rest?"

Honi didn't answer. He looked down and scratched his chin.

"We're starting work on the building soon, and someone has to keep an eye on the workers," Amiram said. "I want you to take it on. You can come in the morning before you go to the radio, or afterward, whatever you prefer. As long as you show your face. The contractor I hired is a professional, but you still have to watch him like a hawk. I want him to know he's being checked up on. I'll explain to you exactly what to look out for. We have building plans, I'll give you the keys to all the new doors in the building."

"Are you destroying everything?"

"*You?* You mean, 'we.' Yes, we're destroying everything. But we're not allowed to touch the exterior walls because it's a preservation site. First they'll attach support rods, then they'll knock down the walls and destroy everything behind the façade, even though Gruzovski keeps threatening to set himself on fire in the shop. He acts like I care. Next time he opens his mouth about a fire, he'll get a visit from the police. Funny thing is, the crazy old Halabi, Laniado, is the only one who isn't making trouble. I think he's happy to get out."

"What about Menashe?"

"Why do you ask?"

"No reason."

"What do you think, Honi?"

"About what?"

"Menashe Salomon. You think he's going to make trouble?"

"I don't know."

"He didn't say anything to you?"

"No." Honi tried to keep calm. "Why?"

"Because you go there and visit him, you sit there, you drink coffee, you listen to all the crap he and that apprentice come up with." Amiram Kadosh raised his voice briefly but then pulled himself together. "A poor man's *Thousand and One Nights* they've got going on there. So I thought maybe he let you in on his plans."

"No."

"Glad to hear it. Because you listen to me: You're a big boy now. A soldier. I can't tell you where to go or who to talk to. But before you go believing any old thing someone tells you, you remember who Menashe Salomon is, and who his father was, and what happened with his father's aunt and my grandmother. Did I ever tell you about that?"

"No."

"Then I'll tell you now. Gracia, who was the sister of my grandmother, Hassiba, was a prostitute in Damascus. A high-class whore, but a whore. You hear me? A *boooor.* True, she had a high-up position in the Jewish community, because of all the rich Arabs she hung around with, who had good connections, and the Jews took advantage of that sometimes when they had to. Those Arabs bought Gracia with their gifts and their gold, and she slowly climbed up the ladder until she got to where she got. But it was a big embarrassment for the community. Even in Turkey they said all the Jewish women in Damascus were whores. Gracia didn't care, as long as she had money and gold and a big house. But one day things stopped going so well for her. She wasn't the beautiful young girl who'd turned everyone's heads anymore. So what did she do? She went and seduced Moussa, my grandfather, who was married to her own sister! And Grandfather, he was only a man, after all, only human. So he went with her, that whore. Whatever she asked for, he gave her. It took a while, but in the end it all came out. You couldn't keep secrets in that place. And a while after it came out, Grandma fell off the balcony. I mean, that was the official story. There were those who said she jumped off, and some people said there was a kind soul who gave her a push. And then my grandfather's brothers went at night and stood under Gracia's window and called for her to come out. Grandfather's oldest brother even brought a gun and threatened to kill her. There was a whole to-do, and Aunt Mona and her family stood by Gracia's side and defended her. And not just that: They bad-mouthed my grandfather and said he'd invented the whole thing, that he hadn't had an affair with Gracia at all, that he was the one who'd killed his wife. Ever since then, the two families have been enemies—except for your grandfather, Shayu, who always stayed friendly with Rafael and gave him a shop in the building for pennies. But I don't forget, and I don't forgive Rafael's family. I heard all the stories and I know exactly what went on there. Now do you understand why I have no sympathy for Menashe Salomon?"

Honi didn't answer.

"And don't think that was the end of it," Kadosh added. "After it was over, the jeweler's family stayed in touch with Gracia like nothing had happened. It was one thing for Mona, Rafael's mother, who was blind, because she was completely dependent on her husband. But him, Rafael—he turned out just like Gracia."

"How so?"

"There was a whole story, don't ask. If I told Rafael's family about it, I'd break up the family. But me, I don't care about that stuff. I just want Menashe out of the building and for the whole thing to be over. Don't want to hear anything more from Rafael Salomon or his family."

"Are you planning to give Menashe any kind of compensation?" Honi asked feebly.

"Are you crazy? Compensation? What about rent for all the years his father sat there in our building scratching his balls? He should be thankful I don't sue him! As far as I'm concerned, we're even now. I'm not asking him to compensate me for all those years his father sat there, so he shouldn't expect anything either. And just so you know, I'm doing this only out of respect for Grandpa Shayu, because I know he loved Rafael, despite everything. But enough is enough, you have to draw the line somewhere. Now look, Honi, I have a little assignment for you."

"For me?"

"Yes. I was thinking of sending Ayelet, but it's better that you do it. You remember Adela, Menashe's mother? Well, I want you to go see her and find out if they have any papers showing ownership of the shop, a lease in perpetuity, anything like that."

"But you said they don't have a lease."

"As far as I know, there's no lease. But I want to dig around a bit, be prepared for any eventuality, in case they take us to court. I don't want any nasty surprises."

"Why on earth would she tell me if there is or isn't a lease?" Honi wondered.

"I don't know. I have a feeling Menashe's cooking up a surprise for us. I'm not completely certain there wasn't some kind of agreement. So you need to go to his mother, ask how she is, have a chat with her, listen to her stories. After all, she remembers you from when you were little. And then you'll find the right moment to ask her about the shop, like you're just curious. If she says there's a lease, ask to see it, and take a picture with your phone for me. Okay?"

When they stood outside the restaurant, Amiram squeezed Honi's cheek and slapped his back. "Cheer up, Honi! Go find yourself a nice girl, have some fun. What are you doing walking around like you're in mourning the whole time? You mark my words, these are the best years of your life. And give my regards to Adela."

## 2

Adela lived in the north part of Dizengoff Street, in the same apartment Rafael Salomon had bought when he came to Tel Aviv. Since her husband's death, Adela had become a hermit, refusing to leave home even for family celebrations, much less funerals. Yet some of her youthful vitality remained. Something was still restless in that body, which, after sixty-some years in a land whose language she had never properly learned, still gave off a whiff of another place and another time.

Physically, Adela was a mere shadow of the animated woman she once was. But those who knew her could tell that old age had actually given her a new determination and even a certain irreverence — the prerogative of those who have nothing to gain in life anymore, but also not much to lose. For the past decade, Adela had shared her home with a Filipina caregiver named Rowena, a woman of forty-five with a husband and three sons in Manila. She had worked as a research assistant at the university in her hometown, but when she lost her job and her husband became the sole breadwinner, his earnings could not cover the family's living expenses.

Rowena's lovely long hair was always tied back, her black clothes were carefully chosen, and her fingernails glistened with red polish. Her face projected the utmost gravity, but at the same time there was something tender and compassionate about her. On the rare occasions when someone entered her orbit and struck up a conversation with her, she would gaze at him with intense scrutiny. Rowena was a good listener, and her conversants sensed it and were not afraid to trust her. They told her everything, even things they told no one else.

When Honi knocked on the door, Rowena looked through the peephole and asked in Hebrew, "Who is it?" Only after Adela gave her approval to allow the guest in did she open the door.

Adela took one look at Honi and his awkward expression, and the distant memories that surfaced made her heart pound for a moment. But she disclosed nothing. She said hello and asked him to sit down. She got up, went to the kitchen, and returned with a cup of Turkish coffee that Rowena had boiled on the stove top, along with some biscuits that looked just like the ones she used to bake herself.

Honi sipped his coffee and nibbled on a biscuit. He was blinded by the sunlight that shone through holes in the balcony bricks. Adela sat silently watching her guest, shaded by a large ficus tree on the balcony. She had not seen Honi for years, since the shivah after Rafael's death. He was still a boy then, and now he was a young man.

Honi looked at the stern old woman as he chewed uncomfortably. She was a hard nut to crack. When she stared at him with her glimmering black eyes, he noticed two lines cascading down from her lips, which gave her face a bitter expression.

Finally Honi spoke. "How many years have you lived in Israel?"

"A long time," the old woman answered.

"Did you meet Rafael in Syria, or was it in Israel?"

Adela seemed surprised. "Syria. Of course Syria!"

"How did you meet him? Was it arranged?"

"No. I'll tell you. I had an aunt, who had a husband who got sick. He had a fever, forty days he lay there with fever. And he had a little son, Yusuf. And me, I was fourteen, and every day I took Yusuf to school because his father was sick. Rafael was a teacher, he taught Arabic and French at the school. And there was another teacher there, a woman called Allegra. She loved him—Rafael. But he didn't love her.

"One day I come with Yusuf, and Allegra grabs me and says, 'Girl!' I ask her, 'What do you want?' She says, 'No, no, you must not bring the boy. His mother must come!' I said, 'His mother can't come. If she could, she would bring him.' She says to me, 'No, no, no. If you come again tomorrow, I'll hit you!' I said, 'Okay, we'll see if you can hit me.'

"I came the next day with the boy. Allegra says to me, 'Girl, again! Again!' I told her, 'Look, his father is sick and his mother can't come.' She says, 'What do I care about his father?' I said, 'If you don't care, I do, it's my uncle and aunt.' Then she starts, she grabs me like this, and she wants to hit me. I told her, 'Look, if you hit me, no, no, no—big trouble for you. Big trouble!' I was little, only fourteen. But I told her, 'Let's go see the headmaster, you and me.'

"I walk in, I say to him, 'Mr. Headmaster, listen. My uncle is very sick and his wife can't leave him alone. Poor little Yusuf. My aunt told me to bring him to school every day.' I told the headmaster, 'Look, I have to. If I tell my aunt I can't do it, she'll think I don't want to.' The headmaster said, 'You come back tomorrow, and if this woman Allegra does anything to you, I'll get rid of her.' He said that right in her face: 'I'll kick you out of school if you do anything to her.' So I left and she didn't dare show her face outside her classroom.

"So one afternoon I go to pick up Yusuf. Suddenly when I walk in, I see Rafael standing there, holding a newspaper. He used to read everything. And he must have said something to Allegra about me, like, 'Look at that girl, look how good she is.' That's why she said those things—he talked to her about me, and she felt he was looking at me, and I was just a girl. So you know what he did with the newspaper? He said, 'Girl, what's your name?' And I said, 'You think I'm going to tell you? I won't tell you my name.' So he says, 'Look here in the paper, see what it says? *Je t'aime.*' I say to him, 'Get out of here! What are you doing, you're starting with me? I'm just a girl, go start with that other one, the teacher.'

"And since then, he got to know me. Every year on Purim we do something nice, like we make a big party, with water guns. So I filled up a gun, I got one and filled it up, just like that, and Rafael looked at me—bang, I squirted him! It was cold, Purim was very cold where we lived. Snow sometimes. It's very cold where we lived in Syria. Weather like on the Hermon. You know how the Hermon is? Like that.

"And since then I got to know him. My friends were so jealous—wow! With us everything was free, you come, you go, girls and boys, you have fun, sometimes you leave the girl after a few years, you walk out on her and go with another girl. Every evening we went out. We'd go to the pictures, we'd go to the bars, oh yes, there were great places there. Believe me, Rafael went to all the places, he ate all the food. Me, I wouldn't taste it, he'd bring me a piece of cake—I'd barely eat one bite. He ate *everything*, didn't care about kosher. Every day he went to eat in the souk. Only when we got married, ah...then...He liked to eat in the souk then, too."

"Where did you get married?"

"Let me tell you. Right before the wedding, his father suddenly died. On a Saturday, and our wedding was on the Sunday. Heart attack."

"The day before the wedding?"

"Yes! One day they came home, and suddenly a heart attack. So we put it off. A whole month. We got married a month later. We wanted it at the Alliance, because they do weddings there with dancing and a band, so pretty. But we didn't. We wanted to but we didn't, we had it at home. Because his father died, and we thought it's not nice to have a big wedding. So we had it at home."

"Well, that's understandable," Honi commented.

"Rafael's parents wanted him to study being a doctor, but he didn't want to. He went to university for a bit, then he told them, 'I don't want to be a doctor, I want to be a merchant!' He left. Where did he work? At the Bourse. Worked at the Bourse, had an Arab partner. This Arab, he was a friend of the prime minister of Syria, the president, I mean. This partner, he said, 'Look, Rafael, whatever you want, just ask, I'll arrange everything for you.' So Rafael said, 'I want to go to Libnon.' The friend says, 'Really? Okay, very nice. Write down what you want to take.' We had a little boy then already. Rafael wrote things down, and the friend said he'd make us a visa. He got us the visa, got us a moving truck, and a taxi, we took our furniture and everything. They let us do it, only us, because we had papers from him. He arranged everything for us. After a year in Libnon, we came down to Metula in Israel. That evening, it was the first independence holiday for Israel, and we heard shots, you know, and they had sirens. What did it mean? Maybe it was a sign for us? So we changed routes. We'd only gone half an hour, then we walked seven hours on foot. There were twenty people there, Jews who came with us, but you know what, Rafael held on to Shlomo, back then he was still called Salim. And my other hand? I gave it to an Arab who took us. There were two Arabs. I told him, 'You hold me so I don't fall.' The whole time I'm with him: 'Don't leave me, I'll walk with you *main dans la main* — hand in hand, together.'

"See, he was an Arab. But they're very good people. They worked with Rafael. He told me, 'You see, you see this road? We're bringing goods here, and it's very difficult, we're afraid they'll catch us.' I told him, 'Really? Then go work in the *jora*, where they clean out the sewage! But you're not going to work in a job like that, are you?' He said, 'You're right.'

"He let me go for one minute — I fell down. I told him, 'Come here!' He said, 'Don't shout, they'll catch us!' I said, 'You left me, I was so scared, I was afraid I'd fall.' I made *main dans la main* with him and we kept going. I told him, 'There'll be big trouble if my husband thinks this is not hard for me, he sees it's hard for me, that's why he lets me go *main dans la main* with you. I never went that way with anyone.' Finally we got to Metula.

"We sat down, we had to, we had the boy and I was pregnant, too. I said to him, 'We'll stay for one week.' They said, 'No, you have family, you have to go to Sha'ar Ha'Aliya.' That's where all the new immigrants go, they stay there, they give them beds, every day Rafael goes, holds out a dish, they give him a piece of bread, some margarine, and a little jam, that's the food. That's it. There was no food! I told him, 'What is this? Where is the food we used to eat? What happened? Not a single banana, no apples, no oranges.' Every day Salim says to me, 'Mama, I want *tafaaha* — apple.' I tell him, 'We don't have any.' He says, '*moz* — banana.' Only later we got to her, Rafael's sister, in a house that belonged to Arabs in Ha'Tikva neighborhood. After that we came here, to Dizengoff. What we went through, I tell you . . ."

She took a sip of water and said no more.

They sat quietly for a long time. Adela stared at the squares of concrete outside the window, Honi glanced at his phone and remembered why his father had sent him. But he didn't have the courage to ask her about the shop and the lease. Finally he said softly, "And what about Sabakh?"

"What did you say?" The old lady raised her eyebrows and pursed her lips.

"The diamond. When was the first time you saw it?"

"*Ya sater* — God help us! They told you about the diamond?"

"Yes."

"Who told you?"

"Menashe and his nephew, Tom."

"Oh . . . He told you?"

"Yes."

"That diamond, I don't remember when I saw it. May . . . no. I don't remember. Why do you want to know?"

"Because Menashe told me."

"Your father, Amiram, does he know you came here?" The old lady was becoming suspicious.

Honi did not answer.

"If he only knew how his father loved Rafael. Like a brother, he loved him."

"I know."

"Who told you?"

"Menashe."

"He told you everything, Menashe?"

"Not everything. He said there are some things I don't need to know."

"No, listen. You need to know everything, but you don't need to *tell* everything. So tell me, Honi, what do you know about the diamond?"

"I know there's a blue diamond."

"Do you know everything about it?"

"No."

"I'll tell you." She looked at him with half a smile but paused for a moment until she finally nodded and told him what was in her heart.

3

"That woman, Rafael's aunt, Gracia, she started it all."

"What did she start?" Honi asked.

"In Damascus, when she was a girl, sixteen, she went to the Muslims' cafés and she sang. She had a beautiful voice, really very beautiful she sang. So she went there and sang, and them, the Arabs, they came. And they came a lot, with their money and their presents—here a gold chain, there an expensive scarf, here precious jewels. They gave her everything. And Gracia, she takes the gifts and sings for them. After the singing, they take her to their homes. Then she had money and she bought a big house in the Jewish neighborhood, and her boyfriend came to her house with his friends, and they all sat around her place. And she sings and plays for him and for his friends. And she smoked a hookah, too, she did. And they were Arabs.

"Rafael's mother was blind, *ya sater.* Can't see anything. And she sits with her sister Gracia, she lives with her, she listens how Gracia sings for the Arabs. She sang for them—they gave her gifts. Then she found a husband for Mona. That was Rafael's father. But she herself, Gracia, she didn't want to marry. She wanted to be, you know, independent. And she had a diamond, the sultan gave it to her. The diamond—this is what she told Mona—it brought a lot of good fortune to Rafael's family. And they all believed her. She's a very beautiful woman and she sings so nice and she has money and she has a diamond. So they listen to her and they believe everything she tells them.

"Only me, I said to Rafael, that diamond, *ya sater,* it must be sold, or even given away as a gift, just don't keep it with us. But he wouldn't listen to me. Never listened to me. His aunt, she holds on to the diamond, and she goes with this man and then with the other man. Then the Arabs start hating us because of them Zionists. And Shayu's whole family speaks evil about Rafael's family for being on Gracia's side. And Gracia, she tries to fix things, but she can't. In the end, Shayu's mother, poor woman, fell off the balcony. She was your grandfather Shayu's mother. What can I tell you..."

Honi thought about the things his father had told him, but he wasn't about to interrupt Adela's story.

She continued. "Me and Rafael, every year in summer we went to Libnon. It's very pretty there in Libnon, in Aley. There's green trees and it's quiet and there's a big house and we rest and eat good food. I tell you, we had a beautiful life in Libnon in the summer. And that's where Rafael met a woman, an Arab from Yafa. This Arab woman used to come with her mother from Yafa every few months. And we're good friends, Rafael and the Arab woman and me. She was a very beautiful woman."

"You mean they were Muslim Arabs?"

"I'll tell you. This Arab woman, her mother wasn't right in the head. Always lay in bed without moving. So her father, Sami, said to her, 'Go with your mother to Aley, stay there, get some rest.' It really was very nice there. But she didn't want to stay with her mother in the room the whole time, she was afraid of her. So she came to us."

"What was the Arab woman's name?"

"What can I say . . . I won't tell you her name. Her father, his name was Sami. And this woman, Rafael loved her very much. He was always happy, Rafael. And he had that, you know, the blue diamond. And I'll tell you something, Honi: That diamond, Sabakh, it gave us a lot of trouble. You know why?"

Honi shook his head.

"I'll tell you. Where did they find the diamond? In India. With the Indians. That gentleman, the Frenchman, he found it. He was a very important man in India, the Frenchman. What did he do? He took the blue diamond out of the Indians' holy statue. Took the diamond, took it out of India, sold it over there in Europe. Forgot about it. But the diamond—it didn't forget! Why did the Frenchman take the diamond from the holy statue in India? Why did he go with it all the way to Europe? He should have left it in India, where it belonged. He took it all the way to Europe, to the kings of France and England, and in the end all the way to the sultan. So I said to Rafael, 'That diamond, it'll bring us a lot of trouble one day.' But he didn't listen. He was always happy, with his friend from Yafa. She was beautiful, she was. But me, I wasn't happy. That's that."

Adela stopped talking, and evening fell, and the bricks on the balcony darkened. Honi rubbed his eyes and looked at her. Even though it was late, she did not ask him to leave.

Honi shook Adela Salomon's warm hand, said goodbye to Rowena, and walked out onto the street.

## 4

"Honi..."

"Yes, Tom?"

"You look troubled."

"I'm okay."

"You sure?"

"Sure, Tomi."

"Okay, if you say so."

"Why do you think I look troubled?"

"Because you're furrowing your brow and you're whistling. When you start whistling, I know you're irritated."

"You whistle, too, sometimes."

"Yes, but it's not the same. I whistle when I'm happy."

"I can't remember ever seeing you happy, Tomi."

"That's not true. I'm happy now, with you."

"Me, too."

"Come and lie here on the couch, I'll scratch your neck."

"With your stubble?"

"Yes, with my stubble. So tell me, how did it go with Adela?"

"Not easy. She's a pretty tough woman, but I got through to her in the end."

"Did she tell you anything you didn't know?"

"Yes and no. We talked about the feud between the families and about the blue diamond. It's pretty amazing that you're writing about all that. Adela told me a few stories I'd already heard about your diamond. But I did hear some things about a young woman from Jaffa, an Arab, who I didn't know anything about until today."

"Who is she?"

"I didn't quite understand. Someone Rafael was in love with once, in Lebanon. Maybe he had a lover?"

"I guess so."

"But it struck me as odd, because Adela talked about it as if she were part of the story, not like he was doing things behind her back. I didn't quite get it. I get the feeling they haven't told us everything about that family. They're my relatives, but the bottom line is I barely know them."

"What did she say this woman from Jaffa was called?"

"She wouldn't tell me. She just said her father was called Sami."

"Sami."

"Yes."

"Sami, Aunt Gracia's boyfriend?"

"What do you mean, her boyfriend?"

"I'll tell you some other time. But look, how's the radio show coming along?"

"We've done loads of interviews."

"Cover your mouth when you yawn, Honi. Have you talked to anyone interesting?"

"I don't know. Everyone I meet tells me the same thing all the papers say. I still haven't cracked this program. I'm trying to find a less chewed-over angle, something new. But maybe the department head is right and I shouldn't have got into this whole thing at all?"

"No, I think you should keep thinking and working, and in the end you'll crack it."

"Remember how we were talking about passion? I mean, about your passion for writing *The Diamond Setter*?"

"Yes. Why?"

"That was the first time we talked, at the café. I was trying to understand why you're writing this story, and you told me the blue diamond fascinated you. But to tell you the truth, I didn't really buy it."

"What's not to buy?"

"I can't figure out the significance of the diamond for you."

"Look, ever since I've been working at the jewelry shop, I've heard so much from Menashe about that blue diamond, and I thought to myself that if I could somehow reconstruct the story, I'd be accomplishing something much bigger. Through the diamond, I'd tell the story of two families that on the one hand belong to two enemy nations, but on the other hand are connected through bonds of love and secrets, from back when the Middle East was—"

"—steeped in love and not only in blood, I know. Okay, great. So have you completed the mission? Have you cracked the code? Exposed the lies?"

"I don't like your tone, Honi."

"Too bad. This whole story is just messing with my mind a little, you know?"

"Well, either way, I think I'm on the right path. And besides, there are two questions on my mind while I'm writing."

"What are they?"

"I'm interested in finding out whether you can love more than one person at the same time. I mean, romantic love. With everything that implies."

"I read an article about that recently. It's called polyamory."

"Yes. The second question is completely different, ostensibly, but perhaps it's connected to all the things we've been talking about. And that is the question of return."

"You mean, like the right of return?"

"Not just the political issue, with the Palestinian refugees and all that. I mean *return* in a broader sense, in every sense."

"I'm not following you, Tomi. What's the question?"

"The question is, can you go back? What really interests me is not the return itself but the place. You know, people always fantasize about a time machine that can transport you back to a different time and place. But my question is, do we even have anywhere to go back to?"

"To me it doesn't seem important whether we have anywhere to go back to. What's important is the place we're in now."

"Look, Honi, I started writing *The Diamond Setter* and I got stuck. One day I read in the paper about that Syrian guy who crossed the border and went on a roots journey in Jaffa. And that little act of his made all these other things come together for me. I realized that for us, the third generation of immigrants, we can't do anything to change the political situation. Our hands are tied. But we can tell a story. And that's a lot."

"Well said, sweetheart."

"Honi . . ."

"What?"

"Can I ask you for something, before you fall asleep?"

"Your wish is my command."

"Okay, well it's just a small thing. I want you to go to the Garden of the Two, in Jaffa. Do you know where that is?"

"Yes."

"Some people have set up tents there recently."

"Like on Rothschild?"

"Kind of, but not exactly. Go and talk to people there, okay?"

"Why?"

"Because I'm asking you to."

"But why?"

"Because it's important to me, Honi. Come on, don't I do things for you when you ask?"

"Okay, I'll go."

"Thanks."

"But now I want to sleep."

"Sweet dreams, my love. Sleep well."

"Sweet dreams."

# CHAPTER SEVEN

# SAMI

## 1

SAMI JABALI WAS BORN ON THE NIGHT OF JANUARY 1, 1900, in the Ajami neighborhood of Yafa. His whole life was affected by this serendipitous birth date. Even the monks at Saint Joseph School were convinced Sami had been blessed with special virtues because he entered the world on the first day of the last century of the second millennium. And so, to be on the safe side, when they lashed the thighs and bottoms of the Christian, Muslim, and Jewish pupils for not speaking among themselves in French, they spared Sami the rod. No one could have predicted that this gaunt, quiet child would grow into a broad-shouldered citrus grower. The seed indicated nothing of the fruit.

Sami had few childhood memories: his grandmother feeding him apple slices, a chicken that wandered in from the neighbor's yard standing on the windowsill looking at him with its head cocked, and one other memory, of a little sister who was born at home after many silent months. He had fleeting recollections of her face and her bed, which was separated from his by wooden slats painted white, and the chain of yellow beads that hung above her head. Sami used to stand beside the bed, stick his head between the slats, and reach his finger out to touch the hollow of the baby's neck, with his eyes closed.

One day the baby wasn't there anymore, and Sami's father dismantled the crib and placed its parts behind the kitchen door. In the weeks that followed, Sami wondered where the baby had gone, but eventually his contemplations stopped, and only her pale pink face, moving from side to side like the head of the chicken on the windowsill, remained dimly engraved in his mind.

Each time he met a relative or friend of his parents, Sami asked how old they were and quickly calculated when they had been born and how much older than him they were. From the age of four he knew to look up every day at the new clock tower that had been built in the square—first two floors, then a third—and look for the two clocks, which displayed local time and European time. Legend had it that one of the city's wealthy Jewish residents, Yosef "Bey" Moyal, who was esteemed by the Ottoman Empire, had grown tired of all the people who were always coming into his shop to ask when the train to Jerusalem left and what time it was. So he commissioned a watchmaker to install two clocks in the tower—one European, which would tell when the train was leaving, and the other a local clock, so that residents would know the prayer times in the mosque.

When Sami was older, he spent his afternoons in a club near the mosque, where he played billiards with his friends, drank lemonade, and ate ice cream, and on summer days he splashed around in the sea at Jabalya beach. The monks at school liked to tell the children about Jonah the Prophet, who was the closest person to God—so close that he tried to run away from him, via Yafa, to a place called Tarshish. And in the Yafa sea, the same sea where Sami rode the waves all summer long, and in whose waters he dunked his head and opened his eyes and tasted the salt, in this sea a great storm rose up around Jonah and the people sailing in his ship. Only when they threw Jonah into the waves—said the monks—did the storm abate. And then came a great big fish and swallowed Jonah.

The story of Jonah enchanted Sami. Over and over again he asked the monks to repeat it, over and over again he listened to the words Jonah shouted at the Lord from inside the belly of the fish: "For Thou didst cast me into the depth, in the heart of the seas, and the flood was round about me; all Thy waves and Thy billows passed over me. And I said, 'I am cast out from before Thine eyes; yet I will look again toward Thy holy temple.' The waters compassed me about, even to the soul; the deep was round about me; the weeds were wrapped about my head."

When Sami emerged from the water, he would walk to the port and then on through the market that led to Saraya Square. The market was lined with fruit and vegetable stands, and a spice stall where the seller piled up colorful towers of powdered spices that tempted one to dip one's fingers in and take them out bathed in red or yellow or green.

People strolled about and prodded the vegetables. A man stopped at the spice towers and asked for a little sumac and some zaatar, haggled keenly with the seller, rummaged through a pocket sewn inside his trousers, pulled out a note, collected his spices in little paper bags, and went on his way.

Near the produce stands was a stall with swatches of fabric displaying gold-plated metal earrings made of several hoops, studded with yellow or orange or purple glass. Women leaned over to inspect the jewelry, tried on earrings, then picked up the copper-handled mirror and glared sternly at their reflections. Next to the earring stands were three scrawny donkeys with their eyes blindfolded and their tails twitching in the clammy air.

Among the shoppers, local residents, and travelers from nearby lands, Sami spotted four men walking tall, with their fingers touching the glistening swords and daggers that dangled from their waists. At that very moment his elbow was pinched by a woman whose face was covered by a black scarf, who tried to sell him pita and salted cheese. He shook her off and went to his favorite place in the market, where scribes sat writing letters of inquiry and complaints to the authorities on behalf of their clients.

One of the scribes sat on a stool in front of a woman in her fifties, who held a little boy by his hand. She had tears in her eyes. The scribe held his quill in one hand, licked the finger of the other to erase his mistakes, wrote something, and erased something again. He dipped the quill in a copper ink pot that was attached to his belt. The woman followed his every move. "Tell them I paid my taxes every year," she said, "but this year I can't pay, I have nothing. Write that they took my husband to the army last month. That very day, a man with a knife came into my shop and stole all the eggs! And tell them that after that, a Turkish soldier took my daughter to Syria and I haven't seen her since then. I only got one short letter. She is the mother of this boy!" The woman rattled the boy, who tried to get out of her grip. "Could you also write a letter to my daughter?"

The scribe nodded.

"Then write this: 'Your son, thank God, is very well. But your father is gone and your mother doesn't sleep at night and she has no money for her grandson. Come back quickly to your mother, and if you can't come back then at least send money for the boy. Answer me quickly. Your mother.'"

The scribe licked his lips and wrote what she dictated, furrowing his brow in concentration. Then he read the letter aloud to the woman and held out both letters. Her eyes roamed from one to the other. She debated, but the young man standing behind her in line prodded her shoulder with his finger to hurry her up—he was eager to have his own letter written and mailed. The woman approved both letters. Sami watched as the scribe scattered fine powder on the ink to dry it, blew gently on the paper, then fold the letters into their respective envelopes and marked a small circle on one of them. "This is for your daughter," he said, "and the other is for the city governor." The woman paid and took her letters, and when Sami turned to leave, he heard the next person in line say, in an urgent, businesslike tone: "A letter to my parents in Cairo, 23 Suliman Pasha Street. 'Dear parents, please inform my fiancée's family that I have decided to stay in Yafa. Praise God, I have found work here in a soap factory, and I am engaged to my employer's daughter. There is no need to send messengers after me; my decision is final. Yours, your loving son.'"

To Sami's right were shops selling perfumes and medicines in little bags, and in the entrance to one such shop, behind an invisible cloud of scent, the elderly shopkeeper sat on a chair with a rope dangling above his head. Whenever someone came in, the old man would take hold of the rope and hoist himself up to welcome the customer. On the left was the Bulgarian's shop. The shopkeeper stood there all day with a sunburned face, handling his merchandise, which was known all over the market: briny *lakerda* fish, smoked hard cheeses, dried sausages hanging from the ceiling, and jars of soft round olives. Near the Bulgarian was a stall displaying bowls of pickles, behind which stood a short, stolid man who never talked, and no one knew whether he was voluntarily mute or if his vocal cords had failed him. All day he picked up pieces of red meat and sliced them into thin strips, which he seared on skewers over hot coals. Customers stood in a long line for pitas filled with the meat, drizzled with a pale yellow condiment he stored in a glass bottle. Around the bend in the road, Sami experienced curiosity tinged with nausea when he eyed the skinned sheep hanging from sharp hooks, surrounded by clouds of flies. Not far away, a man wearing a robe crouched down and urinated, and farther on Sami could see the cafés with their tables spilling out onto the street, where men sat sucking on bubbling hookahs. He was almost at his parents' café. He had only to pass by the money changers who perched on chests covered with glass panes, beneath which lay bills and coins from foreign countries, loudly announcing their wares. People came here to exchange local Turkish currency for foreign bills. The air was rife with smells from the nearby fish market, and for many years Sami always imagined a sharp fishy odor on foreign coins.

When he finally reached his parents' café on Najib Bustrus Street, his mother waved at him from the kitchen to come in. He received a kiss and drank a whole glass of lemonade with fresh mint leaves, then went to his father, who was darting among the patrons, both Yafa residents and travelers from Beirut, Cairo, or Baghdad. In the corner of the room sat Sami's grandfather. This grand old man, whose birth date no one knew, spent days on end huddled in a thick wool cape, sucking the hookah mouthpiece and drinking *yansoon*. When the last of the patrons had left, Sami helped his father stack chairs in the corner, then swept the floor and took the big garbage cans out to the street.

## 2

When the First World War broke out, Sami was fourteen. He had to leave his studies at Saint Joseph and help his parents at the café. The city was bombed and shelled. In between bombings, the men would gather in the café, whose location made it relatively safe. There they listened to the news, told of what had been bombed and who had been injured and whether any property had been damaged, exchanged money and sold various belongings, some of which were pawned until things quieted down. The women gathered in the homes, drank juice made of almond and pomegranate, nibbled on sweets, and with infinite patience wove a tapestry of matchmaking.

When Sami was sixteen, Hassan Bey, the commandant of Yafa, decided to destroy the shops housed in alcoves on either side of the market. He wanted to build a street leading from the Saraya House to the Customs House. He captured army deserters to serve as his labor force, and at night they followed his orders to destroy the shops and throw the bricks into the sea. By morning, there was a street there. Not long afterward, Sami decided to leave the family café. For a few weeks he worked in date and apricot orchards, vineyards, sugarcane fields, and tobacco fields, then he started working for one of Yafa's major citrus growers. He got up early every day, washed his face, drank a cup of tea, packed a pita and a cucumber, and hurried to the orchard on the east of the city, which the Arabs called a *biara*—a well. Nearby stood the well house, which was also known as the *biara*. This grand structure was the home of the orchard owner, an imposing man who looked much older than he was, bald and full-bodied, with one eye covered with a patch tied around his head.

Sami picked fruit all day, and in the evenings he stopped at the café, where his mother served him dinner. After he ate, he went home and dozed until nighttime, then went out to walk along the beach. His ears were attuned to the whispering waves as he watched the fishermen cast their rods: The line cut through the black air and pierced the water with a hook wrapped in bait. The fishermen pulled out their rods and threw them back in, and the little fish—known as "communists," perhaps because they had invaded the Mediterranean from the Suez Canal after the Russian Revolution—flopped about on the sand. Sami looked north and thought of the day when he would have enough money to stop working and travel to Beirut and Damascus.

His quiet, serious nature soon inspired the confidence of his employer, who put Sami in charge of a team of pickers. Then he supervised the workmen who built wooden crates and packed the oranges, and after a few months he was appointed liaison to the administrators in charge of land betterment tax, as well as the property's groundwater and well water. For many hours Sami oversaw the workers, who crouched on the packinghouse floor, in a room neck-high in oranges. Each orange was carefully wrapped in tissue paper and placed in a crate. The finest were sent overseas, to England and France. The rest were sold locally and in neighboring countries.

One day at the café, Sami's mother pulled him into a corner and began singing the praises of Nafisa Said, whose father owned a fabric shop in Souk el-Balabseh. Sami knew Nafisa, and had honestly never given her much thought. But he was interested in her older sister, Suad. When he tried to find out about Suad from his mother, it turned out she was engaged to a man who had gone to study medicine in Cairo two years earlier. Except that further investigation found that all contact with the young man had been lost for the past two months, and his brother had been sent to look for him. Sami did not say anything explicit, but his mother put two and two together and inferred her son's interest. A week later she gave him information about Suad. It turned out her betrothed had fallen in love with an Egyptian woman, a distant cousin by marriage, and had decided to stay in Cairo.

The matchmaking needle abruptly changed direction, and now the women who sipped almond and pomegranate juice put their efforts into marrying off the older sister. The tapestry unraveled and was quickly rewoven. In their first face-to-face meeting, Suad looked even more beautiful than Sami had thought her from afar. She hardly spoke, but something in her silence, which hinted at unfathomable depths, echoed in his soul and enchanted him.

When they left the Hassan Bey Mosque after the marriage ceremony, they were accompanied along the streets by musicians, all the way to Clock Tower Square and on to Ajami. The next day, the orchard owner summoned Sami to his home. "That mosque, where you got married," he said, and Sami imagined he could see his employer's blind eye piercing him through the eye patch, "you should know that we shunned it at first. Who do you think built it for Hassan Bey? Deserters from the Turkish army! They suffered injuries and even death because of him. And he confiscated stones from private houses to build it. But even so, from that mosque, God willing, there will come great prosperity for your family." He smiled, baring his teeth, took a handkerchief from his pocket, and wiped the sweat off his brow. Then he reached into the waistline of his trousers, dug around an inner pocket, and fished out three gold pound coins, which he gave to the new groom.

After the weeklong wedding celebrations, Suad and Sami moved into Sami's late grandparents' home near the sea.

## 3

Years later, Sami asked himself when things had started to go wrong. There were undoubtedly bad omens. Suad appeared to be peaceful at first, but over time Sami began to worry about the black circles under her eyes, her lips that trembled for no reason, and her distant gaze. Again and again he asked if she felt well, if something was troubling her, but the more he probed, the more entrenched she became in her silence. When he finally consulted Suad's mother, he was astonished to learn that as a young girl, Suad had spent a long time lying in bed, refusing to go out, hardly eating or speaking to anyone. When he asked why no one had told him about the episode, Suad's mother replied that it was a long time ago, and that the doctor had said there was no reason to expect it to happen again.

Sami's mother was furious about this secret that was kept from her during the matchmaking process, but her son felt it would not affect his love for his wife, perhaps even the opposite. He was filled with compassion for Suad and did everything he could to appease her. Occasionally, he succeeded.

But one day Suad confessed a desire to end her life, and Sami removed all the knives and sharp objects from the kitchen. When he went to work in the orchard, he was distracted, and he comforted himself by leaving Suad's mother in charge. There was unrest between Jews and Arabs in Yafa at the time, with dozens of people murdered and shops looted. Sami's family was frightened, and he helped his parents break a hole in one of the walls at home and hide their meager savings, as well as a few pieces of gold his mother had inherited from her mother. When the unrest died down and there were a few weeks of calm, Sami thought Suad was recovering from her dark episode. He was twenty-one, and she was two years younger.

By the summer, Sami had saved up enough money for a trip to the north. He told Suad about his idea, and to his surprise she agreed. In fact she seemed happy to leave Yafa for a few days. A week later, they boarded a train that had come from Cairo, and traveled via Haifa to Lebanon. They disembarked in Beirut, and the train continued to its final destination in the northern Lebanese city of Tripoli.

Sami and Suad stayed in a hotel by the sea, and for a while it seemed to Sami that the distance from Yafa was easing Suad's mind. Still, he feared for her and constantly scrutinized her expression. When they went to a restaurant and she left her plate full of food, he was worried. They strolled along the streets of Beirut, sat down to rest under the palm trees, licked ice cream, wandered arm in arm along the beach, and in the evening watched shows. After ten days they returned to Yafa.

Sami often traveled from Yafa to Tel Aviv, and he liked living in both towns, which shared the same sea. In Yafa, bare-chested young boys charged around on horseback, and expert oarsmen dressed in billowing black trousers and white shirts maneuvered small boats all the way out to the huge steamships that could not squeeze into the port. On land, camels arrived at the crowded port, loaded with wooden crates full of citrus fruit draped down on either side of their bodies. The crates were unloaded and dragged over wooden boards onto the boats, where they were lined up, row upon row. With great effort, the oarsmen navigated their cargo out to the ships, across the stormy waters of what was known as "the most terrible of the seven seas."

One day Sami stopped to read a notice posted by the "Young Worker" Zionist organization, and stood deciphering the Hebrew letters. It said that the Jewish immigrants who had recently arrived in Yafa by ship included the following: saddle maker, leatherworker, wood-carver, water-pipe layer, dental technician, draftsman, butcher, two carpenters, stonecutter, electrical engineer, baker, wooden-crate maker, two welders, two pharmacists, teacher, secretary, architect, watchmaker, four gardeners, two typesetters, miller, stocking maker, shoe-polish maker, barber, coppersmith. "Anyone requiring a practitioner of these vocations will kindly contact the Young Worker's office of labor in Jaffa."

When he walked along the beaches of Tel Aviv, Sami saw deck chairs neatly arranged in rows, sheltered from the sun by a swathe of fabric stretched between two wooden posts. Women in bathing suits walked hand in hand on the sand, and every so often the bathers disappeared into huts erected between the beach and the road leading east, to town, perched on little pillars to protect them when the tide came in. At low tide, children crawled under the wooden floors to find a penny or two dropped by the bathers when they took off their clothes.

In between the two cities, not far from the notorious "pickpocket school," where both Jews and Arabs trained, stood the brothel. Its clients included Arabs and Jews, as well as British policemen. The British—who had by now replaced the Turks as Palestine's custodians—lusted after young girls, and sometimes boys. All of Sami's friends had lost their virginity at this institution and were full of stories about the prostitutes, and the rooms decorated with lace, and the strong perfume. Sami alone, of all his friends, had insisted on remaining a virgin until his wedding night.

Indeed, he was tied with every fiber of his being to Yafa. He loved Najib Bustrus Street and his parents' café, which always seemed to be in a state of languor that soaked up the aroma of coffee, with his grandfather huddled in the corner sipping *yansoon*. He loved the clock tower with its two different times, and King George Boulevard bustling with thousands of guests from neighboring countries, the grand houses looking out to sea, with floor tiles in warm colors, the large balconies facing the waves, the little fountain in his courtyard, the fragrance of grilled meat and tomatoes, and the cubes of lamb dipped in flavorful tahini. Yet his feet still led him to Tel Aviv. He heard stories of how crowded the young Hebrew city was, with entire families living in one room, beds rented out for a few hours a day, in cramped and unsanitary conditions. He was increasingly able to appreciate the spacious homes of Yafa, the sea breeze on the balconies, the expansive courtyards where one could sit and rest. Yet despite all this, for most of his twenties—which were also the century's twenties—Sami frequently left Yafa to stroll along Allenby Street and Rothschild Boulevard.

Sami's best friend, Hassan, was a regular reader of the newspaper *Falastin*. The editor warned readers against visiting Tel Aviv cafés and reported on an Arab who had visited Tel Aviv: "When he turned to a street corner to do his business, a Jew stood in his way." The Jew cursed at the Arab and then a dozen more Jews jumped out and beat him. The editor concluded, "We have frequently counseled our youngsters not to visit Tel Aviv, because they spend their money in shops and eateries in order to impress the local women, while they themselves suffer from the financial crisis. The Jews paid for our lands with one hand, but they take back our money with the other—through women, and through food and drink establishments. Now they are also beginning to charge interest on these payments—in the form of beatings." Another article warned unequivocally, "We advise our youths to learn their lesson, as there is no predicting what awaits them in Tel Aviv tomorrow or the next day. We shall leave it at that."

Sami worked hard for another two years, until one day the orchard owner died and his son, who inherited the land, offered Sami a partnership. Sami had no capital of his own, but he was hardworking and responsible, and the offer appealed to him, especially since his family was about to expand.

When Suad's doctor informed her she was pregnant, she received the news with strange indifference. The doctor instructed her to rest in bed and not do any housework. Her mother came to care for her. About two months later, Sami took up his friend Hassan's invitation to accompany him on a trip to Damascus, where he had family.

They set off early in the morning. Hassan was keenly interested in politics and often sent letters to the editor of *Falastin*. While the two made their way north, Hassan lectured Sami about the Sykes-Picot Agreement, which roughly a decade earlier, after the Great War, had divided up the areas of control in the Middle East between the British and the French. He spoke angrily of the British, who encouraged the Zionist invaders and hypocritically pretended to be neutral observers. Sami listened calmly and somewhat uninterestedly, and did not interrupt because he knew Hassan was passionate about these issues; he belonged to a group of orchard workers who had been trained to use weapons in preparation for the next bloody battle. Sami, on his part, was not a member of any organization. His friends in the orchard sometimes mocked him for being a "Zionist," but he dismissed them with a wave of the hand. At first he viewed the political developments impassively, but as things heated up in Yafa and the workers grew furious at the Jewish citrus growers who were robbing their livelihood and their lands, Sami began to fear he might be stretching the rope too thin, and realized he must demonstrate involvement in the political struggle, if only for appearances.

As they traveled north by train, his thoughts wandered to Suad lying at home in bed. Her mother had not rebuked Sami for abandoning his wife, at least not openly, but when he said goodbye he thought she was glaring reproachfully at him.

Hassan noticed that Sami's mind was wandering. His voice softened and he asked how Suad was feeling.

"She's fine," Sami answered tersely.

"I know it's not easy for you," Hassan continued after a pause. "It's good that you're going away for a few days. You deserve a change of scenery. You spend too much time with all those women."

The farther away he got from the Bride of the Sea, and the closer to the city he had never visited but had heard so much about, the more revived Sami felt. They reached

Damascus in the evening, and Hassan, who knew the city well from previous visits, headed straight to his uncle's home on al-Amin Street. It was the street that divided the Muslim quarter from Harat al-Yahud—the Jewish quarter.

"Look here," said Hassan, tapping the wall of a house where the plaster was peeling away. "This is what a fallen city looks like." They strolled through the alleys of the Muslim quarter, each carrying a suitcase. "If you look closely," said Hassan, "you can see the remnants of all the glory that was once Damascus."

"When, during the Abbasids?"

"Of course not. It was only a few decades ago that Damascus was still one of the wealthiest cities in the region. Every year thousands of camels passed through on their way to Baghdad, India, and Persia, loaded with spices, coffee, tapestries and rugs, sesame, olive oil, wax, copper, tobacco, jewelry, and on and on. And what happened? The French dug that canal, the Suez, and just like that the processions stopped going through Damascus and all the goods went through the canal. And I'm not even talking about how Damascus used to be the departure point for pilgrims heading to Mecca. When the city lost its economic standing, everything went wrong. What we see here doesn't even resemble the Damascus our grandparents knew. We can only imagine how it all used to look. You see those Jewish houses?" He pointed at a cluster of homes nearby. "These used to be veritable palaces."

Sami nodded. In Yafa they talked a lot about the wealth of Damascus Jews.

He looked over at the houses on the other side of the street and suddenly longed to visit them. "They really do look incredible. Why don't we go and see them sometime?"

Hassan walked on without answering. When they arrived, Hassan's uncle Ali welcomed them at the doorstep and invited them in to wash their hands and sit in the courtyard for dinner. The air soon filled with the aroma of grilled meat and cooked legumes, and the citrus fragrance mingled with the perfume of apples from the trees in the yard.

They sat with Hassan's family and ate a good meal. After dinner they were served coffee and *ma'amul* cookies stuffed with dates, and Hassan's uncle invited them to sit on the balcony overlooking the garden. Sami sprawled back on the red cushions. His coffee cup grew cold in his hand. He leaned his head back and gazed up at the star-studded sky.

"Did you have time to see any of the city on your way from the station?" Ali asked.

"A little." Sami turned to him. "Hassan told me about the history of Damascus."

"He did?" Uncle Ali smiled. "I didn't know he was a scholar of history."

"I know a lot of things," Hassan said, sounding slightly insulted.

"He's published a few letters to the editor in *Falastin*, you know," Sami added proudly.

Ali reached out and patted his nephew warmly on the back of his neck.

"Let me ask you something," Sami said. "You have Jewish friends here in Damascus, don't you?"

"There are some Jews I work with at the al-Tawil market. Difficult people, but they always keep their word."

Hassan smiled. "I wish we could say that about our Jews."

"Did you notice that the Jewish quarter is very quiet this evening? They have a holiday today."

"Yes, it's their festival of trees," Sami told him, and Ali looked at him questioningly.

"You're surprised he knows their holidays?" Hassan asked glumly. "Do you know what they call Sami in the orchard? 'The Zionist.'"

"Why is that?" Ali inquired.

"Because he likes the Jews."

"I don't like them but I don't hate them," Sami explained.

"You like hanging around Tel Aviv, don't you?" Hassan asked.

"Sometimes. So what?"

"So you're a Zionist," Hassan decreed. "And you should know that you're naïve. Trust me, you'll end up with no oranges and no orchard and no nothing."

"You're exaggerating," said Sami, examining his friend's face.

"And you don't understand anything."

"Since we're on the subject of Jews," said their host, "this evening we're all invited to a celebration at Moussa Kadosh's home. He's a textile merchant I know from the market. His oldest son got engaged and today is their 'lovers' festival.'"

"I'm confused—is it the festival of trees or of love?" Hassan wondered.

"Both." His uncle laughed.

"Then let's go," Sami said, trying not to sound too eager.

They went to their rooms to unpack, change clothes, and wash the journey's dust off their faces. Then they joined Hassan's uncle and aunt.

The four walked along a dirt road in the dark. Ali held a yellow oil lamp, and the light danced on the walls in front of them. They turned off al-Amin Street into the alleyways of the Jewish quarter. Ali stopped outside a door, wiped his feet on the mat, and entered the courtyard. His wife and the two young men from Yafa followed. In the courtyard was a large table decorated with branches and laden with bowls of dried fruit, peanuts and almonds, figs and pomegranates.

Moussa Kadosh, a dark-skinned man of about fifty with a rust-colored mustache and small eyes, hurried over to welcome them. Hassan's aunt joined the women sitting inside, and the men sat at the table in the courtyard. Moussa Kadosh offered them drinks, which Hassan's uncle refused with a faint smile, as per the etiquette. Moussa offered again, and finally Ali acceded to his imploring host, and the three guests were seated and served glasses of arak, dishes of *baluza* perfumed with rosewater, *kadaif*, and *sliyya*—wheat berries soaked in honey.

Sami looked around at the guests. Many of the men looked like members of one family, with similar features and the same short, solid build. They were discussing America, specifically one of Moussa's sons who had immigrated there recently and was living with relatives. A few days before his brother's engagement feast, the son had sent his family an enthusiastic letter in which he told great things about his new country and urged them to join him. He included a photograph of himself in his merchant's outfit, with an elegant top hat, spreading out a handwoven tapestry before an American customer.

They were invited into the living room. Ornate rugs covered the floor, and in one corner stood an old wooden buffet with intricately painted dishes. Next to it was a glass cabinet containing silver knives, forks, and spoons, as well as little goblets and antique coins. A dark wooden grandfather clock stood against the wall. Sami unconsciously adapted the pace of his breath to the ticking clock. The women sat on one side of the room. Hassan leaned against the wall with his arms crossed over his chest. He looked unenthusiastic and tried to signal to his uncle that it was time to go home. In the middle of the room sat a woman with her hair swept up into a high bun, wearing jangling gold bracelets. Her face glowed as she welcomed the guests with a smile and invited them to join her and the other women. It was the lady of the house, Hassiba Kadosh.

The family members carried chairs over and sat with the women, and Moussa Kadosh motioned for Hassan's uncle and his group to join them. Ali said it was late and his guests were tired after their long journey, but the host would not hear of it: "Come sit with us, I will accept no excuses or refusals." He examined his wife's response before adding, "And you should know that very soon a famous singer will come to sing for the young couple."

Sami noticed a slight shadow pass over Hassiba Kadosh's face, but she quickly restored her smile. "You must stay," she concurred. Something in her voice—an attempt to sound cheerful that disclosed a slight tremor—made Hassan sigh, and his uncle accepted his hosts' offer.

They sat down near the women. At that moment the door opened, and two boys burst into the living room, shouting.

"Shayu!" said Hassiba Kadosh to one of the children. "What are you doing running like that? You'll fall!" The scolded boy stopped short, and Hassiba spread out her arms and said, "Come here, Shayu, give your mother a kiss!" The boy ran to his mother and hugged her. The other boy stopped behind him and eyed the people in the room curiously. He gave a sidelong glance at a crystal bowl full of little cloth purses. Sami noted that this boy was not a shy one. The mother glanced over her son's shoulder and said, "Rafael, come and say hello to your aunt Hassiba. My, how you've grown!"

The boy went over to his aunt and stood there hesitantly. She held out her hand and he kissed it, and Hassiba took one of the purses and gave it to him. Rafael peeked inside, then quickly turned a questioning gaze at the door and waited. At that moment two women walked in. One held the other's hand and led her inside.

The first woman was roughly thirty. Her beautiful face was made up heavily, her brows completely plucked and drawn in dark blue pencil, and her light brown hair was piled high and held up with hidden pins. She took off her white coat and gave it to Moussa Kadosh. Sami looked at her thin red dress with short sleeves that showed her bare arms. She wore a string of pearls, and her deep neckline revealed damp, glistening skin. The other woman's face was almost free of makeup and her clothes were long and severe looking, but not without charm. The women's features—they were undoubtedly sisters—were remarkably similar, but they had very different expressions. In fact, the combination of resemblance and difference was so marked that it aroused a vague discomfort in Sami. He could not take his eyes off them.

Mrs. Kadosh stood up halfheartedly to welcome the guests and kiss them. The younger woman, who walked in first, sat on a chair, and her sister followed. Rafael went over to the older one, and she held out her fingers in front of her and stroked his cheek. Rafael smiled at his mother, though he knew she could not see him.

"I am honored to introduce you to Mona and Gracia, my wife's sisters," said Moussa Kadosh. Mona looked up at the guests. Her eyes were lost but her smile was genuine, as though she could clearly see them.

Sami was amazed to learn that the women were Mrs. Kadosh's sisters. Nothing in the way she treated these two women had indicated familial relations. Quite the contrary. When he kissed Gracia's hand, her scent reminded him of a perfume he had known long ago, as a child, but at the same time it evoked a certain mystery, something sealed and hidden. Gracia scanned him for a moment, said hello with a courteous smile, and turned to look at Hassan and his uncle. Out of the corner of his eye, Sami noticed Hassiba Kadosh's frozen expression.

"Please." Moussa Kadosh stood and served his sisters-in-law glasses of pomegranate juice. They thanked him, and now Sami saw Gracia's pearly white teeth and her tongue, and he was seized by a passion to kiss her lips.

Only when Gracia opened her mouth and began to sing for the young couple, about half an hour later, did Sami realize that he had not listened to a single word anyone had uttered from the moment she had entered the room. He was captivated by the tune, although he understood very few of the Hebrew words she sang:

> *Yidad mini dod kedoshi*
> *Ve'gozel shnati mitoch af'api*
> *Mi'yom nudo ye'erav shimshi*
> *Ve'ozel...*

Pained by the sorrowful melody, Sami stared down at his shoes. The scent of Gracia's fingers still lingered in his nostrils, and he smelled it as though he were already missing it, years later.

While Sami was lost in thought, Hassan's uncle leaned over and whispered, "You see that woman? Just the way she sings to us now, she once sang for the Turkish sultan! This Jewish woman was known not just in Damascus, but throughout the Empire. What a voice she had! And how beautiful she was!"

"More beautiful than she is now?" Sami protested.

"When she was sixteen she was as lovely as the bud of a jasmine flower and as wild as a desert foal. She comes from a very poor family, but thanks to her talent they want for nothing, as you can see. She married off her sister Mona to the son of one of the wealthiest Jews in our community."

"And who is her husband?" Sami asked in a whisper and looked back at the singer, whose eyes were now closed, her right hand suspended up above her.

"She is not married." Hassan's uncle chuckled.

The melody suddenly plunged and curled in deep tones, as though the ground had dropped away from beneath the sad love song, but the sounds kept hovering above the abyss that opened up at their feet. Before Gracia climbed back up to the high notes, she lingered for an instant and looked at her older sister, Mona, who sat erect and expressionless. Sami listened to the final notes of the song: "I shall fall silent, my lips are sealed."

When she finished singing, Gracia bowed deeply amid a flood of applause, and the young couple went over and kissed her. When Sami looked away, he felt an inexplicable sense of dread crush his chest. The singer stood beaming at the couple, and they thanked her again profusely. The boy, Rafael, pushed his way between the three adults and looked up proudly at his aunt.

After the guests and hosts bid them farewell, Sami and his three companions walked home. On the way, Hassan's uncle told them about a famous diamond that the Turkish sultan had given the Jewish singer years ago. "A blue diamond," he explained.

"Did you ever see it?" Sami asked.

"No, no one has seen it, except perhaps her blind sister." He laughed. "She keeps it very safe somewhere. They say it brings bad luck, but she doesn't believe in that."

Years later, on Ha'Kovshim Street in Tel Aviv, after a futile attempt to persuade Gracia to sing for him, Sami tried to reconstruct the voice in his imagination. His failure was not due to the many years that had passed, but because of something else, something secret and untouchable.

# 4

After their daughter, Laila, was born, Suad's condition deteriorated. She didn't sleep at night, felt too weak to care for the baby, spoke very little, and when she did she cried to Sami and blamed herself, urged him to banish her, said she wasn't worthy of him, then plunged into a deep silence in a fetal position with her face to the wall.

Meanwhile, events were unfolding around them: The United States closed its gates to new immigrants. A Druze uprising broke out in Syria and Lebanon. And in October, after the French were driven out of Damascus by the rebels, they bombed the city in retaliation.

In 1931, Hassiba Kadosh fell off her balcony into the courtyard. Her death aroused a flurry of rumors in the Jewish quarter, and a bitter dispute between the families ensued. But the cousins Rafael and Shayu remained close. In the mid-1930s, shortly before the Arab Revolt began in Palestine, eighteen-year-old Shayu decided to immigrate to the Jewish settlement. Since he did not belong to a Zionist youth movement, his decision came as a surprise to the family. Still, despite the dangers, no one tried to dissuade him.

At first Shayu settled in a small studio apartment in Jaffa and worked odd jobs. He liked Jaffa more than its northern neighbor, since life there reminded him of his hometown. But when the riots began, in the spring of 1936, he thought back to the pandemonium in Damascus during the Druze uprising and the subsequent French bombings. Fearing a war would break out, he decamped to Tel Aviv. With the money he had brought from Syria, he bought a building on Plonit Alley, in the heart of the first Hebrew city.

And all those years Sami kept thinking about Gracia.

Every year on the Jews' festival of trees, the day he had first laid eyes on her in Damascus, Sami sent Gracia a crate full of oranges he had picked himself. Year after year, he went to the same tree in the orchard and selected the finest fruits. The sweet golden treats hidden in the tree reminded him of the pins embedded in Gracia's hair. With infinite care, he wrapped each orange individually, put a card in the box, and sent it to Damascus. Every year Gracia sent him a terse thank-you letter. Only in 1939, after the Arab Revolt, did she finally acquiesce to Sami's request to meet her in Beirut.

Privately, she could not explain why she had agreed, since for years she had steadfastly refused every suitor, and there was ostensibly nothing about Sami that should compel her to make an exception. She sought advice from Mona, her sister and confidante, who told her it was probably related to age. For it was in those days that Gracia turned fifty.

Sami told no one of his planned meeting with Gracia. He was especially afraid to tell Hassan, as he did not know how his friend would react if he knew he was in love with this woman, who was not only ten years older than him but also Jewish. Back when they had first set eyes on Gracia, Hassan's uncle had told them, "Gracia always says she will never marry. She wants to keep her freedom."

What exactly would Sami offer Gracia when they met in Beirut? He considered this for many nights, as he lay in bed listening to Suad breathing while she slept. He had no answer. Even if Gracia decided to leave Damascus and follow him to Tel Aviv or Yafa, would he leave his wife and daughter? Where would he live with Gracia? And how would he protect her and himself in these days of madness?

Gracia asked her nephew Rafael to accompany her to Beirut. She was afraid to go alone and wanted to take advantage of their time together to tell him she had decided to give him the blue diamond when he married. Rafael had finished school and was working with his father and brother at the Bourse in Damascus, and planning to study medicine.

Sami did not want to travel alone either, and suggested that his daughter go with him. And so, while Sami and Gracia sat in the hotel restaurant, Rafael and Laila met for the first time in the garden café. The first thing Rafael noted was that one of Laila's eyes was blue and the other was brown.

Throughout their evening together in the restaurant, Sami and Gracia gave no thought to the two youngsters. They sat talking for a long time. Gracia wore a long-sleeved black dress and a chain of red gold around her lovely neck. Her face, which was less made up than it had been when Sami first saw her, looked slightly pale to him now, and he longed to caress her cheeks and plant a kiss deep in her neck. Gracia said nothing, but her penetrating gaze bore into him. After dinner they left the restaurant, and Sami took a key out of his pocket and let them into one of the hotel rooms. They did not emerge until much later.

The next morning, Sami and Laila boarded the train back to Yafa. The conductor blew his whistle to hurry the last of the passengers aboard, and Sami felt his heart plunge. Something fateful, he sensed, had almost occurred in his life, but it had changed course at the last minute and dropped away from him.

In the tense years of the Second World War, Sami and Hassan began speaking seriously of marriage between their children, Laila and Abed. Although at first it seemed little more than a whim shared by two old friends, it soon turned out that Abed was interested in the beautiful Laila and that she was not indifferent to him. They decided to wait until Abed finished his medical studies in Cairo and returned to Yafa.

At times, when Suad's depression worsened, Sami would travel with her and Laila north, to Lebanon. He insisted on accompanying them all the way to the convalescence home in Aley but always made a point of returning to his business in Yafa that same day. Suad lay in bed at the resort in Aley for weeks, refusing to get up. It was in this mountain resort town that Laila met Rafael again, this time with his new wife Adela. She spent her days with the couple, and their love eased her loneliness.

When she returned to Yafa with her mother, Laila kept up a correspondence with the Jewish couple from Damascus. None of the letters survived, and one can assume they were lost in the journey from Damascus to Tel Aviv.

When Abed finished his studies, he returned to Yafa as a certified physician. He wanted to be an optometrist in his hometown. Because of the political tensions, Laila and Abed held a modest, almost rushed wedding. They moved into Laila's childhood home near her grandparents' house, on the street that would later be named Sha'arei Nikanor. Abed was besotted with Laila and jealous of her, whereas within months of their marriage, Laila simply loved Abed as a given and inarguable fact, not with any sort of emotion that was to be nurtured.

Around them everything simmered and roiled. It was early 1948, and the city began emptying out. Almost every day there were explosions. People told of riots in Ha'Tikva neighborhood northeast of town, and in Menashiyya, the neighborhood on the beach. At night, snipers fired shots from the southern suburb of Bat Yam toward Yafa and, conversely, from Yafa to Tel Aviv. The Jewish underground movements set car bombs outside cafés, grenades were thrown at bus stations, and when the Saraya House was blown up by the Jewish underground, Sami heard the explosion as he sat in his parents' café nearby.

The Bride of the Sea was gradually becoming a ghost town. First the wealthy families left, and shortly afterward the independent business owners, followed by the craftsmen, the salaried employees, and finally the laborers. Sami stood by and watched the processions of vehicles leaving town. He naturally began considering his own departure but was undecided for a long time. The frightening events began to take their toll on Suad, who until then had been almost completely indifferent. At night she woke up terrified, and Sami tried in vain to reassure her. Even the news of Laila's pregnancy aroused no pleasure in the future grandmother, but in fact only increased her anxiety.

One morning, after another sleepless night, Laila went to see her father. She told him Hassan had decided to leave Yafa and was urging her and Abed to go with him to stay with his uncle in Damascus. At first Sami tried to hide his affront, feeling he should have learned of this plan directly from Hassan. But in light of the situation, he swallowed his pride and gave his blessing to the trip, which he believed would last only a few weeks. As for him, he was now determined to stay in Yafa.

Sami remembered well his visit to Hassan's uncle's home in Damascus in the 1920s, on that distant day when they had been hosted by Moussa Kadosh and he had first met Gracia. That was where his daughter now wanted to go, and perhaps there she would meet her—Gracia.

Laila and Abed helped Sami fill sandbags, and the two men stacked them along the walls around the house and inside. They filled the storage room with food supplies. Sami knocked a hole in the wall with a hammer, right where his parents had hidden their valuables during the riots in 1921. He felt around deep inside and extricated a few gold jewels. After giving the jewelry to his daughter, he took a stack of money out of his belt and handed it to her. Laila and Abed took nothing from their home. They left everything just as it was, knowing that at Hassan's uncle's house their needs would be met, until it was time to return to Yafa.

"When things calm down, we'll come home," Laila assured her father. And Sami repeated to Suad, "They'll come home as soon as things calm down." Suad gave her daughter a long hug, not wanting to let go. Laila and Abed kissed the family goodbye and set off. That was in March.

After the mayor's departure, only a few thousand residents were left in Yafa by April. Sami and Suad moved into the well house in the orchard. Sami paid two men to guard the house in Ajami, and every day he made his way there from the orchard to make sure no one had broken in.

Yafa surrendered to Jewish forces in May 1948. Sami Jabali was among the signatories to the surrender agreement, and although it stated clearly that any Arab who had left Yafa and wished to return could apply for reentry permission, the authorities were unwilling to allow Laila and Abed to return. The military government claimed Abed's application had not been submitted in good faith, having failed to prove that the petitioner did not and would not at any time pose a danger to peace and security.

# CHAPTER EIGHT

# ACHLAMA

*1*

AFTER HER HUSBAND DIED IN THE SPRING OF 2011, Achlama Java-heri inherited a lot near the flea market in Jaffa, as well as the apartment he had lived in till the day he died. For weeks the apartment stood empty and no one knew what to do with it. It was impossible to rent out, because according to the will, the rightful owner of the apartment was now the elderly, grumbling Persian cat that had lived there since it was a day-old kitten. The late owner had been extremely attached to the cat, despite or perhaps because of its selfish temperament. In their own way, the two had maintained a close friendship that had included many tacit agreements. The cat was unconcerned about its future after its owner died, and if any troubling thoughts did run through its mind, they were difficult to see in the vacant, sunken eyes in its squashed face. Either way, since officially an animal cannot inherit property, the executor of the will decided that the apartment would be registered in Achlama's name, on condition she took care of all the cat's needs.

But there was a problem: The new owner of the property adamantly refused to leave her rented apartment and move into the attractive new property she had inherited. Not only because of her memories, or because of her distress at the thought of living in the home of the man who had hurt her so badly, but also because of the cat. More than she feared angering the lawyers, Achlama feared the dead. And more than the dead, she feared cats and their evil nature.

After the will was read, it did not occur to anyone to remove the cat from its home, nor to bring in tenants to live with the cat. Achlama cursed and insulted the cat in every language it may or may not have known, and refused to take up residence with it. She appointed her son to care for its needs. The son did not dare defy his late father or his mother, and carried out his job with commendable precision.

Achlama had immigrated to Israel as a young girl, but her Persian accent still tinged every syllable she uttered. She had spent her whole life hearing jokes about her ethnicity, especially about the Persians' notorious cheapness, but try as she might, she was absolutely unable to get rid of the accent. It was stuck in her throat like a carp bone.

Decades earlier, after her husband left her, Achlama had grit her teeth and begun working as a cleaning lady. She got up every day at five and worked until the early evening. For years she hid her occupation from her daughter, telling her instead that she was employed by wealthy families as a nanny. Only her son was in on the secret.

Her longtime employers were used to her personality quirks. Every week she entered their home like a tempest: First she flung open all the windows, then she put old gym clothes on her slender body and, with rubber gloves on her hands, began throwing away everything she came across: toothbrushes, half-full tubes of toothpaste, old and current newspapers, unused medications, and various other objects she disliked and had no time to ponder the purpose of. When asked how she was, she would answer, "Thank the Lord, thank the Lord," and resume silently cursing the house and its filthy residents who had never heard of a mop or a vacuum cleaner.

Once a week, Achlama went into the Great Synagogue on Allenby Street to thank the Lord personally. She did so almost furtively, like a Catholic slipping into a confessional, and when she left she felt pure and cleansed for a short while. She made a point of regularly donating money to charity, because she knew there were always people more unfortunate than her.

When her children were grown, she began traveling the world, to her employers' astonishment. Each year she signed up for a package tour with National Geographic, and after she had made her way through all of "Classical Europe," she moved on to more exotic destinations. Apart from the trips, Achlama saved every shekel she made and hardly ever bought herself anything—except a piece of jewelry from the shop on Plonit Alley once a year on her birthday—and feared the day when her legs would no longer carry her to the apartments she cleaned and her hands would grow weak.

Once a year she invited her longtime employers to her home for a traditional Persian meal. She set out dishes of rice colored green, white, and yellow, decorated with a layer of potatoes that had cooked at the bottom of the pot; big, moist *gondi* meatballs swimming in chicken broth; and large cuts of meat nestled in green *sabzi* leaves. The guests, who knew each other from previous dinners, were allowed to discuss any topic in the world and could even tell ethnic jokes and gossip about Persian celebrities like Rita, Ahmadinejad, and Moshe Katzav. Only one topic was taboo: the host's profession. The guests were instructed ahead of time not to reveal how they knew Achlama, and although everyone knew very well that she cleaned the other people's homes, her employers respected her wish. They each had a cover story she had rehearsed with them: Some had met her in India, others in Brazil or Vietnam.

She hoped these gatherings would continue forever, but one fine day a lawyer phoned to inform Achlama that her husband had left her his apartment and the lot, along with savings amounting to a few hundred thousand dollars. Overnight, the hardworking housecleaner became a wealthy property owner. After making sure it was not a cruel joke, Achlama hurried to the Great Synagogue to thank the Lord and then walked to work as usual. With a glimmer in her eyes, she told her employers about her newfound fortune, but in the same breath reassured them that she had no intention of leaving her job. She was determined that her unexpected windfall would not even remotely change her life. Except for one thing: the jewelry.

Achlama had always had a soft spot for jewelry. Not for nothing was her last name Javaheri, which means "jeweler"

or "precious gem dealer" in Persian. Even as a child in Teh-
ran, Achlama loved to stare at her mother's jewelry and
secretly wear it, and she knew she could always put her faith
in gold, because gold—even in its raw form, even unpolished
and tarnished—meant strength and power and security. Jewelry was the only possession Achlama's mother had brought
with her to Israel: heavy handmade chains and magnificent
pendants that were works of art, signet rings embedded with
Persian turquoise stones.

When her mother died, Achlama inherited most of her
jewelry, and she fulfilled the vow she had made: Whatever
fate had in store for her, she would never sell or pawn these
jewels. Achlama always kept her word, even when hard times
came and she struggled to make a living. After she caught
her son hovering around the jewelry box, Achlama hid it in
a hole in the wall, in a spot only her daughter knew about.

## 2

After her husband's death, Achlama got rid of the blue diamond as quickly as she could. She gave it back to Menashe
the jeweler, mumbled a hasty apology, and left before he
could say anything about how the stone had come into her
husband's possession. A few weeks later, she plucked up her
courage to visit the jewelry shop on Plonit Alley again.

When she walked into the shop, the jeweler was sitting in
his spot working. I was polishing a ring at the machine, while
Honi sat on the other side of the counter looking at his phone
with great concentration. Achlama stood patiently scanning
the turquoise jewels under the glass until Menashe was free.

Menashe held his torch and put the flame to a red-gold ring. "I want you to know, Achlama, that I kept the jewel for you."

"Which one, the turquoise?"

"Yes."

"But you shouldn't have kept it, Menashe." Achlama felt guilty.

At that moment someone knocked on the door. Menashe's right hand caressed the red button under his workbench. He held up his left hand and signaled, *Closed*.

Honi laughed. "Menashe, you act like you're in the 1970s, back when there was a line of people out the door. Times have changed! People don't like buying jewelry anymore, they're not in the mood for it. So someone finally comes to the shop and you don't let him in?"

"I don't like the look of that character."

"Take my advice—if you want to make a living, you could stand to be a little less snobbish."

"Well, listen to you!" Menashe surveyed Honi through his large safety goggles. "Do you have any idea what happened here in 1991? Let me tell you, it was in all the papers. On the first day of the Gulf War, the buzzer in the shop was broken. And it was precisely then that a young man with a long coat and scarf walked in. He wanted to see some rings, so I showed him a few, and he chose one, but it was too big. And while I start working on it, he pulls a gun on me!"

"So what do you think Menashe did? Pulled a gun, too, of course," I added.

"He almost killed me!" Menashe said. "I escaped by the skin of my teeth."

"You were a big hero, Menashe," Honi said. "There's no doubt about that. Too big a hero, if you ask me. Why on earth did you pull a gun? What is this, the Wild West?"

"Those were different times."

"Do you still walk around with a gun?" Achlama asked worriedly.

"No."

Menashe doesn't carry a gun anymore, but I know very well that he doesn't let just anyone into his shop. He doesn't discriminate: If he doesn't want to let you in, you're not getting in. Doesn't matter if you're Mizrachi or Ashkenazi. And if he does let someone in and things get dicey, he'll hit the panic button, which alerts two places: the pharmacy next door, and the police. The pharmacist will get here first and the police a few minutes later. Most likely, as soon as they arrive the situation will deteriorate, because policemen—unlike doctors, for example—do not follow the imperative, "First, do no harm."

When Menashe brought up the robbery, Achlama kept uncomfortably silent. Because, as Menashe now knew, the notorious robber was none other than her late husband. And this is the story Menashe told us that day:

# 3

It was 1991. January 16. Exactly the day when the ultimatum the U.S. gave Saddam Hussein was expiring. On the news they talked all day about the war that was expected to break out and the Iraqis' chemical weapons. I didn't believe even for a minute there'd be rockets launched at Tel Aviv, but I was a little worried, because not a single customer came into my shop that day. In those situations no one thinks about jewelry.

And another thing—for some reason on that day the security system was broken and the alarm didn't work. I'd moved the workbench the day before to fix something, and a cable must have come loose. When I got here that morning, I discovered the alarm wasn't working. I should have closed the shop and gone home, but I decided to stay. Big mistake.

I didn't think any real customers would come in on a day like that, but I hoped someone might stop in for a repair, and then—if I was in good form—I might be able to palm off some new jewelry on them. Of course all sorts of people came in just to drive me crazy, and like I always do, I told them I don't pierce ears, I don't repair watches, I don't sell candlesticks, I don't buy silver, I don't sell gold-plated jewelry, I don't sell wholesale, and I don't buy equipment from businesses going bankrupt. None of that. At five thirty my mother Adela called, as usual.

"Why are you sighing like that, Menashe?"

"Because people are making me crazy all day."

"What crazy? Haven't they heard there's a war?"

"There's no war, Mom."

"Then why don't you shut down and go home? It's late already."

"It's only half past five."

"Half past five is late. Your father used to close the shop at four and come home. Tell me, have you exercised?"

"Yes."

"I don't believe you."

"Believe me."

"I keep telling you and you won't listen. You just sit there all day long on your chair like a potato. What's going to happen if a hooligan comes into the shop? You have to be in good shape, like my father was. Did you know that Grandpa Menashe killed a man in the Argentine?"

When we finished talking I stayed just where I was. It was one of those days when on the news they say things like, "The police are pleased: because of the security situation, all the thieves stayed home today."

All except one.

He wasn't tall and he wasn't short, my thief. He wasn't black and he wasn't white, didn't look like a square or like a criminal. I had no reason not to let him in, and anyway the buzzer was broken. I remember how he leaned on the door and it slid open like he'd said "Open sesame." I didn't have time to say Jack Robinson and he was already in the shop.

If anything looked strange to me about that man, it was the fact that he wore a scarf. It wasn't an especially cold day. When did I really start getting suspicious? When he asked to see rings. Men almost never come in to buy a ring without their girlfriend or wife. Doesn't happen. Still, I got up from my chair. When I turned around to the safe—one eye on the safe and the other on the guy—I saw him lean on the counter, looking around and whistling to himself. He wore blue jeans, a black button-down shirt, and a black coat. He had a little scar next to his eye. There are some things you never forget.

He kept whistling to himself while I took out the tray of men's rings and put it on the table. My thief held the tray with his thick, hairy hands and glanced at his reflection in the mirror. He noticed the dish of candy and asked if he could have one.

"Of course," I said.

He chose a ring and held it up to his eyes. "Is this gold?"

"Everything you see here is gold."

"Eighteen karats?"

"Fourteen."

"All of it?"

"I have some eighteen-karats, and some that are less. The ring you're holding is fourteen. That's the standard in Israel."

"How do you tell the difference?"

"In eighteen-karat gold, the ring will be slightly more yellow."

"Did you make this ring?"

"I made everything you see here."

"Talented man." He smiled. "Did you learn, or was it a God-given talent?"

"A little of both. Do you want to try on the ring?"

"Wait a minute," my thief said, "don't rush me. Let's see this one." He put the first ring back and took another. "When did you open this shop?"

"At nine this morning."

He smiled. "No, I mean how long have you owned it?"

"It's a family business. My father started it in 1950."

"Did your father make you work hard?"

"My father didn't like to work. He was just a tradesman. He didn't make jewelry himself."

My thief said, "I used to work with my father, too. He was a plumber. Every morning I went with him to work in people's houses. I was his assistant, I brought him all the tools from the truck, I got him falafel in pita when he was busy with clogged toilets, but he never said a kind word to me. Always complained: Why did you do this? Why didn't you do that? One day I just got sick of it and I left. I decided to go work on my own. You have some very nice jewelry here. And your father, did he make jewelry, too?"

"No, I told you."

"That's why you wanted to make jewelry. It's like me and my dad. Everything he did, I didn't want to do. But I didn't study and I didn't have diplomas, so I went to be a handyman. When you're a handyman, you go and knock down walls in people's homes, and they don't make your life easy. Treat you like you just picked up a hammer and broke down their walls without even asking them. I was at one lady's once, rich as Rothschild, and she had loose floor tiles. But I didn't touch her floor, because they asked me over to install a sink, not to fix the floor. Long story short, the next day the police come to my house. I open the door, ask them what happened, and they don't answer but they take me to the police station and a cop tells me, 'You saw the floor tiles were loose, so at night you broke into her apartment because you thought she was hiding dollars under the tiles.' Didn't matter what I said. They put me on trial and threw me in prison. You ever been in prison?"

"No. So what did you do?"

"I waited patiently in prison, killed time. And one day they found the real thief and let me out. That was a week ago. And here I am today."

"Who sent you to my shop?"

"My wife once told me about your shop. You mark my word, one customer in the hand is worth a thousand in the bush. Bottom line, why am I here today? Because I want to treat myself to a ring. So what do you say?"

"About what?"

"About the ring I chose."

"It's very nice, and fashionable. But it's the wrong size for you."

"It is?"

"Yes, it's too loose."

"So what? Are you afraid it'll fall off?"

"Yes."

"Can you resize it for me now? You don't look busy."

I could have sent him on his way. Could have told him I don't resize rings, I don't have time for him—basically, all the things I do when someone drives me crazy on any other day. But that day was not like other days. It was a day not a single customer came in, and mostly it was a day when I did not sit on my chair like a king and make pronouncements: This one comes in, that one does not. Whether I wanted him or not, my thief was in, and I figured if he was already in and I'd already let him tell me his whole story, I might as well fix the ring for him. So I sat down to work.

"How long will it take?" he asked.

"I don't know, depends if anyone disturbs me."

"No one's going to disturb you," my thief said. "They'll wait patiently." And as if to show me he was serious, he lifted his shirt up a little and I saw a pistol in his waistband. I remember, that was the moment I felt around under the table for the panic button. With the other hand I made sure my gun was in my pants, too. I took the ring and marked delicate parallel lines on the inside, then picked up the hacksaw and got to work.

My thief sat on a chair while I worked. He spread his legs out in front, took out a cigarette and smoked. After a few minutes he said, "You could tell me a story meanwhile."

"What story?"

"I don't know, something interesting. Did your father use to tell you bedtime stories?"

"He always told me the same one."

"Go on, tell it."

I carefully threaded a string through the ring and placed it on the parallel line, and to the sounds of the hacksaw screeching, I began speaking:

"It's the story of a very rich man who went and bought himself a slave. He bought him because he wanted a personal servant who would go everywhere with him, but also because he wanted someone he could consult with or just talk to, to ease his loneliness. Anyway, one morning he goes to the slave market and finds a boy he likes. He takes him home, and the boy is pleased because his new owner seems like a good man."

"Go on," said my thief.

"At night the man can't fall asleep. He goes to his servant's room and finds the bed is empty. The boy is gone."

"Ran away."

"Maybe. Anyway, he's not in the room. The man looks all over the house and in the yard, but he can't find him. Later that morning, he suddenly hears the door open. His servant is back. He goes over to the kid like a father whose son was lost and he doesn't know whether to slap him or hug him. But before he can make up his mind, the boy takes out an antique coin from his pocket and gives it to him. The master looks at the coin and realizes it's worth a lot of money."

"Where did the servant get the coin?"

"There's no way to know, and the master doesn't know either. He asks the servant, but the servant offers him a deal. He says, 'I will give you a valuable coin like this every day, but you must not ask me how I got it. And you must not follow me. If you ask me even once where I find these coins, I'll stop bringing them.' The man agrees, of course, because rich people never get tired of making more and more money. And also he knows that even if he orders the servant to stay at home at night, it won't do any good. Anyway, he takes the deal. And so every day the servant disappears in the middle of the night, and in the morning he comes home and gives his master a coin."

"So what, he never sleeps?" asked my thief.

"It's a fairy tale, my friend. In fairy tales people don't have to sleep. Anyway, the master doesn't dare ask questions, but at some point rumors start to fly. One day one of the rich man's friends says to him,

'They say your new servant is connected to a gang of grave robbers.' The master doesn't want to believe this, he's convinced there's a different explanation, and he decides to solve the mystery himself."

"How?"

"He breaks his promise. At night, when the servant leaves the house, the master sneaks after him. He follows him for miles and miles. They leave the city, get to a desolate area, and there the servant takes off his clothes, puts on a Sufi cloak, and starts praying. He prays for hours, almost till morning. At the end of the prayer he shouts, 'God, give me what I deserve!' And suddenly a coin falls from the sky and the boy picks it up. When the master sees this, he's so happy his servant isn't a grave robber that he decides to set him free."

"And then what?"

"When the servant hears the man wants to let him go, he is so excited that he picks up a handful of sand and throws it into his master's lap. And they each go their separate ways, but with a heavy heart. The man goes home alone, and when he gets there, he finds that in his lap are many dinars made of pure gold."

"Is that the end?"

"Almost. The man is happy with the gold dinars, but more than he is happy, he is sad, because he misses his servant very much. And then come all the people who told stories about the servant, and they mock him and say, 'What did you do with your servant?' And he tells them the whole story."

"And what do they say?" asked my thief.

"They regret all the stories they made up and they repent."

"Nice story," he said. "But you know, that master shouldn't have followed the servant."

"You think so?"

"Yes, trust me, there are things you're better off not knowing." He looked at his watch, considered for a moment, then asked, "So tell me, how's my ring coming along?"

"It's almost ready."

Then he asked out of nowhere, "Tell me, what's the most expensive thing you have here?"

I put the ring down on the bench and looked at him. I felt dizzy for a moment. And that's when I realized I was really done for. I repeated his question: "The most expensive thing?"

Then he asked exactly the question I was fearing: "Yes. Is there something here you hide deep in the safe, something you never take out?"

I decided that when he drew his gun, I'd pull mine, too. I'd draw my weapon, and whatever happened would happen. If it's written above that today is my day to die, that today a criminal will put a bullet in my stomach, then so be it. I wasn't afraid, because the dizziness passed and then I saw him for what he was: a thug with a scarf and a big mouth. And good taste, because after all he'd chosen a nice ring.

My thief didn't wait for me to answer. He wasn't interested in the ring anymore, wasn't interested in anything. He repeated his question like a parrot: "What is the most expensive thing you have here?"

My father always told us to take good care of Sabakh. He said, "That diamond is the most precious thing we have. Thanks to Sabakh, everyone in our family will eat well, and get an education, and marry well." And now the diamond belonged to Menashe Salomon from Plonit Alley. And I suddenly got so frightened by his gun that I told him about Sabakh.

My thief was confused. "What do you mean? One single diamond?"

"It's not just any diamond," I told him. I was covered in a cold sweat that made the safe key stick to my skin. It was too late now. From the minute I'd let that man into the shop, everything was decided: the conversation, the ring, Sabakh. So I told him how they'd stolen the diamond out of Shiva's third eye in India, how it had reached France and been sold to the king for 147 kilos of gold, and how it was embedded in the royal crown for Marie Antoinette, and how King George IV of England had worn it at his coronation, and how the diamond wandered on and took revenge on anyone who bought it, until it got to Sultan Abdul Hamid II, who ordered that it be split in two, and he named the little one Sabakh. And how Sabakh came to my family because of my great-aunt Gracia, and since then it was our secret possession, the only souvenir from a life long gone.

"Show it to me," my thief said.

At that stage I could have told him to go to hell. After all, he hadn't pulled his gun on me or threatened me, he hadn't even talked rudely. On the contrary—he was polite, just a bit nosy.

"Will you show me this Sabakh?" he asked again. He didn't even order me, he just asked quietly, like we shared a secret, like he was dependent on me now and nothing else interested him. Just him and me and Sabakh.

I turned around to the safe. I thought I could still pull my gun and finish him off, like my mother's father finished off that man in the Argentine. Just one thing stood in the way of my plan. I don't know whether to call it curiosity, or maybe superstition, but it was clear to me that I absolutely could not pull my gun and kill him, or worse—let him go—without knowing what Sabakh had in store.

So I took out the keys from my pocket, opened the safe, then unlocked the little safe inside the main one, and took out the box with Sabakh. But when I turned back and put the box on the table, a minute before I put the key in the lock, I saw out of the corner of my eye that someone was standing at the door. It was Dalia, the pharmacist from next door. She waved at me and smiled. I looked at my thief: His face was blank. I sighed and motioned for Dalia to come in. That day everything was wide open, it was all lawless. She pushed the door and walked in.

"Are you busy, Menashe?" she asked.

"I'm with a customer. Anything in particular?"

"There's a registered letter for you, it came this afternoon." She put an envelope on the table with my landlord's name and address on it.

"Thank you," I said.

Dalia didn't leave. She smiled at my thief and asked, "Wedding ring?"

He said, "Something like that."

"You're in good hands," Dalia said. "He has hands of gold."

"Thanks for the letter," I told her.

"No problem." She stopped for a moment and looked back and forth—at me and my thief, at my thief and me. She furrowed her brow, held up a finger and tapped one of her teeth, but after pondering for a minute she smiled again, turned around, and left.

Now I didn't waste any time. As soon as she left, I put the key in the lock and turned it, but before I had time to open the box, my thief put his hand over mine and slammed the box shut.

"Wait a minute."

"What's the problem?" I asked.

"No problem, just a question. Didn't you say this diamond was cursed?"

I sighed. "I didn't say it was cursed, just that people *claim* it's cursed. And anyway that's not this diamond but the original one, the one they cut Sabakh out of."

"So if there's no problem with this diamond, why did everyone want to get rid of it so badly?"

"I don't know." I was getting annoyed. "Maybe they just wanted to be kind to other people, and that's why they passed the diamond around. Did you ever think of that?"

"That doesn't make sense to me," he said. His hand was still on mine.

"What doesn't?"

"It smells fishy, your story. Forget it, I don't want to see the diamond. Forget I asked. Give me the ring, tell me how much I owe you, and I'll be out of here."

"No."

"What do you mean, no?"

"Don't start up with superstitions now. You're not leaving before I show you Sabakh."

"Excuse me?" He stared at me. "What do you mean? You can't tell me what to do!"

"Whether or not I can, I just sat here for half an hour working on your ring without getting a penny. I told you stories, you drove me crazy with your questions: What's the most expensive thing here? What do I put in the safe and what don't I put in it? And now you start with the superstitions? So please, I'm going to show you the diamond now."

He nodded, then looked up until his eyes met mine. "You're crazy."

I moved my hand out from under his and started turning the key in the lock.

And then he drew.

And the minute he drew his, I drew mine, and we were facing each other with our pistols aimed.

"What are you doing?!" he shouted. "Have you lost your mind?"

"Why didn't you listen to me?" I was breathing hard. I remember thinking that if he ran away I wouldn't be able to chase him, and it was the first time in my life I regretted not being in shape.

My thief said, "There are some things in life you're better off not knowing. I told you that before, when you told me your story about the grave robber."

"He wasn't a robber! Did you even listen to the story?"

"That doesn't matter now. You calm down. Put that gun down, god-damn it."

"God damn *you*!"

"No." He took a step closer to me and I could see that his eyes were bloodshot. "God damn you and your lousy diamond. I don't need any-thing from you, I'll tell everyone this is a lousy shop with crappy service, I'll give you bad publicity, you'll regret the day you let me in."

"I didn't let you in, you came in on your own," I said.

"Put the gun down! Nothing's going to happen, put down the gun and I'll leave."

I put the gun down on the table.

"Very good," he said, and started backing out toward the door. He reached out behind him and was already touching the handle. But a second before he left, I picked up the box and decided I wasn't giving in: I was going to show him that diamond.

"What are you doing?" He let go of the handle and walked back to me.

Now the two of us were holding the box with Sabakh. He held his gun in one hand, and with the other tried to stop me from opening the box.

"Don't you open that box!" he yelled.

"Don't tell me what to do."

"You're forcing me to take the diamond. I don't want it, but I'll take it if you don't let go of the box and put it back in the safe."

I wouldn't give in. In the end he managed to grab the box and get to the door.

"Wait!" I said before he left.

"What now?"

"You forgot your ring."

"I don't need your lousy ring," he practically whispered. Then he slammed the door behind him.

I leaned against the display window and watched him hurry away. I waited a minute or two and then pressed the panic button. Dalia came running from the pharmacy. When she saw me she let out a shout. I pointed to the gun lying on the table and said, "I've been robbed."

"Was it the man who was here, Menashe?"

"Yes."

"Why didn't you say anything when I came in before?"

"He had a gun."

When the police came, they fenced off the place and told me not to move anything. They took fingerprints and asked me loads of questions. They verified over and over again: "He only took the diamond?"

"Yes."

"Did he know it was a famous diamond?"

"Yes, he had information. It's a miracle he didn't shoot me." That's what I told them.

Today, when I think about it, it seems to me that I had to do it that way. It's like a genie got into me and I simply had to get rid of that diamond. That's how it seems to me today. Anyway, at night the war broke out and Scud missiles fell on Tel Aviv. The next morning, when I got to the shop, there wasn't a dog on the streets. I waited an hour, two hours, and in the end I went to visit my parents. I didn't want to tell them about the robbery over the phone, especially on a day when missiles were falling.

When my parents heard about the robbery, Mom said to Dad, "Rafael, go to synagogue and say a *gomel* blessing. That diamond is cursed, I always knew it would kill us in the end." But Dad refused to say the *gomel* blessing. He said, "You don't understand anything, Adela. That diamond saved your son's life. There's nothing to get angry about. Just as Sabakh left, it'll be back one day."

## 4

When Menashe had finished telling us the story of the robbery once and for all, from beginning to end, he was interested in only one thing: "What's going on with your book, Tom?"

"My book?"

"Yes. *The Diamond Setter.*"

"First of all, I'm not sure that's going to be the title anymore."

"Why? It's a good name."

"I was actually thinking of calling it *The Diamond.*"

"*The Diamond* is too general," Honi interjected, "it sounds a little meaningless."

"But it's not just any diamond," I reminded him.

"Then how about *The Blue Diamond?*"

"To tell you the truth, it doesn't matter what you call the book," Menashe announced. "*The Jeweler, The Diamond,* for all I care you can call it *The Third Hand.* Whatever you decide. But I want you to know that there's a whole shelf in this shop waiting for the book. And I hope your piano teacher didn't steal my thunder. After all, it's a book about a jeweler, not a pianist."

"Don't worry, Menashe, you have a place of honor in the book," I told him.

"I'm glad to hear it. So tell me, Tom, when can I read it already?"

"I'm doing revisions now. And then all I have left is the end."

"Don't get too bogged down with these stories," Menashe advised. "Remember what my thief said? You don't have to know everything. And my mother always said you have to know everything, but you don't have to *say* everything. That's the whole thing."

I wasn't going to argue that point with him. I myself hadn't decided what one needed to know and how much, and if there really were things better left unsaid. The farther I got in the book, the more I knew about certain things and the less about others. Every time I uncovered a secret, another, larger one turned up behind it. Eventually I started doubting even the smallest facts.

"Tom," Honi said with a laugh, "I think Menashe's afraid you're going to give away his deepest secrets."

"Who told you such a thing?" Menashe raised his eyebrows.

Honi ignored him. "Well, whatever you decide to do, I would advise your readers to be suspicious. Always be suspicious: Every time they get close to the truth, it runs away from them."

"What difference does it make anyway?" Menashe asked. "I mean, in any case it all comes from your imagination, doesn't it?"

"Precisely," said Honi. "Remember, we're talking about a work of literature, not the Channel 2 news. So let's settle it: Everything the reader believes is the truth. Maybe not the absolute truth, but the Diamond Setter's truth." There was a brief silence, and then Honi gazed at me with his beautiful brown eyes. "What are you thinking about now, Tom?"

"I'm thinking about my characters. And about the book, and the ending, which I haven't written yet. It always seems like a momentous battle: Who will finish off whom first—me the book, or the book me?"

"Maybe both?" Honi suggested.

"Maybe."

Menashe went back to his work, Honi to his cell phone, and I adjusted my safety glasses, pressed a button on the machine, and began polishing the pile of rings I had to get through. After work, Honi and I walked to the café, as usual.

Honi was contemplative. "Are you thinking of spending your whole life working at the jewelry shop?" he asked on the way.

"If your father doesn't throw Menashe out first. Why do you ask?"

"Why don't you come to Berlin with me?"

"And leave the jeweler on his own? Just like that?"

"I'll speak with Kadosh. Maybe we can do something about it."

"Like what, exactly? Your father will never give up on his boutique hotel."

"I'll think of something."

"From your lips to Kadosh's ears. So tell me, did you go to the Garden of the Two in Jaffa?"

"No, why?"

"But we talked about it!" I gently slapped the back of his neck. "You're a lost cause, Mr. Hanan."

"We did? When?" He stopped and looked at me, befuddled.

"And you have the gall to boast about your phenomenal memory?"

"I swear, Tom, I have no recollection of talking about this."

"All right, never mind. You promised me you'd go to the Garden of the Two and talk with the people who set up tents there. Will you do that for me?"

"If it's important to you, then of course. Although I want you to know that I'm getting a little fed up with this social protest. I don't have enough material for a program. I mean, I have lots of material, but nothing that can hold together a show."

"Go there, and then we'll see," I said. "Maybe we'll even kill two birds with one stone."

"Okay."

"But listen, Honi. I don't want you to just go there."

"What do you mean?"

"When you get to the park, turn on the app."

"What app?"

"Grindr."

"But you know I don't use it anymore now that we're going out, Tomi…"

"I know. But I'm asking you to log in. And not just that: If someone contacts you while you're there, someone located very close to you, answer him. And if he wants to meet up, arrange it."

"I don't get it. Are you trying to set me up with someone, or have you started pimping me out as a side gig?"

"Very funny. Just do this for me, okay? I'll explain afterward."

# CHAPTER NINE

# LAILA

*1*

ON THE DAY FAREED TURNED NINETEEN, he went to visit his grandmother Laila in the Almaza neighborhood of Damascus. She served lentil soup on the balcony, and while they ate she told him about his grandfather, Abed. Her eyes grew distant as she talked about the man she had lived with for over fifty years until his sudden death, and it was clear her thoughts were sailing far away.

"I told you how every summer I used to go with my mother to Aley, right?" she asked her grandson.

"Yes." When he was a child she had told Fareed how she looked forward every year to those trips, and about her Yafa days, when she would sit on a rock by the sea and look out north.

"Do you know how beautiful Lebanon was? Back then they called it 'the Switzerland of the Middle East.'"

Fareed nodded. "And what about Yafa? Do you miss it?"

Laila thought for a moment. "No," she said finally.

"Really? But you grew up there—how can you not miss it?"

"When a tree is cut down, does it miss its roots?" she asked contemplatively.

"What sort of a girl were you, Grandma?"

"I don't know. Just a girl."

She said those last words with a childish smile and a nostalgic tone, and Fareed could suddenly see her as she once was. And he felt very close to her, even more than usual.

"Are you angry?" he wondered.

"At who? The Zionists? No, I'm not angry."

"How can you not be angry?"

Laila did not answer. She thought about the day she'd left Yafa with Abed and his family, and about their arrival in this foreign city. They had managed to integrate in Damascus over the years, thanks to family connections and Abed's flourishing career.

It was not long after their arrival that Laila had learned of her mother Suad's death. After that, she met with her father, Sami, in Paris every year. Sami gave Laila all the news from Yafa, which had changed unrecognizably. He told her about the Jews who lived in the homes she knew, the new neighborhoods they were building, the houses that had been destroyed, the orchards now owned by the Jewish National Fund. He described in great detail his struggle to keep the house on Sha'arei Nikanor Street in the family. The house was locked up now.

Laila listened to her father's stories. She gave him a picture of her son, Shaker, so that Sami would have a souvenir from his grandson. Finally, she could not resist asking about Rafael and Adela.

Sami described Rafael's jewelry store on Plonit Alley, and told her about Menashe, their dreamy little son. Finally, and not without trepidation, Sami confessed his relationship with Gracia.

At first Laila said nothing. Sami examined her expression curiously and wondered if she understood what he was saying.

"Have you kept in touch with her all these years?" Laila finally asked.

"Yes."

"So you met with her while Mother was still alive, after our trip to Lebanon?"

"No, we corresponded by mail."

"Does her family know about your relationship?"

"Only Rafael's son, Menashe. He's exactly Shaker's age."

Laila thought about Shaker, whom she had been carrying when they left Yafa. She pursued her train of thought: "And Rafael . . . Did he ask you about me?"

"I never see him. Gracia doesn't want her family to know me. Rafael's son came to visit one day when I was there and surprised us together. Apart from him, no one knows."

"What about people in Yafa? Do they know you visit Gracia?"

"No."

"Do you want to live with her?"

"I don't know, Laila. All those years I lived with your mother, I was alone. She wasn't really there with us. Gracia is the only woman who was always there when I needed her."

Laila's eyes glistened for a moment. It was difficult for her to hear these things about her mother, though she knew her father was being truthful.

"If you only knew how difficult it is to be far away," he said, and she didn't know if he meant the current distance between him and his daughter and grandson, or the years when Gracia had been far away from him.

They said goodbye, Sami returned to Yafa, Laila to Damascus. The following year, Laila brought Shaker to Paris to meet his grandfather.

## 2

In those years when Laila met her father in Paris, Gracia lived near Yafa, Laila in Damascus, and Rafael and Adela in Tel Aviv. It all fell into place almost as though an invisible hand had intervened. Now, at the age of eighty-five, on her grandson Fareed's birthday, Laila felt she had the opportunity to revisit those times and places, to ruffle things up a little, to disrupt the natural course of things and wipe away the borders, at least the ones in her mind's eye. She felt a burning urge to talk openly with her grandson, although she feared the conversation. She looked at him and asked, "Fareed, tell me, do you have a girl?"

He blushed, looked down, and fiddled with his cell phone. "No," he finally said. He took a pack of cigarettes out of his pocket and lit one.

"When I was twenty, I fell in love for the first time," Laila said. She finished her soup, leaned back in the chair, and gazed out at the high treetops in the courtyard. "Up until then, men had fallen in love with me, but I had rejected them all. My first true love was a slightly peculiar love. But what can you do, that's how things happened."

Fareed said nothing, only looked tenderly at his grandmother.

It was hard for Laila to imagine what was going through her grandson's mind, and she decided to pick up his original question. "Do you really want to know what I miss, Fareed? It's difficult to say exactly. Sometimes a person can miss themselves. Do you think that's possible, to miss yourself? After all, you could say that you are the closest you can be to yourself—you don't even have to reach out very far. You never leave yourself even for a second! And yet you can be very distant from yourself. And one day you can discover that you have grown so distant that you can no longer go back. You have nowhere to return to. The place you left behind is no longer the same place: the smell, the air you breathe, the things you touch, even the sights. Nothing is the same."

Fareed looked at her questioningly. He reached out and put his fingers in her hand, and she softly kissed his fingers with her warm lips. Then she told him stories he had never heard before: about her trips to Aley and her meetings with Rafael and Adela, the long nights in their hotel room, the blue diamond. Laila spoke firmly and somewhat urgently, and Fareed leaned back in his seat and listened.

After some time, Laila got up and went into the living room. She opened one of the glass cabinet doors, took a box off the top shelf, came back to the balcony and sat down next to her grandson. When she removed the lid, Fareed saw a bundle of photographs tied with elastic thread. She untied the knot and placed the pictures on the table. Fareed looked at them silently.

The first picture showed a very young woman sitting in between another woman and a man. Behind them was a window showing a strip of sky and a few treetops, and above the window was a rolled-up screen, open just enough to reveal a different landscape. It seemed the photographer had not had time to roll down the artificial landscape, or perhaps this was a practice photograph. Fareed looked at the people in the picture. The young woman in the middle had a necklace twinkling on her chest, which he immediately recognized: It was the pendant his grandmother always wore, with three delicate lines engraved horizontally.

"Is that you?" But he knew it was, having also noticed that the girl in the picture had one eye that was darker than the other. "Who are they?" he asked, although he could already imagine.

"Those are Rafael and Adela."

In the picture, Rafael sat on his chair with a stern expression. His brow was furrowed and his lips pursed, with one hand on his knee and the other in Laila's hand. Rafael's wrist was folded in a gentle position that contrasted with his severe look. On Laila's other side sat Adela, her shoulders slightly hunched, with a questioning, somewhat suspicious face, small black eyes, fairly short-cropped hair, one hand on her knee and the other in Laila's hand.

"Look how we were dressed!" Laila said to Fareed. "With sleeveless dresses, and above the knee, like they wear in Paris. And our heads were bare, you don't see that anymore."

Fareed studied the women and man holding hands, and he suddenly perceived a tension, a restlessness: Adela's hunched shoulders, Rafael's lost look, Laila biting her lip.

"Why did Adela give you that diamond?" he asked after a few moments. He lit another cigarette.

"It was the last time we met. She wanted me to keep it for her."

"Why?"

"Because she was afraid to have it, but she didn't dare give it to anyone else."

"What was she afraid of?"

"What can I tell you, Fareed? She was a complicated woman. And she loved me. Maybe she wanted me to have a souvenir."

"Did you love her?"

"I think so."

"What do you mean, you think so?"

"It was a long time ago."

"What about Rafael, did you love him, too?" He spoke candidly. It was hard for him to imagine the situation, but ultimately he felt he did understand. One thing still bothered him: "If you say Adela loved you, then how can you explain the fact that she gave you a cursed diamond?"

"I didn't believe in that."

"But Adela believed in the curse, didn't she?"

"I think she did."

"After all, you told me yourself that she spoke to you explicitly about the diamond's curse and said she was afraid to keep it."

"Yes, but I thought it was nonsense."

"Maybe she gave it to you because she actually wanted to hurt you?"

"Are you mad?"

"Maybe. I mean, after she gave it to you, you had to leave Yafa."

"At that point we didn't have to leave yet. We decided to go away until things calmed down. It was only a few months later that people started leaving Yafa because they had to."

"That doesn't change the fact that you left your home after meeting Rafael and Adela in Aley, and then you weren't allowed to go back."

Laila looked at Fareed as though she were seeing him for the first time as he really was. "That's a very unkind thing to say."

"What?!"

"The things you just insinuated, Fareed. It's not kind. I just told you some very personal things. Maybe you don't understand this sort of matter—" She stopped short because his look told her he was all too familiar with the things she spoke of.

"No, I'm glad you told me," Fareed said. "But this issue bothers me. Would you rather I just listen without saying anything?"

Laila was lost in thought. Perhaps she regretted being so open with him. But it was too late. Now he knew. Although in fact, he didn't know everything. And she felt she had to defend Adela and Rafael, or at least try to distract Fareed from the diamond. She told him about their last night in Aley, about the pregnancy in Yafa and the difficult birth of Shaker, his father, in their new home in Damascus, in 1949.

Fareed was confused. "Why are you telling me this?"

"Because you need to know."

"But why?" Fareed wanted to know and yet he didn't.

"You already understand," Laila said, and her voice was low now, "that the baby I gave birth to in Damascus..."

"My father."

"Yes, your father. Well, his real father was..."

"I don't believe you." Fareed got up and sat down again, trying to maintain his composure. "This is a made-up story, a thousand and one nights."

"You could look at it that way," she said, and tried to take his hand. "In fact maybe it's better you did. It doesn't matter anymore, and maybe I shouldn't have told you. But I've kept silent for so long."

Fareed leaned back. After a moment he stood up. "Who else knows about this?"

"No one, only you."

"Mother doesn't know?"

"No."

"And Father?"

"No."

"That diamond..." Fareed's voice was low and ominous. "Where is it now?"

"Why do you ask?"

"I want to know."

"I've already decided that when the time comes, you will get the diamond."

"Me? But why?"

"Because that is what I want."

"But where is the diamond now, Grandma?" He turned to her and his voice cracked.

"Fareed," she tried to calm him, "everything in life has its time."

She was fearful upon seeing him so upset and deeply regretted the things she had told him. But it was too late. She bowed her head in defeat. Her shoulders shook. She hardly noticed Fareed standing up. He leaned over and was about to kiss her forehead, but at the last moment he turned around. He walked inside and went to his grandmother's bedroom. Laila heard him open the closet drawers and dig around, and imagined him finding the box with the blue diamond. She did not move and did not say a word.

### 3

Adela and Rafael did not speak of it between themselves. In the months they spent at home in Damascus, everything proceeded ostensibly as usual: Each morning they led the animals from the farm to Adela's family's slaughterhouse. The *shochets* slaughtered the beasts with a sharp knife, and at midday they sold chunks of red meat to their customers. The poor young men whose job was to inflate the sheep carcasses with air in preparation for skinning walked back and forth between the butchers and the slaughterhouse with blood congealed on their lips and glazy eyes. Every day Rafael went to work at the Bourse, ate lunch with his friends in the souk, and went home to Adela in the evening.

Laila sent them a letter from Yafa every week. They read her letters together, and then sat down to read them again separately. Adela shut herself in her bedroom for a long time, her fingers still damp from cooking. Her eyes delved into Laila's words, and she tried to decipher the meaning behind them, or perhaps to imbue them with what she longed to find.

Laila did not explicitly mention the date of their next meeting in her letters, although she did on rare occasions admit to missing them both, and said she thought of them often. Adela was not sure if one could really miss two people equally, and she wondered if Laila truly thought of them both, or if perhaps she sometimes loved one and hated the other, yearned for one and not the other.

She did not dare discuss Laila with Rafael. She loved him now even more than before, and felt she had enough love inside herself for both Rafael and Laila. Neither of them was deprived, and in fact quite the opposite: The more she loved, the greater her capacity to contain the love, and she filled up with love as one can become filled with memories.

This is how it began: One summer, Laila traveled to Aley with her mother, Suad. The day after they arrived, she came upon Rafael with his wife, Adela, in the café. Rafael was resting his head on his hand. A newspaper was spread out beneath his saucer, and he read comfortably while he sipped coffee. Adela sat opposite him in an airy light blue dress. Her hair was curly and black. She sat straight up and looked far away. Rafael said something to her, and she looked back at him and answered.

What were they talking about? Laila wondered. She longed to go over to them but she was embarrassed. Finally her curiosity got the better of her. She got up and went over. Rafael looked up at her, said hello without any apparent embarrassment, and introduced Adela. Rafael could not conceal his smile when the two women shook hands.

He asked for the check and paid, and the three walked out and strolled the streets side by side. Rafael told Laila that his father had died shortly before their wedding, and so the glorious celebration they had planned was canceled and instead they had a modest meal. He told her about the relatives, especially those who came from Turkey and Iraq, and about his aunt Gracia who sang traditional wedding *piyutim* for the young couple.

While he talked, Adela looked at Laila. A breeze blew in and ruffled her hair. She swiftly ran her fingers through it and braided it loosely. Laila smiled.

Rafael kept talking about the Bourse and his in-laws' slaughterhouse, about Adela who refused to eat meat ("Only vegetables and chicken for her, she feels sorry for the cows"), about the days of war in Damascus and the shocking events in distant Europe. Eventually they reached the hotel. Rafael looked at Adela and smiled with his bright eyes. He told her to go up to their room and promised to join her soon. Adela did not object. Perhaps she was happy to be alone. She said goodbye to Laila and lightly touched her shoulder. Rafael kissed Adela on the lips and she turned and left.

Rafael and Laila walked toward the place they had first met, a few years earlier, when Rafael had come with his aunt Gracia and Laila with her father, Sami. Time seemed to have stood still in the café, with its lush garden and tree-shaded benches, where lemonade was served in tall glasses garnished with thick sprigs of fresh mint.

"How was your journey?" Rafael asked when they sat down.

"So-so," Laila replied. "It was hot on the train and I was nauseous from the dry air. Perhaps also from the excitement. How was it for you and your wife?"

Her emphasis did not escape him. "It was a pleasant journey. We were happy to get out of Damascus for a bit. The last few months have been too busy."

There was another silence. Laila looked down at the ground. Rafael studied her expression and tried to read in her eyes the way her life would unfold without him, far away from him.

When he had first met Laila, he had noticed something that made her face unique: One of her eyes was blue and the other brown. It was clear to him that these eyes suited her capricious nature, a very stable foundation tinged with delusion and changeability. How different was Adela, with her black hair and small black eyes and the constant skepticism and judgment on her face, as well as unspoken mockery.

Laila was as curious as a little girl, although her life was already sketched out almost completely: She was about to marry, she would have a family with Abed in Yafa, she would probably soon be a mother, in charge of a household and the children's education. They knew nothing yet of the nomadic life in store for her and Abed.

To overcome his awkwardness, Rafael asked a lot of questions about Laila's fiancé: What sort of man was he, what kind of doctor did he want to be, how did he treat her, did he care for her well? And how many children did they want? And what were things like in Yafa, after years of violence? What did they think about the situation between the Zionists and the Arabs?

Laila gave Rafael a distant look. She was clearly not especially bothered by the political situation. Her feet were planted in the present so firmly that she did not believe things could change, even though in recent years it was impossible to deny that violence was looming over the entire land. Her thoughts were preoccupied by completely different matters. Burning with curiosity, she asked Rafael about Adela. What sort of woman was she? Did she like summer or winter? What was her loveliest quality, in his opinion, and what sort of relationship did she have with her mother and father? And how had their wedding night been?

Rafael answered all her questions, and then there was another silence. Was she satisfied? It seemed that his forthright answers were paradoxically making her restless. She wanted to get up and say goodbye, but just then Rafael gently touched her hand, and she fell back against the back of the bench.

He took out a little box from his pocket and looked around to make sure none of the café dwellers was watching. Rafael opened the box, and Laila beheld a diamond with a bluish tone that danced in the sunlight. "I've never seen such a beautiful diamond," she said after a long silence. She studied Rafael's face, which turned grave. He began to say something, but after a few truncated syllables he fell into a heavy silence again. When he finally opened his mouth and began telling his story, Laila gaped. This was not what she was expecting. Instead of explaining the origins of the diamond, he began telling a strange tale about his aunt Gracia, his mother's sister. Rafael wished to know if there were chanteuses in Yafa, too, but he discovered that

Laila did not even know the word. He paused awkwardly but continued his story and allowed her to read between the lines.

Back when Gracia was a young girl, Rafael explained, she was known for her delightful voice and wonderful singing. Rich men came from near and far to hear her sing and enjoy her beauty and company. Gracia became famous throughout Syria, Rafael recounted with a hint of pride, and one day, "You won't believe this, she even met the Turkish sultan!"

Laila looked at him in astonishment.

"The Turkish sultan bought the diamond in 1901," Rafael continued, ignoring Laila's dubious look. "But the diamond you see here is actually only part of the original one. It came to Europe from India in the seventeenth century. The sultan paid almost fifty thousand dollars for it."

When he finished telling the story of how the diamond ended up being gifted to his aunt Gracia, Laila carefully took the box, removed the diamond, and held it in her hand to examine it.

The next day she dined with Rafael and Adela in one of the restaurants that looked out on the mountains. After dinner they invited her to their room. The two women sat on the sofa. Adela inhaled the scent of the unfamiliar body—the body that later, when its limbs were so familiar, she would find traces of in every blouse or pillow or even walking down an alleyway. And then her fingers were in Laila's hand. The windows, veiled with yellow curtains, were open to the valley. Rafael sat on a wooden chair to the side. His face was flushed after a morning spent out in the sun, and he stared at the curtains. Then his eyes rested on the two women. They asked him to come over and sit with them. Together, they asked him. And he came.


At night Laila lay between them on the wide bed. Her head rested on Rafael's chest, and he felt his heartbeats imprinting her cheek. Adela lay with her back to them, facing the window, with the back of her foot on Laila's shin.

That long night sustained Rafael's thoughts for a whole week. Over and over again he remembered the long hours the three of them spent in each other's arms. He looked forward to their next meeting but did not count the days. It was not the anticipation of a man in love but rather a vaguely distorted sense of time, as though the three of them existed in a time and space that were measured differently. The anticipation of fulfilling his passion imbued him with pleasure but also instilled in him a constant disquiet, and his spirit—which he had controlled so finely in the past—was uneasy most of the time. His mood swung back and forth like a pendulum: happiness, dulled senses, restlessness. And above all—yearning.

In the morning, Adela leaned over Laila, who lay curled up under the sheet with her head beneath a pillow, uncovered her cheek, and kissed her. "Are you awake, Laila?"

"Yes," came a low, steely voice from under the pillow.

"How are you? Did you sleep well?"

"I slept all right, but I'm not all right today," Laila answered.

"Why not?"

"I'm asking for trouble today."

Adela looked questioningly at Rafael, who lay on the other side of the bed watching them. "What do you mean?" she asked, trying to keep her composure.

"We'll see," came the answer from under the pillow.

Adela pulled away. She covered her eyes with her hands and wondered what she would do today.

A few moments later, Rafael got up and went to the bathroom, and Laila said to Adela, "Rafael showed me the blue diamond."

"Did you tell anyone you saw it?"

"No."

"Very good. No one must know about it. It's a secret, you know."

"I know, and I won't say a word."

"I'll tell you something: I don't like that diamond."

"But don't you think it's beautiful?"

"It's very beautiful," Adela said. "There's no denying that. But its story... It'll bring us nothing but trouble, that diamond."

"If you're talking about the curse, then you should know that I don't believe in that kind of nonsense." Laila grinned. "That's a Turkish superstition."

"How can you not believe it? They cut off the head of the queen of France in the guillotine—don't you believe *that*? And the king of England, are you saying he had a good life? And the Turkish sultan—did you hear what happened to him in the end?"

"I don't believe that stuff," Laila said ponderously. "What can I tell you? A thousand and one nights... You can't blame a little stone for every trouble."

Adela turned to look at Rafael, who had come back to the room with a glass of *yansoon*. He sat down by the window and sipped quietly.

The following night was long, and Adela had disturbing dreams. All three shared the bed again, and again she saw on her right Rafael's large back, rising and falling to the rhythm of his slow breaths, and to her left Laila's body huddled against the wall, her head buried between two pillows and one foot reaching back, as if probing for something. All night long Adela tossed and turned in the gap between the two, afraid of the moment when dawn would come.

As soon as the sky took on a pale white color, the horrible screeching of the chickens came from beneath the window, and it grew louder and louder, as though the dawn were about to wring their necks. When the sky was finally captured by a pale blue, the chickens were spent. Between the bushes lay a dozen eggs as an offering, their shells soiled with mud.

They sat on the balcony and ate scrambled eggs with pieces of onion, and vegetables the cook had picked from the garden, drizzled with olive oil. Laila filled her glass with more and more lemonade, and after every sip she chewed the sprigs of fresh mint to extract every drop of their essence. Adela concentrated on her eggs and dipped slices of fresh bread in the olive oil. Her forehead was wrinkled in concentration, and it seemed she had to make a great effort.

Rafael perused the French newspaper under his coffee saucer, as was his habit, and tried to guess at the hidden fragments of headlines. After their meal, he sat in the big armchair and sipped *yansoon* while he wrote letters. The two women stayed on the balcony talking, and after a while they joined him. There was total silence outside, and they could hear the curtains rustling against the open windows. Adela thought of their imminent parting and wondered when they would meet again. As soon as the memory of separation rose in her consciousness, she was eager to reach the moment and cross it, as one traverses a difficult path.

Rafael took a small box from his pocket and gave it to Laila, a gift from Adela and him. Laila opened the box and found an eighteen-karat gold chain with a pendant engraved with three delicate lines, curling and intertwining with each other.

It was time to say goodbye.

They kissed in the hallway, and Laila went into her mother's room. Rafael and Adela turned back and disappeared into their own room, and the door shut behind them.

CHAPTER TEN

# FAREED

*1*

IT HAD BEEN FOUR DAYS since Fareed's return. He'd visited Shami Bar twice, joined one mass protest in Tel Aviv, and snuck out to glimpse the sea of Yafa several times.

When he stood looking at the sea, Fareed's gaze skipped over from the pale rocks to the sand, from the sand to the shallow waters, and out to the spot where the earth drops away and subterranean currents color the sea in dark turquoise and black. He was never bold enough to wade into the water, and was surprised at the children splashing around in this sea that could wash over all of Yafa at any minute, and the young boys climbing on each other's shoulders to make pyramids in the water.

Rami worked every night to save money before the semester started. He kept warning Fareed never to tell anyone where he was from and was privately starting to wonder about the visitor's intentions. When they had corresponded, Rami was able to discount the borders between them, and the whole land seemed to him one entity. But here in Yafa, he felt a certain foreignness between him and the young man from Damascus, and for the first time in his life he began to contemplate those distant days of early 1948. Had the Jews expelled Fareed's family? Perhaps they left when conditions became intolerable? He knew they'd lost their home and much of their property in the war, but they had survived without any physical harm. Their ears had not been deafened by bombardments, their vehicles were not confiscated for the war effort, and they escaped the days of panic and fear.

And what if Fareed were to ask Rami why his own family had stayed in Palestine all these years? But those who stay in their homeland—Rami would reason defensively—don't owe anyone explanations or excuses. Those who left were victims of war, and they should not justify leaving by blaming the ones who stayed behind. No one in the whole Arab world wants to take us in, Rami would say. We're viewed with contempt and hatred, we're ugly.

He looked at Fareed, who was a handsome man: purplish-red lips, long soft curls, large and smiling dark eyes. He was fairly short, his body solid and well proportioned, his skin smooth, fingernails nicely shaped. He disliked his stocky thighs and tended to wear pants that hid their shape. Rami, in contrast, was tall, thin, and dark skinned, with thick black stubble and tiny eyes. The gold chain he wore was visible on his smooth chest. They were incompatible, and not just physically. Their eyes did not gaze at the same places.

Their thoughts did not coincide. They spoke at the same time, or else were given to long silences.

After a few days, Fareed realized that Rami's hospitality was standing in the way of fulfilling his mission. Rami, on his part, missed his privacy and also began fearing that Fareed's secret would be discovered and get him mixed up in a world of trouble. If his parents knew he was sheltering an illegal alien, they would accuse him of endangering the entire family.

After a long conversation with Rami, Fareed packed up his bag, stood on his tiptoes, and kissed Rami on the cheeks. Rami gave Fareed a bear hug and his scent flooded Fareed's nostrils. Then he quickly pulled away, thanked his friend, turned, and left. Rami watched him walk down the steps and shut the door behind him after he'd disappeared.

The streets were languid. Fareed's shirt clung to his skin in the humid heat, and when he turned to look at the sea, he saw nothing but a blinding yellow spot. Voices swirled around in his mind, and for a moment he did not know if they were coming from the street or from inside him. Only now, without a focal point or center of gravity in Yafa, did he see the city through the eyes of a true illegal alien rather than a tourist. He felt nauseous. He stopped at a street corner, leaned on a utility pole, and spat onto the crumbling wall. A few cats circled around him in some sort of incomprehensible dance, their tails erect and their heads bobbing like snakes. He took a few sips from his water bottle, then walked on without knowing where he was headed. He walked down Yefet Street, the route he had taken when he first got here.

Fareed did not know a single person, nor did anyone know him. A local said something to him in Hebrew, and he panicked. But when he spoke up in Arabic, he was answered in his language. He was afraid to talk to anyone, suddenly convinced he would be pegged as a foreigner by his features and expression. The blue diamond rattled in its box inside his pocket, and every step reminded him of its presence.

He stopped to look at a little park among the houses. There was a hammock hung between two trees. Tents had been set up on the grass, children ran among them, and birds flitted under the branches. A few men sat on plastic chairs smoking a hookah, with a little hill of mineral water bottles piled up behind them. Fareed stood some distance from the tents, breathing in the air.

"*Khalas*—it's enough! People are exploding here," he overheard one of the men say. He was smoking a hookah and speaking into a microphone that a soldier was holding. "How much longer can we keep quiet?" The man told the soldier he was twenty-eight years old, married, the father of a five-year-old boy and a four-year-old girl. He worked as a painter, rented a small one-bedroom apartment on Yefet Street, and made 3,400 shekels a month. "My parents were born in Yafa, my whole family is from here. We didn't run away in the war, we stayed despite everything. But today I can't buy an apartment, I can barely make ends meet. I have nightmares every night, I only think of one thing: money. My wife is afraid I'll start stealing or dealing drugs. We don't want to leave Yafa, and anyway we can't. Where would we go—Tel Aviv? Ramat Gan? Where will my kids go to school? The city said young couples will be able to buy an apartment in Yafa soon, but how many couples are they talking about? Thirty? Forty? That won't help us."

An older man sitting next to him added, "This has nothing to do with Jews and Arabs, it's about the rich against the poor."

Then someone spoke to Fareed, in Hebrew, "Do you live in Jaffa?" When he didn't answer, she repeated the question in English, and he said he was from New York.

"Tourist?"

"Yes."

She asked how he was spending his time in Israel, whether he'd visited Jerusalem, the Negev Desert, the Carmel forests. Fareed said he'd only arrived the day before yesterday and didn't know anything yet.

"Where are you staying?" she asked.

"In a hostel in Tel Aviv," Fareed answered. "But I want to save money, so I thought I might couch surf."

"Why don't you just sleep here with us?"

"Where?"

"In the tent camp. You're welcome to."

"But I don't have a tent."

"That's okay, we'll figure something out."

And so Fareed settled in the tent camp in Yafa.

They spoke in languages he understood and in some he did not. The new tent settlers sat around talking all day and all evening, in Arabic and Hebrew, and at night they kept sitting there because they knew the earth would not run away beneath their feet. Every morning they gathered in a circle on the lawn, conducted debates, and declared in two languages: "We are the new Israelis."

This was how Fareed became, for the first time in his life, a worker, and for the first time in his life he demanded social justice. He sat in the circles and took part in the debates and made odd gestures with his hands. Sometimes they let him talk. He discussed alienation in the capitalist society, the generation gap in contemporary culture, the Arab Spring, and other affairs that troubled the tent dwellers in Yafa and in Tel Aviv and in all of Palestine.

He knew what he was talking about. He knew about the Arab Spring, and about social justice. He had not experienced any of it firsthand, but in recent months he'd read the newspapers a lot, chatted online with acquaintances in Egypt and Tunisia, and above all spent a lot of time in contemplation. When he lay in his room in Damascus, he would sink into thought for many hours, and from the day he arrived in Yafa and was master of his own time, he spent whole days ruminating and making plans.

Soon after he settled in the tent camp, Fareed walked over to a nearby convenience store. He bought a SIM card and put it in his iPhone. He snapped a photo of himself and uploaded it to Grindr, where he appeared first in the series of pictures on the screen. And he chose a username: "diamond20."

Sometimes Fareed disappeared from the camp for an hour or two. When he came back, he quickly reintegrated in the discussion circle, reinforced tents, shook out blankets, dusted off armchairs, stared at his camp mates, rekindled the hookah flame, and whispered advice to his new friends. Fareed gave good advice, and they liked to listen to him. When comrades from the Tel Aviv encampment came to visit, usually in the afternoon, Fareed would step aside and disappear into his tent until the coast was clear, or engage one of his Arab friends in conversation. Sabakh was always in his pocket, reminding him that, after all, he had not come to Palestine to deliver news of the Arab Spring to the region. He had a less ambitious task, and although he could have left the diamond in the tent and blindly trusted his friends not to take Sabakh, since after all they were there to support one another, he still walked around with the box in his pocket, as if to constantly remind himself of the very existence of the diamond and the fate it had dealt him.

One day, while he was flipping through the app, Fareed became curious about another user: "hameagel21." He sent a short message and got a quick response. The conversation was conducted in English. After a while, Fareed apologized and said he had to log off. He went back to the encampment and welcomed a delegation of Arab activists from southern Israel. That afternoon he was tired and lay down to sleep in one of the small tents at the edge of the park. He opened the app and saw that hameagel21 was online. They picked up their conversation where they'd left off. They exchanged a few more blurry pictures, and after chatting for about half an hour they arranged to meet at the falafel stand on Haj Kahil Square.

When Fareed got to the meeting point, he couldn't see anyone except a soldier with blue ribbons on his shoulders. The soldier held a small microphone and looked around awkwardly. Fareed recognized him: It was the soldier who had been interviewing people at the tent camp. What was he doing here? Fareed ordered a falafel, in Arabic, and stood eating at the counter, looking around for his date. The soldier glanced at him, but he didn't look dangerous and Fareed wasn't alarmed. Still, the looks bothered him, so he walked a few feet away and leaned on a car. In the middle of the small square was a traffic island, with vehicles all around it, honking, driving onto the sidewalks, stopping in the middle of the lane to pick up passengers. Arabic music blared from a car double-parked nearby. The driver got out and asked for five orders of falafel. The vendor sliced open pitas, spread them with humus, stuffed in falafel straight out of the hot oil, added fries and salad, and finished off with a generous squirt of tahini in each pita. The driver paid for his food, thanked him, and disappeared into his car. The music faded down the street like a curl of smoke.

It was hot. Fareed bought a bottle of water, then leaned on the car again. He was wearing a white undershirt. The soldier, oddly, did not seem to be suffering from the heat, despite his uniform. But he finally went over and bought his own falafel, then leaned on the next car over. Now they were close, and conversation seemed inevitable. Still, another minute or two passed. And although they had chatted at length on the app, it took a while for the conversation to gain momentum.

They finished eating and tossed their paper napkins into the trash. They crossed the square and walked up Yefet Street, where they turned right onto one of the side streets that lead to the sea. Honi asked Fareed why he had picked him, and Fareed said he was curious about his username. Honi asked if he knew what *me'agel* meant, and Fareed said no, but he knew what 21 meant. So Honi told him the legend of Honi the Circle Maker.

Fareed thought about it. "So when you log on to Grindr, you're kind of like him, aren't you?

"Why is that?"

"Because it's like you're drawing a circle around yourself. And not just that—your circle can go beyond walls, beyond borders, even."

"It's a *virtual* circle, remember."

"I know, but it's a concrete one, too. And here's the proof." Fareed pointed at himself.

Honi blushed. Staring at this charismatic, confident young man, he felt something he could not explain in words. For reasons he didn't fully understand, he was reminded of his conversation with Adela. He quickly explained that he was already spoken for, and Fareed smiled and said he was only here for a short time, and anyway he wasn't planning anything serious with a soldier.

By the time they got to the beach, they were each lost in thought. Fareed stared at the waves and thought about his grandmother, Laila. What would she say if she knew he was standing in Yafa now, looking at the sea, the same sea she had told him so much about?

Honi turned on his iPhone and sent a message.

"Stay with him," I texted back.

"But why?"

"You'll understand everything later," I typed. "For now, keep talking to him and don't leave him, no matter what. Trust me."

When evening fell they made their way back to the Garden of the Two. But when they got there, they saw a police car near the park and kept to the other side of the street.

They walked farther down and stood at a safe distance away. A few policemen were walking around the park, shining flashlights into the tents. "Come with me," Honi said.

They walked down Yefet Street. There were police vehicles everywhere, and police officers walked around the side streets with walkie-talkies, looking for something. They stopped passersby to ask questions and occasionally huddled together to consult. Honi and Fareed managed to slip away, but they kept encountering more police. When they turned onto Yehuda Ha'Yamit and kept walking toward the radio station, the tense atmosphere dissipated slightly. Except that a police car was parked right outside the station, and two officers stood in their way. One of them was about to question Honi, but he quickly stepped aside and rang the buzzer to get into the station. Fareed hesitated, and Honi pulled him into the building. Fareed's heart pounded as they walked in, but something about Honi seemed trustworthy. And he reasoned that if this was how his visit to this country had to end, then so be it.

"What's up, Honi?" said the female soldier at the front desk.

"It's all good, Stav," Honi answered. "They're working you like dogs, eh? When are you going to have time to do the news flash?"

"Don't worry, I've already said it twenty times today: 'The social protest began on the Internet...' Who's that?" She jerked her head at Fareed. "Let me guess, he's working on the show with you."

"You're the queen!" Honi exclaimed.

"Look who's talking."

A second later, the two men were inside the station, climbing up to the second-to-last floor. Honi looked into an office to make sure it was empty, and led Fareed through to the next room, which was under construction—the same room where I had first kissed Honi. He brought a chair in, sat Fareed down, left, and came back a minute later with two Styrofoam cups of tea.

"Sugar?"

"Why not?" Fareed answered. "Tell me, who do you keep texting?"

"My boyfriend."

"Did you tell him about me?"

"He knows you're here. But don't worry, he's cool."

They sat next to each other drinking tea and calming their breath. Police cars honked out on the street, and their horns blended with the sounds of the muezzin. After about half an hour, Honi's phone beeped, and he told Fareed, "Don't go anywhere, I'll be right back." A few minutes later he came back to the room, out of breath, with me close behind.

Honi introduced us and I shook Fareed's hand. "Nice to meet you," I said. "You look exactly like I pictured you."

## 2

The police came back to the Garden of the Two a week later. They dismantled the tents, loaded their contents on a truck, and threw the whole lot in the trash. The activists, who had been expecting this for a while, took over an old Yafa house that same night, not far from the Scottish Church. It was one of the houses that had been abandoned in early 1948, a few months before the war. A small, pretty stone house surrounded by a low wall, with a fountain in the courtyard. In the 1960s, the house was rented to Arab tenants from Yafa, who paid rent to the State of Israel through the Custodian of Absentee Property. But for the past two decades, after the patriarch of the family died and his children couldn't pay rent, it had stood vacant.

The activists walked through the gate into the courtyard and easily broke open the back door to the house. Inside, they were met by darkness and dust. They opened the windows and began scrubbing and cleaning. As dawn broke, they hung a banner from the second-story bedroom window: THE PEOPLE'S HOUSE. Photographers and journalists came to capture the moment, but the protesters paid little attention to them. A few had their pictures taken and gave interviews, but most darted around preparing the space for habitation. At around eight in the morning, the police banged on the door. Even though they knew there was a temporary stay of execution on the evacuation order, thanks to their pro bono lawyers, the activists did not open the door. They continued to move around the house making themselves at home.

Fareed did the same.

Indeed, he had returned. Without a key, through the back door, he had nevertheless returned. His act of return was neither a political statement nor a national movement. It was conducted, as was most everything he did, unobtrusively, unselfconsciously, with the same sense of mystery that seemed to characterize practically all his actions: He simply found his place between the walls of this house, which had once belonged to his grandfather Abed and grandmother Laila. And what if someone were to stop and ask: Whose idea was it to pick this particular house to squat in? Why this house on Sha'arei Nikanor Street, out of all the abandoned houses in Yafa? Well, then, someone else would soon ask a different, more burning question, and the issue would be dropped.

This was the house they had chosen, rather than any other, and who was he to judge? Return occurs in mysterious ways. You think you've given up something and then it sneaks up on you through the back door. You comfort yourself over a life long gone, and a new life forms right in front of your nose.

Fareed had spent many long months in his room in Damascus contemplating the notion of return. And he knew if he returned, it would not be to the same place, because that place had changed and become something else. He knew that people had lived and died here, and had been replaced by other people. And yet something remained. And now, against all odds, he had managed to find that something in Yafa. And for one elusive, rare moment, he was happy.

All he had left to do now was to seal the fate of the blue diamond.

# CHAPTER ELEVEN

# RAFAEL

## 1

IN MAY 1945, French military planes bombed Damascus. Some four hundred people were killed and thousands made homeless. The next day, Adela gave birth to her first son, Salim-Shlomo. The baby had trouble breathing and coughed all night. Adela, exhausted and depressed, begged Rafael to get the diamond out of the house.

Rafael left home, and when he came back at daybreak he found the normally unflappable Adela sitting in bed, sobbing with despair.

"The bombings are over," he reassured her, but she was inconsolable. After a difficult pregnancy, she now found herself surrounded by relatives, with a tiny, ravenous baby constantly at her breast. The noise of the bombardments, the cries of her neighbors, the smoke coming in through the windows, the thought of the land to their south, of the closed border, of faraway Laila—all these horrified Adela and rattled her nerves. She looked at Rafael in utter exhaustion and did not say a word.

Rafael sat down on the bed and kissed his wife's forehead over and over again. He picked up the baby and looked at him: His little face was covered with red splotches and surrounded by a damp, warm head of hair. His little eyes were torn, black, glassy. His upper lip was swollen in the middle with a tiny blister. Rafael stood up and carried the baby to the window. He breathed in the infant's smell and searched for his own reflection in his eyes. But the baby wrinkled his face, parted his tiny lips, and screamed. Terrified, Rafael immediately handed him to Adela. It took several minutes before they were able to calm him.

In the silence that now engulfed the room, they were finally free to examine each other. Traces of anger and anxiety were still evident on Adela's face, but a certain comfort now softened her. And perhaps there was something else there now, a new emotion in the way she looked at Rafael. He thought about what his father had always told him: Childbirth changes a woman—it turns her into a completely different person.

Ten years later, when Rafael was living far away, surrounded by his children and his silence, he would remember that night and Adela's changing face.

The baby kicked his father's elbow as hard as he could with his tiny feet, and Rafael looked at him fearlessly, but also without pride or satisfaction. This baby was evidence of his own existence, an assurance that something would remain in the world when he left it, and he was now responsible for quieting the creature's hunger and satisfying all his needs. A faint stench came from between the baby's legs, and Rafael recoiled and stood up. Adela called for her sister, who came to help. Rafael left the room without a word.

There was no longer any point in denying it: Things had gone wrong, both inside the home and outside. They had planned to meet Laila that summer in Aley. Rafael gave the authorities six hundred Syrian pounds to be allowed to travel, and they set off with little Salim. When they finally met, Laila wore the gold chain they had given her. She stared at the baby for a long time. She was afraid to touch him, but Adela asked her to hold him while she went to rest. Laila sat on the sofa with the baby in her arms, unable to detect either Rafael or Adela in his features. Evening started to fall. When the baby fell asleep, she gently placed him in his crib. Then she shut her eyes and waited for morning.

But when it arrived, it was a difficult, disquieting morning. It was hard for the three of them to bridge the time they had spent apart. Rafael told Laila what he had said to Adela the night before: If things continued to deteriorate in Yafa, Laila would have to leave.

"But what about you?" Laila asked. "Doesn't your family want to leave Damascus?"

"My younger brother, Yosef, wants to go to Tel Aviv, and he's trying to persuade us to go with him."

Laila thought about this. Living apart for so long meant that the chasm between them was growing deeper. Would they meet in Yafa? It was hard for her to imagine the three of them strolling the streets she had known so well in her childhood. Adela and Rafael belonged to a different part of her life, outside the familiar daily bustle. The idea of them moving to live so close to her was not appealing.

"A few weeks ago, in Damascus," Rafael told the women, "I met a young man named Rachmo, who was a school friend of my brother's. Rachmo was fired from his job in the market, and since then he's just been sitting around all day and wandering the streets. He has a sick father and three younger brothers at home. Anyway, he told me he was on his way to 'gather children.' I asked what he meant, and he explained: A Jewish Agency representative goes around town recruiting young unemployed Jews to visit Jewish families and convince them to send their children, or at least their oldest sons, to Palestine. They receive one lira for each child they bring to the agency representative."

Adela looked at Rafael uncomprehendingly. Rafael was not sure what was going through her mind when she heard this story, but her look expressed disbelief. Laila, on the other hand, had several questions: Did this young man manage to persuade any families? Where would the children live? How would they manage without their parents? And what did Rafael tell him?

Rafael explained that when families were reluctant to part with their children, the recruiters had a winning argument: "Today your children are wallowing in the mire, but when they immigrate to Palestine they will be cheerful, healthy young Israeli men. They will live a life of freedom and labor in their homeland."

"What do they mean, their *homeland*?" Adela asked angrily. "Their homeland is Damascus, not Palestine. That's where those children were born."

Leila smiled. She was thinking about a future in which the three of them would live in Yafa, her own homeland.

Adela continued: "Besides, what is all this about children wallowing in the mire? Is that what the Jews in Palestine really think of us? Do they know anything about our real lives in Damascus?" There were tears of anger in her eyes. But she was not only upset by what Raphael had said. She, too, was picturing their shared future in one space. And the idea made her extremely anxious, which in turn aroused a great deal of guilt.

They spent the next two days together. Everywhere they went, at least two of them were together, if not all three. Adela liked to gaze at the pendant on Laila's neck, with its three delicate intertwined lines. The gold square had perfectly straight edges, and the shape left a damp square on Laila's skin.

Rafael thought about Laila's eyes, one blue and one brown. He tore a page out of his notebook and started writing:

*It takes courage to fall in love — the courage to deliver your soul into the hands of a woman, the courage to be exposed to her with all your flaws, to reveal the traces of time engraved on your face, the inevitably deteriorating body, and above all, the cruel fact of your needing her presence and her love. It is a need that is comforting yet also somehow terrifying, for it is inextricably and eternally bound with one question: Can love exist even when all external circumstances stand in its way? Even when social norms and acceptable mores mean that it stands no chance?*

He gave the page to Laila.

Later that evening, Adela and Laila sat on a couch facing the window. "Perhaps we can set a diamond in the pendant we gave you, Laila?" asked Adela. She stared at the young girl's white, unreadable face. There was a pair of deceptive eyes in that face, and when her pursed lips parted and revealed her slightly prominent front teeth, it gave her a childish look. Her tongue would protrude every so often and prod her lower lip, and she would frown.

"Why a diamond?" Laila spoke slowly and her thoughts were distracted.

"It would look lovely."

"But I like the pendant just as it is."

"It would still be the same, but with a diamond," Adela explained.

"And what if I replaced this pendant with something else? Would you be angry at me?"

"Try it and see." Adela smiled with great effort.

"How long will it be before we next meet?" Laila wondered out loud.

"It might only be a few months from now, if everything turns out well."

"How could everything possibly turn out well?" Laila asked. But even the dim possibility that things might improve, that perhaps the devastation would not reach them in the end—even that was a comfort to her now.

"I don't know..." Adela bit her lip. "I've spent a lot of time in Damascus thinking about you these past few years. I didn't even know if we'd ever see each other again. I looked at my body, at my face in the mirror, and I asked myself what would happen if I died. But it wasn't death that troubled me. It was other things. For example, that we wouldn't have enough food or water, or that there would be no roses for the rosewater. I know it's ridiculous: Who needs rosewater when there's nothing to eat? But that's what I thought of. And mostly, I thought of you."

Laila sat quietly.

Adela studied her for a moment and went on: "On Saturday mornings Rafael goes to synagogue, but I didn't always go with him. It was early on in my pregnancy and I felt unwell, so they let me be. And in those moments I suddenly felt the distance that stood between me and you. Do you know how you can feel that distance, Laila? It does many things, distance. After all, if I can't see you anyway, what difference does it make whether you're all the way in Yafa or just in the next neighborhood? But that's not how it is. Knowing you were far away from us, breathing in different air, meeting different people, and seeing different landscapes, knowing that your food was grown on different lands—knowing all that had the power to change me. You wouldn't believe it, Laila! I'm capable of changing my skin and almost becoming a different person. And in my mind I can also turn *you* into someone completely different. All because of the distance."

Laila still said nothing. Her fingers caressed the sharp edge of the pendant.

What was she thinking? Adela wrinkled her forehead. Perhaps she should not have spoken to Laila about the distance. Yet she could not hold back any longer.

"One Saturday morning when the house was empty and I lay alone in bed, I heard someone call out through the silence, *'Mash'al naar, mash'al naar!'* When I got up and went outside, I saw Taher, the young man who works in the market. He goes around the Jews' houses on Saturdays to light their fires, and the Jews give him a silver coin. He stood outside the doorway looking at me, surprised to find I hadn't gone to synagogue. He must have thought no one would be home at that time of day. I called him in to light the fire because I wanted to drink some tea. The next week I stayed home again, and again I heard him shout, *'Mash'al naar, mash'al naar!'* and I let him in. The third time he came, we sat drinking tea together. It was just the two of us. And then..." Adela hesitated. "Then I showed him the diamond."

Laila looked up at her in surprise. "Why did you do that?"

"I don't know. Taher was stunned at first. He held it up close to his eyes, and then he did something strange: He stuck his tongue out, licked the diamond, and put it in his mouth."

"That's what he did?"

"Yes, and I was afraid he'd swallow it. But in the end he gave it back to me."

"You shouldn't have shown him the diamond, Adela."

"It's too late now. You have to understand, Laila, I was so lonely in those days. And scared. I'm scared now, too. I had to tell someone about it. Maybe it was a mistake..."

"Where is the diamond now?"

"I have it. But I must get rid of it. Perhaps I'll give it to you..." she said, thinking out loud.

"To me? Why would you do that?"

"Yes." Adela frowned at Laila. "After all, you're not afraid of the diamond, are you? You're not afraid of anything. And I can trust you to keep it for me."

"Adela, you've lost your mind. Where would I keep it in Yafa? Do you know what's going on there?"

"I know, but I trust you to find a safe place."

"Why don't you just sell it?"

"I don't have the courage."

Laila thought about this. "But what will you tell Rafael?"

"I'll think of something. I won't tell him I gave it to you."

Just then, Rafael came into the room. His eyes were red from sleep. The two women smoothed their fingers over the creases on his face. Laila's hand ran against the direction of his stubble, and she said, "You have a beard already, Rafael. When you're an old man, you'll have to grow a long white beard. It'll suit you." She smiled at him and he frowned and tried to imagine that faraway day, when he was old.

It was time to say goodbye again. They stood in the hall-way with their luggage at their feet. This time Adela and Rafael had no gifts. But the polished pendant glimmered on Laila's chest just as it had the day they'd given it to her. They hugged and kissed, then went their separate ways and traveled home.


# 2

They met one final time before the war. It was very difficult to get from Syria to Lebanon, and once again Rafael had to deposit a large sum of money to be allowed to leave the city and cross the border. Rafael fretted about Adela while they traveled. In recent weeks a certain distance seemed to obscure everything she did, and even the way she spoke was peculiar. When he tried to find out what was wrong, she gently pushed him away.

Each evening at home, when Adela lay down, Rafael sat on the armchair cradling Salim. He kept searching for something in the baby's face, something he could not put into words, and time after time he counted to himself the number of years between them and calculated how old the boy would be when he himself was an old man. On particularly gloomy evenings he also pondered the boy's old age, when he, Rafael, would no longer be alive.

Rafael knew many things would change soon, and that the birth of his son was only the first hint: He knew with certainty that he could expect separation, departure, and many years of silence. He had trouble imagining how he would feel on the day he toppled his life with his own two hands, packed it up in bundles and crates, and relocated. But he no longer thought of the future with fury or astonishment. What must be done, would be done. Still, a sense of disquiet gnawed at him.

In the late evenings, Adela would wake up and take the baby in her arms. She would shut herself up with him in the bathroom for a long time and allow no one to enter, not even her mother or sister. When she emerged, the baby was stunned by the water and soap, and lay waving his hands and feet on a sheet spread out for him on the rug. Sometimes he smiled and sometimes his lips curled and he cried an almost adult cry, an experienced cry, as though he were lamenting something. Adela looked at the baby and then at the window. She nursed him and fell asleep on the couch. At midnight, or later, Rafael woke up and came to look for her. He shook Adela gently and led her to bed, then put the baby in the cradle at his mother's side.

Adela fell asleep as soon as her head touched the pillow, but the minute the fragments of her first dream lit her eyes, she awoke in dread. She reached out for the baby, felt his face and checked his body temperature, held a finger to his lips to feel his breath, then got up quietly and went to the living room. There, in a box hidden behind a picture frame in an alcove in the wall, was Sabakh.

Adela took the diamond out of the box, held it carefully, and sat down at the table. She turned on the lamp and closely studied the glowing stone. She tried to delve into the diamond's dark depths, to follow its curves, to see its blue refractions. What would an identical diamond look like? She wondered if Sabakh's deceptive refractions would be visible in a replica—a real diamond, just not this one, not the cursed Sabakh. And she counted the days until the twin she had commissioned was ready.

In the meantime, she would have to stall Taher. One Saturday when he walked past her on his way out of the house, his fingers stroked her thigh. Adela froze but did not say a word, only silently led him to the door. At night when she thought about him, she was filled with shame. She was afraid of the day he would ask to the see the diamond again.

Still holding Sabakh, her thoughts wandered to Laila. She was far away. Perhaps fast asleep. Adela took out a portrait of Laila from a drawer and looked at it. Through the cobwebs of sleep, Laila's face seemed blurry. Adela closed her eyes and the portrait left her heart. The night was long and black. In her dream, Adela went into every hidden corner and shone light into it. When she awoke, she thought about the darkness here and elsewhere. Darkness was darkness.

The wind blew outside and shook the windows. For a moment Adela thought someone was knocking at the door. She grew tense and thought perhaps Taher was trying to get in. She quickly turned off the lamp and sat in the dark. Large raindrops struck the window, and the door rattled against the lock. Adela put the diamond back in the box and locked it in the alcove. She went back to bed and lay down next to Rafael with her hand resting on her sleeping baby's head.

In the car on their way to Lebanon, Rafael scanned Adela without saying a word. She turned her head away from him, and the landscape traveled before her eyes. Shaking off her exhaustion, she asked, "Have they arrived yet?"

"Yes, this morning."

"Is Laila waiting for us?"

"She might have gone for a walk."

Adela sat quietly. Over and over again she thought back to the many nights since their last meeting. She felt angry at Rafael, at this calmness of his. Perhaps I'll find myself someone in Lebanon, she thought. The idea comforted her for a moment. She would slip away from them both, from Rafael and Laila, and at least for a while she would not be dependent on them. She would be free. Free of them both. Adela sailed away on her fantasies and found comfort in them. What would he look like, this man she would find? One thing was sure: He would not be Taher. That man belonged to her life in Damascus. He was a fantasy never to be fulfilled. Besides, she was too fearful to be truly attracted to him. No, she would find a new man. He would be younger than Rafael.

His skin would be dark and his hair black. His arms would be large, and he would have long fingers. He would have dark lips, almost purple, and black eyes. He wouldn't be tall, quite short, even, but solid. He would have a deep voice. He would know how to touch her, and they would hardly speak. What would she tell him? She wouldn't say a word. They would meet once, and when she went back to Rafael she would be carefree and peaceful. It would be her secret.

But the deeper she went in her imaginings, the more Adela withdrew into herself. She remembered Taher, and wondered what Rafael thought. Was there any chance he knew Taher came to their home on Saturdays, when everyone was in synagogue?

"When will we next meet Laila?" she asked.

"But we haven't seen her today yet. Let's wait for this meeting and then we'll see."

"I don't know if I'll even want to see her again." Her words were measured.

"What do you mean?" Rafael gave her a surprised look, and she thought he narrowed his eyes angrily. She wondered if it was anger or panic.

"I mean..." Adela tried to speak thoughtfully, but exhaustion gripped her and she forced the words out. "I mean...maybe I just don't want to anymore."

"Why would you say that now?" Rafael sounded furious.

"Because that's how I feel."

"I cannot understand you." Then he softened his voice, trying to stay calm.

"What is there to understand?" Now it was Adela's turn to be angry. "She just walks into our room whenever she wants to, she gets to decide when she feels like being close, and a second later she wants to be far away from us! Well, I'm telling you, Rafael, I have my opinions, too."

"No one said you didn't, Adela. But you know she comes with her mother, it's not up to her."

"Are you trying to tell me how to feel?"

"I'm not telling you how to feel, and it angers me that you would say that. You're very tired. I suggest we try to calm down before talking any further. When we arrive, we'll rest."

"I can't rest."

"I know." He touched her shoulder. "You've been through a difficult time."

"And you?"

"I have, too," he admitted. "But not exactly for the same reasons."

"Don't you wonder what's going to happen?"

"We have no control over it, Adela."

"I think we do. We have to make decisions, but I'm tired the whole time. I don't have the strength for anything. You don't know that feeling, Rafael. You always know how to do what needs to be done, how to say what needs to be said, and how not to do what should not be done. Sometimes I think you never make mistakes."

"If only that were true." He smiled.

"Well, it doesn't show on you when you're wrong. You always know what must be done."

"I certainly have no idea what must be done now."

"Then I'll tell you, Rafael. You know as well as I do that we'll have to leave Damascus soon. You must start thinking about what we can take with us and what we'll have to leave.

Then sell what we must, and talk to whoever must be talked to. I don't want to be taken by surprise."

Rafael considered. "I see you've already thought of everything."

"Not everything. For example, I find it very difficult to imagine what it would be like to live near Laila."

"In Yafa?"

"Not Yafa, Tel Aviv. But that's very close to Yafa."

"We don't know what's going to happen. Doesn't it make more sense to move to Beirut? What will we do in Tel Aviv? What language will we speak there? Are you saying we'll have to learn Hebrew? And where will I work?"

Adela scanned his face without saying a word.

"On the other hand, maybe we really will live near Laila." His eyes were dreamy now, as he stroked the stubble under his chin.

"I think about that a lot," Adela said, "and I'm not sure I want it to happen."

"You're back to that again?" He leaned back and glared at her with his green eyes.

"I'm saying this because it's important for me to say, and also so that you're not surprised later. Don't think it's easy for me, but I don't know if I can take it, living near her." Adela's voice cracked and tears came to her eyes. "I'm trying to explain to you that I don't have the strength. I won't be able to do it. I'm worried."

"Listen, Adela." He took her hand and cupped it in his. "There is a lovely young girl here, a rare pearl, who loves us and whom we love in return. You know that at first I constantly asked myself what people would say . . ."

"I know." She looked at him with red eyes.

"But now I don't care anymore. I don't think about it. I only think about us—the two of us, and the three of us—and about our happiness. Everything else matters less. But what is most painful to me—"

"Is to lose her?"

"No. What hurts me most is that you are willing to let her lose you. That you think you can be lost just like that, so easily. That you are willing to let her pay that price because of your fears. That's what pains me most."

She rested her head on his shoulder and her body shook. "I'm just trying to protect myself." Her choked-up voice was muffled by her damp hair. "This takes a lot of courage, and sometimes I think I'm not courageous enough. I worry..."

"I know. And that's why I think we should leave it for now, until we get to Aley and meet Laila. We don't know what the future will bring, Adela. There's no point guessing or making plans. Nothing is clear yet, anything could happen. We just have to live our lives and that's that."

"It's not that simple." She sat up straight. Her face was damp and red.

"I know."

They traveled on in silence.


The door to Suad and Laila's room was shut. Rafael was impatient, but after debating, he decided to go back to his own room. "They must be resting," he told Adela. They lay down in the bed they had not slept in for months and fell asleep immediately. The curtains were drawn, and the room was thick with an early, unnatural darkness.

There was a knock at the door, then another slightly louder one. Adela woke up with a start, glanced at the curtains, and dropped her head back on the pillow. Rafael also woke and jumped out of bed. He put on his robe and went to open the door.

Laila. He let her in and shut the door behind her. She gave him a short, fervent kiss on the lips, then pulled away. "Where is Adela?"

"She's in the other room. We just woke up." After looking at her again, he asked, "Is everything all right?"

She nodded. Rafael led her to the bedroom, where Adela had fallen back asleep.

"She hasn't slept for weeks," Rafael said.

"Because of the baby?"

"That, too. She just can't sleep. She's troubled by all sorts of ideas. She thinks..." He wondered whether to bring it up now.

"That you should leave Damascus?"

"Perhaps."

They watched Adela. She must have been sleeping lightly, because she felt their gazes and half opened her eyes.

"Good morning." Laila smiled softly.

Adela closed her eyes without answering. Laila looked questioningly at Rafael, who raised his eyebrows. Laila sat down on the bed next to Adela. "How are you?" she whispered. Adela seemed to be trying to answer, but no sound came from her lips. With her eyes closed, she reached out and hugged Laila. It was a long, desperate embrace. Laila, still in Adela's arms, looked at her worriedly. "Are you happy to see me or sad?" she asked.

Adela didn't answer. Her eyelids trembled, and two large tears rolled down her cheeks. Laila kissed Adela's face. Rafael sat down beside them. "I suggest we rest together, we're all too upset now." He took off his robe and lay down. Adela lay on her back on the other side of the bed.

Laila undressed and without saying a word slipped into the gap between them. She lay her head on Rafael's chest. She was always amazed to hear his rapid heartbeat, so contrary to his tranquil temperament. Laila took Adela's hand and placed her fingers on her own lips. She blew softly on Adela's fingers. Adela was appeased, but a moment later she pulled away, turned her back to Laila, and lay facing the wall beneath the large window.

They finally fell asleep.

In the morning, when Laila opened her eyes, she found Adela sitting by the window staring out at the view. Her face was impassive but peaceful. She turned to look at Laila and came over to her. Was she happy or sad? Perhaps both? She put her face close to Laila's, looked straight at her, and said, "I'm very closed, Laila. It will take me time to open up. But I love you very much."

"I do, too," Laila said with a smile. She kissed her. There was still sleep in her eyes.

Adela left the room, arranging her hair on the way out. A moment later Laila heard water running in the bathroom.

In the late morning, the three emerged from the room and went for a walk. Adela was quiet at first, but after they sat down for a cup of strong coffee, she felt revived. She told stories about Damascus, the bombings, the food shortage, the animals her brothers slaughtered while she insisted on eating only rice and vegetables, and the baby who cried for nights on end. It was a welcome respite to have left the baby in a nanny's care.

As she sat talking, she looked back and forth from Laila to Rafael. Laila wondered where Adela had left the blue diamond, but she did not want to ask. Adela put her hand out and held Laila's, and Laila silently leaned her head on Rafael's shoulder. They sat quietly, retreating into their own thoughts, exhausted from the anticipation. Or perhaps they had nothing to say to each other.

At the edge of the garden sat a young man, watching them. He wore an elegant suit and there was a bowler hat on the table next to him. A thin curled mustache stretched out above either side of his mouth. He had deep green eyes and a very delicate scar down his forehead, accentuated by the sunlight. In his right hand he held a monocle, and every so often he put the lens up to his eye, which became—Rafael noticed from his seat—extremely large and gave his handsome face a slightly distorted look. He spoke French with the waiter, and Rafael tried to identify his accent. Greek, perhaps? Or Italian?

When the three got up to leave, Rafael turned back and his eyes met those of the young man, who kept watching as they left the garden and walked down the street, arm in arm. A church bell rang nearby, and Rafael took out his gold watch. "Are you hungry?" he asked the two ladies.

"Very!" Laila answered.

Adela said nothing. She pursed her lips, and a slight tremor went down Rafael's back upon seeing her altered expression, now suddenly gloomy.

Laila went up to her room to change for lunch.

"Is everything all right?" Rafael asked Adela. He spoke to her in French.

"Absolutely fine," she answered in their language, and looked away.

"How do you feel so far with Laila?"

"I don't know. How do you?"

"Excellent," Rafael declared. "I think our reunion with her is very moving. Don't you?"

"I don't know, Rafael." Adela looked at him. "Imagine: We may never see her again."

"Is that really what you want?"

"Perhaps."

"Then I must tell you," he said, trying to remain composed, "that she is very dear to me and I do not want to lose her."

"More dear to you than I am?"

"You know that's not true," Rafael answered drily. "God, why must you be so difficult?" He was trying not to shout.

"Maybe I'm not the one who's difficult," Adela said reproachfully, though it amused her to see his renowned coolheadedness finally crack. "Maybe it's you who are the difficult one in this whole story, Rafael, despite all your quiet tenderness? Did you ever consider that?"

"Adela, you're very tired. You're not making any sense. There is a lovely girl here who loves us..."

"She really does love us, there's no arguing that. But she is only faithful to one thing in the world: whatever makes her feel good."

"I'm not willing to continue this conversation," he said angrily. "You're behaving destructively, both to yourself and to the three of us. I ask that you compose yourself."

Adela let out a snort of contempt and fell silent. When Laila reappeared, she found them standing with their backs to each other. Rafael glared at a tree while Adela kicked at some gravel on the sidewalk. They walked silently to the restaurant.

After lunch they happened to pass a photography studio, and Rafael suggested they go in and get their picture taken together. Laila happily agreed, Adela conceded grudgingly, and next thing they knew they were seated on three chairs in front of a window, while the photographer hid behind his large camera.

After the photograph they went back to their room. Rafael undressed and put on his robe. Adela lay down on the bed fully clothed, staring at the ceiling with her hands crossed behind her neck. Laila took off her dress. She felt heavy after their meal, and suddenly ashamed. She squirmed this way and that, and finally covered herself with a thin blanket. Under the covers, Rafael touched her body on one side, and Adela's on the other.

Laila acquiesced. Rafael gently kissed her body, then Adela's. The two women looked into each other's eyes. Rafael took off his robe, and his heavy, warm body covered Adela's stomach. His shoulders hunched up slightly on his way to Laila and he stretched his neck out, but when Laila moved her face closer and kissed him, his head suddenly fell forward in defeat.

They were flooded with longings from head to toe. It seemed to Adela that she had never felt such tension. She ran her fingers through Rafael's hair, touched Laila's eyelids, stroked her own body as though acquainting herself with it for the first time. Rafael turned his head to one side, then to the other, and Adela felt even more keenly than before that this situation was beyond her strength. She forced herself to think about different places, far away and barren. But the tide rushed in again, and with terror she envisioned her own limbs floating high above the bed and then slamming back down to the ground.

Rafael threw the entire weight of his body onto hers, as though he wanted to punish her for the way she had treated him. But even if he wanted to hurt her, his moves were quiet, focused, and wondrously gentle. She surrendered to his tenderness and to the slowness with which he melted the tension in her limbs and pushed his way into her. She looked to her side and saw Laila watching them, caressing her stomach with wide circles. She held her hand out to Laila with what seemed like a desperate reach, but Laila caught her fingers, kissed them quickly, and moved them away from her body. Adela was overcome by nausea. She gripped Rafael, who kept boring into her with rhythmical blows, and tried to crush his heavy, foreign body. When she could not do it, she pushed him off with a grunt, and from her throat came low, deep sounds. He finally let her be, but there was something violent in the way his body disconnected and abandoned her there, pent up and breathless.

But then he came to her again. Adela closed her eyes and thought about Taher, about his large hands, his eyes, the smell that came from his shirt. She stomped her feet, a shudder ran through her body, and again a deep growl emerged, and she suddenly wanted Rafael again and grabbed the back of his neck and dug her trembling fingers in. It had been a long time since their movements had been so coordinated. But just as she opened up, she suddenly felt him shift his weight aside and fall away from her. She opened her eyes a slit and saw his fingers stroking Laila's outstretched arm. In a turmoil of emotions, she opened her eyes wide and saw him kiss the chest and neck of the woman lying next to her, climb up to her lips and cheeks and cover her face with kisses. She tried to pull him back to her, but his body was now completely directed at Laila, and he lifted off Adela's body with a painful thrust. She moaned and felt the cold air on her body.

She remained lying on her side, feeling that something of Rafael was still inside her. But he was far away now, lying on Laila. His arm reached back and felt for Adela, and they both motioned for her to come closer. She did not. She pulled the sheet over her cool body and stared at the wall. Close to her, Laila swallowed a scream. Her lips clung to Rafael's and made sucking sounds, and Adela plugged her ears with her fingers. When the kiss ended and their lips sought out other places, Adela turned to watch them with great attention and concentration. Her fingers hovered above their bodies for a moment, tracing an imaginary line in the air, and her lips made a very faint whistle that she thought only she could hear, but Laila turned and smiled at her, her face twisted in pain.

Their two bodies moved together in the darkness. Adela thought about Laila and Rafael's first meeting in Lebanon, even before she herself had met Rafael. Her breaths were heavy now, the sweat that had covered her chest and shoulders had evaporated, and she closed herself up and finally reached the barren, faraway places. But suddenly Laila screamed, as though someone had died in her arms, and Adela opened her eyes just in time to see Rafael pulling away quickly from Laila. He shifted his body onto Adela and gently spread her thighs, which the sheet had fallen off. He held her for one more moment, she felt him inside her again, and after a few breaths he let out a final, desperate sigh, and collapsed wearily.

The room was quiet. Adela pushed Rafael off and he fell heavily on the mattress. Laila stared at the ceiling, her fingers mussing her damp black hair. Adela felt a pain between her legs and wanted to get up. Rafael lay on his stomach between the two women, one arm spread out on Adela's body and the other on Laila's thigh. His rapid breaths gradually slowed, until the only sounds in the room were the ticking clock and the curtain rustling against the open window.

They spent the next morning together as well, lying in bed in each other's arms.

At midday, Adela slipped away from the room and disappeared. After about an hour, Rafael went out to look for her. He searched in the café, in the garden, on the beach.

He asked the newspaper seller if he'd seen her. No one knew where she was. Finally he decided to go back and wait for her in their room.

She did not return until the early evening, and she looked distracted and secretive. They did not scold her or even confess to having been worried. Laila put her lips on Adela's neck and kissed her. Then she looked into her eyes for a long time. Adela said to herself: Remember that face and that look. Her chest was crushed with pain but also with a certain relief. Rafael looked at his wife, opened his mouth to say something, but sighed and kept quiet. Afterward he lay down to rest, and the two women quietly left the room.

They walked along the street. Adela's steps were brisk, and Laila had trouble keeping up. Finally they found a stone bench hidden among cypress and pine trees. They sat down close together, with Laila's hand on Adela's lap. Adela took a small box out of her bag and gave it to Laila.

"What is this?" Laila asked, although she knew.

"It's the blue diamond. I'm giving it to you."

"Do you want me to keep it for you?"

"Yes." There was a bitter taste in Adela's mouth.

"Until when?"

"Until we meet again."

"All right," Laila said after a pause.

They kept sitting for a while, then got up and left. There was a stubborn silence between them all the way back to the hotel.

When it was time for Laila and Suad to leave Aley, Laila was pregnant.

# CHAPTER TWELVE

# THE RETURN

✦

## 1

AMIRAM KADOSH SPENT MONTHS supervising the renovation plans for the building on Plonit Alley. After the internal walls were knocked down and the space redivided into new rooms, it would be time for the interior design: Damascene rugs on the floors, as long as the decorator confirmed that they matched the hotel's "décor language"; a white grand piano set out in the lobby; rocking chairs in some rooms and in others ornate leather armchairs. All the rooms would have shelves with design and art books in English, French, and Russian.

Kadosh had studied the reports that appeared regularly in the financial sections of the newspapers about the flourishing boutique hotel scene in Tel Aviv. He was informed that there were four or five such hotels in the city, with no fewer than seven new ones in the works. He learned that it was easier and cheaper to convert an existing structure into a hotel than to build one from the ground up. The hotel owners interviewed in the articles said that opening a boutique hotel required an investment of a few million dollars, which they estimated would be recouped within fifteen or twenty years, perhaps less. ("God willing, and Ahmadinejad also," said one of the hoteliers, "we'll be ahead of schedule.")

"The main idea," Amiram Kadosh told anyone who would listen, "is to build customized units that are each different. The guests have to feel like they're spending a few days in someone else's home. It should feel like a real apartment, not a hotel. A home away from home." He was optimistic about the project: "The location is ideal, a ten-minute walk from the beach, five minutes from Dizengoff Center, close to the trendy streets like Shenkin and Rothschild. It's the beating heart of Tel Aviv, but it's also a quiet alleyway with a village feel. The building is from the early 1930s, and it represents the epitome of Tel Aviv architecture."

He went on to describe the luxurious wall hangings, the art in the rooms, the exhibition space in the lobby, the flat-screen televisions, the flower arrangements that would be replaced daily, the urban landscape viewed from the windows, the mirrors flown in especially from New York and Tokyo, the bar and restaurant and, of course, the jewelry shop.

He had a plan, Amiram Kadosh.

To set himself apart from all the other boutique hotels popping up in the city, he knew he needed something unique. He thought and thought, and finally found it: jewelry. He would retain the jewelry shop on the ground floor of the hotel, but it wouldn't be Menashe Salomon's shop—not that claustrophobic little space with the elderly fixture of a jeweler, the very mention of whose name aroused unpleasant feelings in Kadosh. No. That shop would have to be destroyed and a replacement built from scratch. A new beginning. Kadosh suffered from no pangs of conscience on this point. Had Menashe Salomon invented the concept of an artisan's workshop that was also a store? Of course not. Would he not be adequately compensated for vacating the premises? He would. Probably.

Either way, his plan was ambitious: He was going to display a large diamond in the shop window, but not just any diamond. A famous one. Perhaps one that had belonged to a Japanese emperor or the queen of England or some glorious sultan. People would come from all over the world to see his diamond. They would make pilgrimages from New York and Moscow and Tokyo. It would be the first boutique hotel in the world that tourists came especially to see.

But the day before the renovations began, when he was perched on a ladder to reach the top shelf of the closet in his apartment, Amiram Kadosh felt a sharp pain in his chest. He'd been suffering from various aches and pains for days but had assumed it was from the stress. He lay down in bed, and the pain spread to his shoulders and neck. His head felt dizzy. He thought his left arm was starting to hurt, too, and he was sweating—from pain or panic. The sweat, in any case, was real, and it felt unpleasant. He opened the drawer next to his bed with his right hand and took out a box of aspirin, chewed one tablet, as he had once read one should do, and phoned his daughter.

Ayelet said she was calling an ambulance immediately, and a few minutes later she arrived at her father's home in a taxi. She met the paramedics outside the building and led them to the apartment. They found Kadosh lying in bed, groaning. A minute later they carried him out on a stretcher, and on the way to the hospital Ayelet held her father's hand and called her brother.

Honi rushed to the hospital and found Ayelet standing alone in the hallway while a doctor examined Kadosh behind a curtain. They felt their mother's absence now more than they ever had before. They had to do everything on their own: talk to the doctors, make decisions, sign papers, and wait. At night, after a cardiac catheterization, they sat next to their father in his hospital room. Every so often Kadosh opened his eyes and looked silently at his children. He was clearly distressed to find himself in a strange white bed, in a place that did not obey the rules of day and night. His fingers were warm, as always, and he squeezed his daughter's hand even when he seemed to be asleep. They spent the night that way. A week later, he was sent home.

A few days after the discharge, Ayelet managed to persuade Kadosh to see a renowned Arab cardiologist who treated patients with hypnosis. There was a very long waiting list to see this doctor, but Ayelet sweet-talked one of his secretaries, who was a regular at the Shack, and managed to get him an appointment. Kadosh told his daughter he didn't believe in all that stuff, but eventually he gave in to her nagging.

The cardiologist seemed to work miracles on the stubborn Kadosh, and he soon began to get better. After a few weeks, for the first time in his life, he bought a gym membership. Upon Ayelet's advice, he postponed the renovations at the building until he was fully recovered. One day at the gym, Kadosh met a psychologist, originally from Montevideo, who was roughly his age and was also a recent widow.

They started going out, and after a while they adopted the custom of walking along the beach almost every evening, from the defunct Dolphinarium nightclub all the way south to Andromeda's Rock, and on to the newly revived Jaffa port. They surveyed the construction progress on the boardwalk, which was being extended as far south as Bat Yam. Then they climbed the steps to the Maronite neighborhood and wandered among the glorious houses on Ha'Tzedef and Ha'Shachaf Streets. Finally, they strolled down Sha'arei Nikanor Street to Yefet Street, and back to their car up north.

While they wandered around Jaffa, Kadosh started to think about buying a house there. He liked the neighborhood, and felt comfortable there, and he knew Ayelet and Honi would be happy if he had a house in Jaffa by the sea. He told no one of this plan, not even his new girlfriend.

Every day, he visited Ayelet at the Shack and revived himself with a nourishing smoothie. One afternoon, he became an accidental witness to a conversation between Ayelet and Honi. It was in the early afternoon, and not a single customer was at the Shack at the time. The two siblings sat chatting on barstools, with their backs to the doorway. Before Ayelet noticed her father and turned to greet him, Kadosh had time to overhear a few things that sounded very strange to him.

His children were discussing a young Arab man whom they called 'diamond20.' Honi told his sister he had met this diamond20 online. From the snatches he overheard, Kadosh learned about a night that his son and diamond20 had spent together, and about a certain blue diamond.

"What language did you talk to him in?" Ayelet asked. "Does he even speak English?"

"Better than you do," Honi answered in a slightly insulted tone.

Kadosh felt awkward and wanted to leave, but he pulled himself together and was suddenly overcome by an inexplicable sense of closeness to his son, for perhaps the first time since he'd been born.

When Honi noticed his father, he looked down and seemed very embarrassed. But something about Kadosh, perhaps the change that had occurred in him since the heart attack and the new girlfriend—whose presence in his life softened his usual toughness—encouraged Honi to talk with his father for the first time since childhood without feeling alienated. He glanced at his sister and briefly considered letting Kadosh in on his experience of the past few days. But he didn't dare.

Ayelet went behind the counter to make her father's regular smoothie. She served him the drink and kissed him on his warm forehead. After a few moments of silence, Honi plucked up the courage to come out to his father: He told him, quite simply, that he was attracted to men. Privately, Kadosh wondered if Honi had told his mother when she was alive, but decided he had not. She would have told him. He stirred his smoothie and calmly took a few sips, but his eyes were burning. Although he still felt this new closeness to his son, as if out of habit he blamed himself for what he had just heard. He thought back to all the drama classes and flute classes they'd sent Honi to, and wondered if he should regret not having insisted on something more masculine, like soccer. His thoughts kept wandering, and now he felt a certain embarrassment when he remembered Honi's attraction to the family's Damascus stories, which contained neither heroism nor courage nor a firm grip on reality.

He asked himself where he'd gone wrong. And he knew the answer: He'd always been wrong. The fragments he'd picked up from Honi's story came back to torture his thoughts at night. Who was this man, diamond20?

## 2

The apartment was immersed in the darkness of dusk. Outside, the days were growing shorter. Achlama—the kitten I'd adopted a few days earlier—stood on the table holding up a hesitant paw and gauged my mood. I smiled at her, but she hopped off the table and leapt onto the two bodies sprawled on the sofa. Honi opened his eyes, which were bleary from his siesta.

"Do you think we're crazy, Honi?" I whispered.

"Crazy? Why?" He watched Achlama getting tangled up in the blanket.

"I don't know. Don't you care what people say about us?"

"Not really. But ask Fareed. Actually, don't, he's sleeping like a baby."

"It's been two hours already. Don't you think we should wake him?"

"You do it."

"I don't have the heart to."

"Well, he worked hard today . . ."

"Look at him sleeping. See how he folds his wrists, just like a cat," I observed. "Speaking of which, how's your dad?"

Honi sat up straight and started playing with his hair. "Seems like he's completely recovered. A new man. Did I tell you he went to a hypnotist? Some Arab cardiologist.

Anyway, I know I shouldn't say this, but if you ask me, this whole heart attack did him a world of good. You know what they say about this kind of thing: It's an opportunity to turn over a new leaf in life."

"Of course."

"Oh, and get this — Kadosh is moving to Jaffa! He just told me yesterday."

"Why's he moving to Jaffa?

"I don't know. He's got this thing about the port. It's all because of his new girlfriend, you know, the therapist. He wants to buy a house on Sha'arei Nikanor."

"So Fareed and Kadosh will be neighbors. How convenient."

"Yes, exactly. And that's not all. I'm not sure how to tell you this...I think my dad overheard a conversation I had with Ayelet."

"A conversation about what?"

"About us."

"What do you mean, us?"

"*Us*. The three of us."

"Wait a minute, you told Ayelet?!"

"Tomi, you know I don't keep secrets from my sister."

"What can I tell you, Hanan...You're something else."

"Well, it's not like your family, where everything's all a big secret."

"What do you expect? My parents were in the security service. They met when they were working for the Shabak."

"The forces of darkness."

"Exactly. You come from warm people, Honi. Everyone in your family is always in each other's business. Still, I can't believe you told Ayelet about us!"

"Calm down, Tom, it's not a big deal, she's cool. But what if Kadosh heard everything?"

"He'd never understand this, don't worry, he's too limited."

"Hey, don't talk like that about my dad!"

"Excuse me, honey. I forgot that you're not allowed to criticize first-degree relatives with you people." I gestured at Fareed. "Is he waking up?"

"No, just grinding his teeth." Honi picked up Fareed's cigarettes from the table. "What do you think's going to happen to him?" He lit a cigarette. "How is this whole Israel chapter going to end?"

"I have no idea."

"Give it a try."

"God knows, Honi. So what do you say, what about my uncle? Is your dad going to let him go back after the renovations?"

"That's not the point now, Tomi. You can't change the subject every time I bring up this guy who came into our lives."

"I'm not changing the subject. I mean, it's all connected."

"You sure as hell are changing it. Every time you have trouble dealing with something, you reroute the conversation to my sensitive spots. It's time to grow up."

"I'll take that into consideration, Honi. May I just remind you that when I was shaving, you were still playing with Transformers."

"I'm sure you mean Biker Mice from Mars."

"Whatever, honey. Now come over and give me a kiss, here."

"Seriously, do you really think this story is going to come to an end?" Honi crushed his cigarette in the ashtray.

"I don't know. I think Fareed's done everything he came here for: He saw Jaffa, he went into his grandparents' house, he even reenacted his grandmother's love life!"

"That's awesome, but what about us?"

"What do you mean?"

"What's going to happen with us after he leaves?"

"Our lives will go on," I said. "Just like they did before we met diamond20."

"I find that difficult to imagine. I know it's hardly been two weeks since we met him, but it all happened so fast that I can't even think about ourselves without him."

"I didn't think I was jealous until now . . ."

"Then don't be jealous now either, because there's no reason. This story is about the two of us together, and you know that very well."

"Shhh . . . I think he's waking up," I whispered.

"No, he's talking in his sleep. Can you understand what he's saying?"

"It's in Arabic—don't you understand any of it?"

"No. Let's record him on the iPhone," Honi suggested.

"Have you lost your mind?"

"No! We'll tape him and play it back for him when he wakes up."

Half an hour later, when Fareed woke up and translated the words he'd said in his sleep, it turned out he was mumbling verses from *A Thousand and One Nights*:

"Maruf said to him: Can you take out everything contained in this treasure and bring it to the surface of the earth? Said he: But there is nothing easier! So he said: Take everything out and leave nothing behind! He pointed at the ground, which opened up. The slave of the ring descended, and after a while out came handsome young boys carrying baskets full of gold, which they emptied out. They descended again and returned with more baskets. Again they unloaded gold and precious stones. Not an hour had passed when they said: Nothing is left of the treasure."

Honi and I looked at each other, then back at the foreigner.

"That's beautiful," Honi said.

"It's amazing that you know all that by heart, Fareed," I added. "I can barely remember my phone number."

Fareed paused. "It's strange that I didn't say the last sentence in the book: 'Here our tale ends. Praise be to Allah, Creator of the World.'" Then he retreated back into his thoughts.

### 3

—Why did you decide to write about the issue of return?

—I wasn't even planning to write about it. I was writing a story about jewelry, diamonds, Tel Aviv, Jaffa. All kinds of things.

—Then where did you come up with the idea of this Arab crossing the border?

—But that happened in the past, you know. In real life it happened a few months before my story takes place. I didn't make it up.

—What do you know about the incident?

—You're acting like it's a state secret. I read about it in the paper! I think it was a teacher from Damascus, he was about thirty. He crossed the border into Israel and went on a roots journey to Jaffa. He walked around, talked with some locals, had lunch at a Bulgarian restaurant, gave an interview to the press, then turned himself in. And they sent him back to Syria.

—Did you meet him in Jaffa?

—The Syrian infiltrator? No!

—Then what's your connection? What made you want to write about it?

—I found it interesting, you know? A man suddenly decides to cross one of the most heavily guarded borders in the world, and with one little step it's like he completely erases it.

—All of a sudden it just interested you? You spend your life writing about other things, and then this, out of the blue?

—I don't know if I've always written about other things. At the end of the day I always write about the same themes.

—What were you trying to achieve in this book?

—Achieve? Nothing.

—What are you trying to prove?

—Look, are you a Mossad interrogator or a literary editor?

—Maybe I'm both. Or maybe I'm neither, and this is all inside your head—did you ever think about that? Have you ever tried to get into someone else's mind?

—I can try to get into *your* mind. My father did exactly what you're doing.

—What makes you think I'm interested in what your father did?

—In his day, people were more polite around here. Can I leave now?

—I can't say for sure yet. You haven't said anything.

—I have nothing more to add.

—Oh, but I thought you had an opinion about everything.

—Not everything. About you, for example, I don't yet have a decisive opinion.

—I couldn't care less about that.

—Good.

—Are you a homosexual?

—Are you?

—You know what I'm asking.

—If I'm gay?

—No, I want to know where he is.

—Who, the Syrian teacher? I told you, the papers said they took him back to Syria. It was ages ago.

—You know very well who I'm talking about. Where is Fareed?

—I have no idea.

—How can that be possible? Are you telling me you knew exactly where he went every second in Israel since the minute he crossed the border, you got into his pants, you knew what he was thinking and what he was saying and where he was staying, but now you simply have no idea where he is?

—Exactly.

—How do you explain that?

—Only Allah can explain.

—You're still being a wiseass.

—Actually, I'm not. It's the truth—I knew everything about him, or almost everything, and now I know nothing.

—How can that make sense?

—I don't know if it makes sense, but it's the truth. But you know what? When I think about it, there's something about this whole story that bugs me, and maybe you can enlighten me. It has to do with that Syrian teacher. All the papers wrote about what he did in Israel—where he went, who he talked with, even where he had lunch, but then suddenly they said he was back in Syria. Abracadabra.

—What are you insinuating?

—I'm just saying I find it odd. How did he get back there so quickly? And anyway, didn't they arrest him? All of a sudden your guys thought it would be best to just send him back home and leave it at that? Not even a little bit of enhanced interrogation?

—What do *you* think?

—I don't think anything. I'm just wondering. Anyway, I have nothing more to say.

—That is clearly not true. You have to write an ending to your story. What are you going to do, write that you have no idea?

—You're right, I really do need to puzzle this out.

—You know what, maybe I can help you.

—This should be interesting...

—For example, you could write about what happened to the Arab after he gave back the diamond.

—I see you're very familiar with the story.

—It's an interesting story, except that I still don't understand what he came here for. Just to give back the diamond? After all, he could have FedExed it. A guy doesn't risk his life for that.

—FedEx from Damascus to Tel Aviv?

—Oh, so it's easier to be an illegal alien?

—Okay, so why do *you* think he come to Israel?

—If you ask me, there was another reason. I imagine it had something to do with his grandparents' house in Jaffa.

—I'm listening...

—Maybe he wanted to set some sort of a precedent.

—You mean a legal precedent?

—Maybe. Or a political one.

—But the whole political story wasn't of much interest to him, I don't think. It was more of a personal matter. A roots journey, coming full circle, whatever you want to call it.

—Then listen to my opinion on the matter.

—Your opinion as what, a Shabak investigator?

—As someone who wants to give you some friendly advice. I'll tell you how I see it: When he sat in his room in Damascus planning the trip, it seemed like a good idea. Guys his age have all kinds of weird ideas, you know. Omnipotent fantasies.

—I see we've been reading psychology textbooks...

—What's for sure is that afterward, when he'd already crossed the border, he discovered that things weren't quite as simple as he thought.

—Meaning he was disillusioned.

—Something like that.

—So what's he supposed to do now?

—If you ask me, he has to leave the country.

—How exactly? By sea?

—By land. He has to go and turn himself in. He doesn't have to worry, they'll treat him well. No one here has any interest in letting this guy become a symbol. Our people will ask him a couple of questions and send him back home alive and well in a few hours. At most a few days.

—That's nice to know. But you can tell your guys it won't be the end of the story. Even if Fareed goes back to Syria, something has to happen.

—What has to happen?

—Something, I don't know exactly what. It's hard to predict these things. But what's certain is that something will happen.

—Let me understand: Is that a threat?

—Not at all. It's an estimate, a gut feeling.

—I suggest you take care of your Syrian soon. You know what they say: First catch your hare. I'm talking very candidly with you. And I'll tell you something else. You take good care of him, that Arab. You don't want him pulling a fast one on you.

—A fast one?

—I've said my piece. Be alert, control your story. A still tongue makes a wise head, as they say.

—I appreciate that. So I'm just supposed to tell him everything will be fine?

—You can promise him that if he cooperates with us and doesn't act like a wiseass, he has nothing to worry about.

—But what about the jeweler?

—What about him?

—He knows everything, after all. And he's going to find out that he has relatives in Syria.

—Cousins.

—Worse, a half brother. Aren't you afraid he'll open his mouth?

—Menashe Salomon doesn't worry me. He's a good Israeli citizen. What's he going to do, tell everyone that half a century ago his parents lived a double life in Syria? That he was brought up on a lie? That what he thought was the blue diamond was only an imitation, and all the stories he grew up on were a big bluff?

—So you really think he's going to keep his mouth shut?

—Yes. He has too much to lose. Believe me, he'll be the first to try to convince himself that this whole story never happened.

—But what is he supposed to do with the diamond?

—There are two diamonds, remember? One belongs to Achlama, the Persian woman, and the other is Fareed's.

—That's true.

—Which is the real one?

—Fareed's.

—Interesting. How can you be so sure?

—Because I know. Adela replaced Sabakh with a different blue diamond, and she secretly gave the real one to Laila in 1948.

—I see. And what if that's not how it happened?

—What do you mean?

—Well, who told you that's what really happened? And even if it is, how do we know that crafty diamond didn't go through another few incarnations on the way? I recommend that you be suspicious, my friend.

—Okay . . . I'll think about it. Anyway, what is Menashe supposed to do with the diamond now, whichever one it is?

—He has to get rid of it. Sell it. Make a few bucks and buy a new shop instead of the hole in the wall he has now. They're opening a hotel there anyway. Besides, that diamond's done enough damage, hasn't it?

—Maybe he could donate it to the security services?

—Bravo, very funny.

—You could frame it behind bulletproof glass and hang it on your wall. All your colleagues would come and see it, you'd be famous.

—I'll keep that in mind.

—So is that it?

—That's it.

—Can I leave?

—After you promise me that Fareed will turn himself in, I'll even call you a taxi.

—Generous. What do I get out of it?

—Out of what?

—If I make sure Fareed shows up here, what do I get in return?

—That's obvious, isn't it?

—No.

—You get a story.

—A story?

—Yes. And that's a lot.

—Let me think about it.

—Go ahead.

(. . .)

—Okay.

—Do we have a deal?

—We have a deal.

—You have a firm handshake. I like that.

—So you'll call me a taxi?

—I gave my word. Where should I tell him to take you?

—Jaffa.


# 4

Rowena looked worried when she opened the door. There were black circles beneath her eyes. Honi looked past her to the spot where Adela had sat the last time he visited, next to the window, beside the large ficus tree. But the armchair was empty.

When he'd visited the shop earlier that week, Menashe was sitting in his usual spot behind his workbench, but his face looked different. He told Honi that his mother had had a stroke. She'd fought for her life all night in the hospital, and in the morning she'd woken up with half her body paralyzed.

When Adela realized she couldn't move half of her face, that one leg was shaking and full of life while the other lay there like a log, and that she couldn't speak or even smile, didn't have the strength to put food in her mouth, and could hug her son with only one arm—she went wild. The commotion she kicked up brought a team of nurses running. They tied her wrist to the bed railing with a strip of fabric that was the same pale blue as her hospital gown, injected her with a tranquilizer, and set about restoring the machines she'd damaged.

Menashe sat next to her bed looking stunned, while the old lady watched him with a mixture of reproof and hurt pride for allowing them to tie her up. They both knew there must come a time when children care for their parents as though they were the babies, but even when Menashe was an unruly boy who disobeyed his mother, even when he misbehaved, she had never allowed her husband to grab the boy's wrists and tie them to a bed. Not her husband and not anyone else.

No one saw the tears in their eyes. One of the nurses had left to care for a teenage boy hooked up to a ventilator a few beds away. His chest rose and fell with a regular, artificial rhythm. His mother stood quietly next to his bed. The boy's eyes were wide open but there was no expression on his face. Menashe looked at the boy for a long time and wondered what had happened. An accident, probably. He noticed the boy's cheeks were meticulously shaved.

Menashe looked back at his own mother. Adela's eyes were staring into space, and her healthy hand's fingers fumbled around with the fabric strip that bound her thin wrist. He sat there for a few minutes longer, then finally got up and said goodbye. She tried to say something, but her lips pulled to one side and a strange gurgle emerged. He leaned over and kissed her forehead. Her furious eyes followed him out into the hallway.

Two days later, Adela was brought back to her apartment on Dizengoff Street, but she came home inchoate: half a living, breathing body stuck to half a dead one. Her eyes were alive, her skin glistened—especially on her shins, which were delicate and beautiful like a girl's. Rowena lowered her carefully onto the bed and placed a towel over her midsection so as not to expose her private parts and to cover the plug that blocked the hole in her gut.

Honi followed Rowena into the bedroom and found Adela lying in bed with her face as smooth as a baby's and her hair neatly combed. A clear tube connected to an oxygen machine was inserted into each nostril. She opened her eyes when he came in. That was all she could do. When he sat down, she began mumbling unintelligibly. Did she remember who he was? Was her mind lucid? Was she angry to find him, of all people, sitting there, practically a stranger, and a descendant of the hated Shayu? Honi didn't know, and he was about to make an awkward exit when Adela giggled to herself with half her mouth, and he decided to stay.

Rowena came in with a cup of water, dipped a cotton swab in the cup, and moistened the old lady's lips. "Maya called today," she told Adela in a perfect Israeli accent. "She's in London. She asked how you were and sent you big kisses."

When Rowena said her granddaughter's name, something seemed to move on the old lady's face. But when Honi looked at her again he realized the words had made no impression. There was a vacant, almost demented expression on that smooth face that had once been capable of such anger, as well as occasional tranquillity.

"Has Menashe been here today?" Honi asked Rowena.

"No, he'll come this evening. Maybe in an hour. The only visitors were Shlomo with his wife, and yesterday evening Mona and her husband came with the grandchildren. This morning there was no one."

Honi looked at Adela and didn't know what to say. He had come to talk to her about what he'd found in the attic at home the day before. He wanted to see her response. He'd climbed up to look for a pair of speakers he'd stored when he moved in with Ayelet, but while he was standing on the ladder feeling around in the depths of the alcove, trying to reach the speakers, he noticed a stack of stapled papers wrapped in a plastic bag. He took the pages and climbed down.

They were written in Arabic, in dense, neat handwriting. Honi went to his room and sat down on his bed. He leafed through the yellowing pages and strained his eyes in an attempt to decipher the words on the first page, based on what he remembered from high school Arabic. But he couldn't understand anything. The letters were too crowded, and some were crossed out with curvy lines. In the evening, he asked Fareed to help. The title was clearly legible: "Love Triangle." Farther down the page, Fareed deciphered the following words: "Cast of Characters: Laila—born in Yafa, twenty-one; Adela—born in Damascus, twenty-two; Rafael—her husband, born in Damascus, twenty-seven." Fareed spent a long time reading the text out to Honi, translating into English as he went.

When he got home, Honi went into his room and locked the door. He lay in bed for a long time, brimming with thoughts. He had never heard that his grandfather Shayu had been a writer. He pondered the story Fareed had translated for him, which was about Rafael and Adela—none other than Menashe the jeweler's parents. When he came out of his room, the apartment was empty. Ayelet was at the Shack. Next to the kitchen sink was a pile of empty plastic cups she'd washed and dried. Honi climbed up the ladder, shut the wooden door to the storage unit, got dressed, and went out.

Ayelet stood behind the counter cutting ginger root into thin slices. She wore a tank top and her skin glistened with sweat. Her long hair, tied back in a ponytail, was damp, and her eyes were red from the heat. An older customer stood waiting for fresh-squeezed orange juice. Ayelet cut the oranges into halves and used a manual citrus press, rather than an electric juicer where the fruit slides down a chute and comes out the other end as juice. "It's not about the money, it's about the muscles," Ayelet explained with a grin when Honi asked why she didn't get an electric juicer.

When Honi was six, his father gave him a Passover gift of a battery-operated toy made of yellow and black Lego bricks. It had a conveyor belt, which Honi liked to place nuts on and watch them rattle down the slide.

Ayelet added an emptied-out half orange to the pile towering up on the counter and wiped the sweat from her forehead with a paper towel. "Ginger?" she asked. The customer nodded. She threw two little pieces of ginger root into the cup, put a lid on, and handed it to the man. After he left, Honi took his spot at the counter and Ayelet gave him a glass of water. "What's going on? You look a little worked up. Is everything okay with Tom?"

"Yes." Honi sat down on a green wooden stool.

"And with Fareed?"

"I think so."

"What about the radio show?"

"We've almost finished editing. It'll be on next Friday."

"So what's up? Did you find out something new about the jewelry store?"

"No. I mean, not exactly."

"I talked to Kadosh," Ayelet said. "He claims he doesn't owe the people who work there anything. You know how he is—as far as he's concerned, if there's no signed lease, there's nothing." She gave Honi an interrogative look. "He's been a little tough on you recently, hasn't he? I'm glad you told him. But..."

"But what?"

"Never mind. So what's up, Honi? What's new?"

"It's about Grandpa Shayu."

"I'm listening."

"I found a story he wrote. Did you know he wrote stories?"

"Now that you mention it, I remember hearing him talking about it once with Grandma. Kadosh was there, too."

"What exactly did he say?"

"He said there was something he'd wanted to write about for years, and he'd finally found the courage to do it. Grandma didn't take it very seriously, but I remember it was Kadosh who told me, afterward, that he hadn't seen his father like that for a long time. Anyway, wow, that was ages ago, I was maybe ten. It's coming back to me now: Grandpa wanted Kadosh to read it, and Kadosh said yeah yeah yeah, but of course he didn't."

"Did you?"

"Of course not! I was a kid. Anyway, he wrote in Arabic."

"And that was it, no one ever talked about the story again?"

"Why are you asking so many questions, Honi?" Ayelet wiped the counter with a damp yellow cloth. "What's the story about, anyway. Have you read it?"

"Fareed translated part of it for me. It's about a triangle."

"A triangle?"

"Yes. I mean a man and two women."

"Grandpa wrote about a love triangle? Awesome!"

"You have no idea the stuff that goes on there! It takes place in Lebanon, in the '40s, and there's a Jewish couple from Damascus and an Arab woman from Jaffa."

"Ooh, naughty Grandpa!"

"Oh, you haven't heard the half of it. Do you know what this couple from Damascus are called?"

"What?"

"The woman is called Adela and the man is called Rafael."

"I don't believe it. He used Menashe's parents' names?!"

"Yes."

"That's getting a little weird, don't you think? Would it have been so hard for him to make up names? Was it some kind of revenge? That's not like him."

"If you ask me," Honi said, "it's not revenge at all."

"What, then?"

"To my mind, it means the story is real."

"I don't understand. Plenty of writers name characters after real people they know, don't they?"

"Look, I mean he could have made up different names, but he didn't. I think he purposely used Adela and Rafael's names because it's a real story, and it was important for him to document it. Or maybe he was planning to change the names later but he didn't."

"Why not?"

"I don't believe it just slipped his mind. Maybe he wanted someone to read it and find out. Or maybe he just didn't get around to it."

"You're talking like a detective again, Honi."

"Listen, lately I keep discovering things I never knew about."

"Well, anyway, it's not our story. They're distant relatives, it's a different family."

"They're a family with very, very close ties to ours, let me remind you. And don't forget something else: Our father is currently laying into Menashe with full force."

"He's not laying into him with full force; he just wants to build his hotel, and the jeweler is sitting there like a thorn in his ass. So he's kicking him out. That's what he knows how to do, it's not out of malice."

"So you think it's acceptable?"

"What do you want me to say—that's the way the cookie crumbles? That we have a capitalist pig for a father? You know that just as well as I do. But what can you do? We have to accept Kadosh for who he is. You don't get to pick your family."

Honi didn't respond.

"Honi, what's the matter with you?"

"Nothing."

She gave him a look.

"What?" he asked awkwardly. "What are you looking at me like that for?"

"I think you're a little stuck," Ayelet said hesitantly. She gazed at her brother and wondered if this was the right time. Privately, she had decided that come what may, she would speak to him candidly at some point. "And if you ask me, you're suffering quite a bit from this stuckness. It has a lot to do with your place in the world. Where are you really standing today, Honi?"

"What do you mean where am I standing?"

"I don't mean where do you stand physically, honey. It's not something you can define with latitude and longitude, like in some iPhone app. I mean where is the place you're really in right now—it doesn't have to be on any time axis, but it has to be a real point. I want to know: Here stands Honi."

"Honestly, Ayelet? I don't understand what you're getting at."

"Remember what I used to call you when you were little? Honi the Circle Maker. Remember how you used to get mad when I did that?"

"So?"

"So I'm starting to think you really are a little bit like Honi the Circle Maker. You've drawn this kind of circle around you and that's that. You're standing inside it and you won't budge."

Honi smiled. "So you think I'm waiting for my prayers to be answered?"

"You can laugh, but I'm totally serious. I'm waiting for you to get out of that circle already. Or, you know what, not even get out. I just wish I could look at you and know exactly where you stand."

"Again with that...Where do I stand? I don't know what you want from me, Ayelet."

"I don't know. This whole thing with Fareed...I don't want to sound like some puritanical preacher, it's totally fine with me what you're doing, but I do have to wonder what it means about you and Tom. It really worries me, if you must know."

Honi said nothing.

"You know what, let's drop all that for now. You were going to tell me about Grandpa's story."

Honi was clearly relieved to change the topic. "Well, I only read the beginning. Fareed has translated almost the whole first chapter for me. But there are more. I have to go over it with him, it's not easy figuring out that handwriting. Fareed says it's like hieroglyphics, and the Arabic is archaic, too. But I intend to figure this thing out, I'm curious about it."

"I have to tell you," Ayelet took his fingers in her wet, beet-stained hand, "I think you're better off letting go. Don't you have enough on your mind without messing around with old stories Grandpa scribbled down? You're acting like a kid in junior high doing a family tree project. What good will come of digging into the past like this?"

Honi looked down and blew air through his straw.

"If you ask me, Honi, you're just looking for distractions. It's time to find *your* story." She gave him a meaningful look, then kissed his forehead and turned around to wash the dishes in the sink. Honi got up and walked out.


## 5

Menashe sat down next to his mother's bed. Adela's dress was hiked up over her knees. She looked at him with her small, seemingly peaceful eyes. Her lips drooped and moved slightly to the left, but she couldn't make a sound.

Menashe was about to say something, but he reconsidered and in the end said nothing. He knew she wouldn't be able to respond and that they would both end up extremely frustrated. He felt guilty, again, about her lying there unable to move, and he remembered the terrified look she'd given him when she woke up in the hospital with her wrist strapped to the bed. He looked down, but her face followed him and he could see it from the corner of his eye. Her fingers were warm, soft, and very thin, and she pressed her son's hand in an irregular rhythm, sometimes powerfully and sometimes almost imperceptibly, as though she were trying to remind him of something distant that could be awoken by the mere touch of her fingers. Adela's eyes suddenly welled up with tears. Her lips crumpled to one side, and now she seemed to be laughing.

Menashe held her face and touched her tears. "Listen, Mother, I have something to tell you."

She looked at him with curious, damp eyes, but Menashe was unable to talk. He was too emotional. Long years of guilt prevented him now from telling his mother what had happened. Instead, he took a small box from his pocket and opened it. Adela looked down and examined the contents.

"It's the diamond they stole from me, Mom!" he said excitedly. "You remember what happened during the Gulf War? Remember that burglar who didn't take anything except the diamond? Well, they found it! Here it is."

Adela breathed rapidly and blinked nervously. No words came from her mouth, but her eyes said one thing: *No!*

"Did you hear what I said, Mom? It's our diamond, it's Sabakh. What a pity Dad can't see it now. He would have been so proud of me for finding it after all this time!" Menashe felt sad again. His mother clearly couldn't understand what he was telling her. If she could have, she would surely have been happy for him and for the family. Perhaps she was still afraid of the diamond? But no, she didn't look fearful, in fact, she looked rather indifferent. Menashe shut the box, bitterly disappointed, and put it back in his pocket. He sat there for a few more minutes, then kissed her forehead and left.

## 6

The next day, before opening the shop on Plonit Alley, the jeweler sat down at Phantom on Allenby Street and ordered a cup of coffee. Life at the café went on as usual. The regular customers were all in their places: the stamp collectors, the antique coin dealers, the loafers, the gluttons. The couple that had recently relocated to a new apartment in Ness Tziona was there, too. They told the others about the quality of life in the squeaky-clean neighborhood and the convenient train to Tel Aviv, and admitted that the big city, with its noise and pollution, was less and less appealing since they had grown accustomed to the green park near their new home.

In the corner of the café sat a dignified man of about seventy-five. Menashe knew him well: It was Zevulun, the Persian gemstone dealer. He wore a three-piece suit that was old but immaculately cleaned and pressed. There was a white handkerchief in his breast pocket, and every so often he used it to wipe his glistening bald head, which was topped with a yarmulke. Zevulun wore one single piece of jewelry: a thick gold band inset with a fine turquoise stone.

Menashe sipped his coffee slowly and looked at Zevulun. The latter nodded his head in acknowledgment. The jeweler was tempted to show his diamond to the elegant Persian gentleman. Who knew how much money he might get for it? Finally, he got up and went over.

"How are you, Mr. Zevulun?"

"Praise God," answered the gemstone dealer. "And you, Salomon? How's business?"

"Day by day."

"I heard that Shayu's son wants to throw you out of the shop."

"So he does," Menashe said. "And what of it? I want lots of things, too. It's not going to be easy for him, you can be sure of that."

"I trust you. If you end up in court with him, you let me know. I'll go down there and I'll tell them his father was your father Rafael's closest friend."

"Thank you, Mr. Zevulun, I'll remember that." Menashe paused awkwardly.

"What's the matter, Salomon?" asked the Persian, worried. "Do you feel well?"

"Yes."

"Have you had your heart checked recently? You have to take care of these things."

"I'm fine," Menashe answered, and wondered for a moment if everything really was in order. He thought about his landlord, Kadosh, who had only recently had a coronary stent put in. "I'm fine," he repeated, pushing away the thought. "Listen, Mr. Zevulun," he said as he took out the box, "I want you to make me an offer on this diamond."

Zevulun removed a gold-framed magnifying glass from his pocket, took the diamond from the jeweler, and held it up to the glass. "Very nice. They did very nice work on this."

"It's antique. Not like the goods those Georgians on Allenby Street sell."

"You don't have to tell me that." Zevulun passionately despised the recent immigrants who were giving the jewelry trade a bad name, as he put it. "But why do you want to sell it?"

"I don't have a need for it."

"Make a nice piece of jewelry with it."

"I won't be able to off-load it on any of my customers," said the jeweler. "It's out of fashion."

"Then give it to your daughter."

"Do you know how many years it's been since I saw my daughter? She lives in London. She found religion, she lives with a Hassid."

"All right, let me think." Zevulun furrowed his large, glistening brow. After a moment of silence he picked up a pen and scribbled a number on a napkin. Menashe took the pen, crossed out the number, and wrote another one beneath it. Zevulun crossed out Menashe's number and wrote a third one. The two merchants did this several more times, until they reached a happy medium. Then the dealer took a sheaf of bills out of his pocket, counted them, and handed a bundle to the jeweler, who counted them in turn. Menashe put the blue diamond in the Persian's hand, stashed the money in his pocket, shook Zevulun's hand, and walked out of the café. He took a few steps down Allenby Street, and near Gruzenberg Street he stopped walking and let out a great sigh.

When he reached the shop ten minutes later, he found a young man by the door. "May I help you?" Menashe asked. To be on the safe side, he did not take his keys out yet.

"I'm looking for Menashe Salomon," the man said in English.

"Who are you?"

"Fareed."

"Have we met?"

"No, but my grandmother knew your father, Rafael, in Lebanon."

"My father lived in Syria, not Lebanon." The jeweler debated his next move.

"But he used to go on holidays to Aley, didn't he?" Fareed spoke in Arabic now. "That's where he met my grandmother, Laila. If we go into the shop, I'll tell you the story."

Menashe stood in his spot for another moment. He felt extremely tired after selling the blue diamond to Zevulun. It was a feeling he had not had since the day the diamond was stolen, and it was difficult for him to comprehend. But just like on that distant day in 1991, when he deposited his story in the thief's hands, today he also felt an inner force urging him to proceed contrary to all reason. He raised the shutters and walked into the shop with the young Arab man behind him.

Menashe pressed the code to neutralize the alarm: 1948. "Coffee?" he asked the infiltrator. The Arabic flowed naturally, as though he conversed with every other customer in this language.

"I'd love some," Fareed said.

The jeweler filled his stainless steel *finjan* with water at the tap and lit the torch he used for welding gold. He held the flame under the *finjan*, and when the water boiled, he turned off the flame, put a large scoop of Turkish coffee in the water, and brought it to another boil. "So what was it you wanted to tell me?"

"I'll get to that," Fareed said, looking around. "How long have you been in this shop?"

Menashe looked up and examined the young man and realized he'd made a big mistake letting him in. But the coffee was already bubbling. The jeweler put a little china cup on his workbench and poured in the boiling-hot coffee, added two spoonfuls of sugar, stirred, and handed it to Fareed. "We've been here since 1950, but we might be moving soon."

"Yes, Tom told me."

"Tom? You know Tom?" Menashe was confused.

"Yes."

"Tom doesn't work mornings. He'll be here in the afternoon."

"I know."

"How do you know him?"

"It's a long story," Fareed said. "But that's not why I'm here." And without a further word he took a box out of his pocket, put it on the jeweler's bench, and announced, "Here you go."

Menashe frowned. "What's that?"

"A gift."

"For me? But why?"

"It's something your mother gave my grandmother."

"Jewelry?"

"Something like that."

"Where are you from?" Menashe was getting suspicious.

"Damascus."

"Is this a joke?" But his heart told him the young man was telling the truth.

"I'm not joking. Beautiful city, Damascus. Maybe one day you'll be able to come visit."

"I don't understand. Are you working for the Mossad or something? What's this all about?"

"No Mossad, no nothing. But it's a long story, don't worry about it now."

"Damascus . . . I don't believe it. My father always told me about Damascus. He loved it so much. And it was his dream for us to go there together, me and him. But he died long ago. Wait, I don't understand. How did you get here from Damascus?"

"By bus."

"Bus?" Menashe started doubting the man's sanity.

"Open the box, Menashe."

"What if it's dangerous?"

"Do you think I put a bomb for you in that little box?" Fareed laughed. "Okay, if you're not going to open it, I will." He picked up the box, but at the last minute Menashe grabbed it and opened it himself.

And there he saw a diamond. A blue diamond.

The jeweler turned to look at the young man. Fareed's eyes glimmered. A satisfied, almost triumphant expression took over his face. And then he told Menashe everything he knew. The jeweler sat there, stunned, and listened to the man with a mixture of disbelief and extraordinary fascination.

"Here our tale ends. Praise be to Allah, Creator of the World," Fareed said finally.

Menashe remembered hearing that line as a child, from his father. And indeed, something in the face of this young stranger reminded Menashe of Rafael Salomon as a young man, in the old photographs he remembered from his parents' picture albums.

Fareed stood up. "Okay, I have to get going. Tell Tom the eagle has landed."

7

That evening, Fareed slipped into one of the rooms in the house on Sha'arei Nikanor Street. The big house was full of activists and journalists, both Israeli and foreign, speaking in a cocktail of languages. Doors opened and shut. Cooking smells came from the kitchen. Young men and women sat on colorful rugs in the courtyard with big pots between their legs, peeling potatoes. The activists sat talking late into the night. The generator rattled, bulbs hung from the branches, the air smelled of the hookah and of Turkish coffee cooking on the gas ring. A packet of wafer cookies was passed around, growing emptier by the minute. At midnight they turned off the lights, leaving only a small lamp lit in the hallway. Sounds of sleep came from the rooms, with doors either shut or wide open: fragments of dreams, tossing and turning, teeth grinding. Fareed rummaged through his bag and took out a notebook. He sat down and composed a letter in English, then typed it on his cell phone.

Darlings,

This evening I began to suspect I was being followed in the house. I looked around a bit and realized I'm not paranoid: someone is really on to me. I locked myself in a room. I had a lot of time to kill. I lay in bed with my eyes closed and thought a lot about my life in this place, which I only came to a few weeks ago, without being invited by anyone. In fact, when you think of it, it's amazing no one has followed me until now. And they say your intelligence service is the best in the region...

I thought about you all evening. It hasn't been long since we met, but I feel like I've known you for years, and I'm connected to you as if we'd been living together forever. I already miss you. Actually, I don't miss you: I already feel your absence.

All sorts of questions troubled me tonight: Will you stay here, in this strange country? Do you feel part of it? Of its people? And if not—where will you go? Where will you live?

What language will you speak? Will you always stay together? Will you remember me?

As for me, I want to go home, to Damascus. Not that I'm happy there, not at all. But that's where I was born and where my family is. And afterward? I have no idea. Maybe I'll go back to the U.S., maybe to another country. Maybe I'll stay in Syria. Everything's open. What's clear is that my life after meeting you will not be the same.

Since coming here, I've often felt rattled by an enormous wave of contempt. Not so much for this place, although I did feel that quite a bit, too, but in a broader sense. Contempt for what? Perhaps for all of human existence, if I can put it that way. At first I was alarmed by my thoughts, but then I realized perhaps there is nothing bad or wrong about them. Perhaps it's even appropriate to feel contempt for yourself, for your life. Because life itself—its futility, its monotonous simplicity—deserves a certain amount of contempt. There are moments in life, after all, moments of mental and physical elevation, which we live for, aren't there? And if that is the case, then contempt is an important motivation for those moments. But there must be courage, too.

I'm really not worried about you, because you don't lack courage. Perhaps what you need is a little more grace. You must nobly bear the heavy burden of life, constantly aspiring to certain moments, which may come when you are alone or with company, but they are always lonely and also slightly painful. And on the way to these moments you feel both pleasure and displeasure.

These are just some of the things I thought about. I've learned a lot in the past few weeks. The things I saw and heard here are completely different from what I imagined before I crossed the border. Different for the better? For the worse? That's not the issue. What's certain is that I don't know if there's enough room for the three of us in this space. I look at this house I'm in now, my grandparents' house, and I really don't feel that I belong in it. I don't miss it and I don't belong. Still, this is my city, this is my family's house, this is the sea my grandmother looked at for many days.

The room I'm sitting in now might already be surrounded by armed soldiers, just waiting for me to open the door so they can rush at me and kill me. Before I came here, Ramadan told me there's nothing Israelis fear more than an unarmed Arab. But here I am: an Arab armed only with pen and paper. And that really is a dangerous thing. Far more dangerous than a gun.

The only thing I have left to do now, really, is to decide how this story will end: Do I have no choice but to turn myself in? Perhaps I must find a way to slip away and leave this place. Leave, but who knows where to . . . Maybe I should just surrender. There is a certain pleasure in defeat, in knowing that you're delivering yourself into its safe arms, that you've lost the battle. I don't mean defeat in the sense of the opposite of victory, but the more common kind of defeat, the kind that gives rise to insight: There was something here that got the better of me, that was more pleasurable than me, more attainable. Sometimes it just happens incidentally, on a particular day of the week: Sunday, Thursday, Saturday.

I look at you, Tom, and I think about how writing dictates your life and not the opposite, as people usually imagine. But when you suffer defeat in life itself, writing will be your consolation, because you will write about the defeat and you will immortalize it on a particular day at a particular time — Thursday,

Sunday, or Saturday. That is your bordered domain. No one has access to it. That, in fact, is the only thing you have. The only thing left. All the rest—passions, jealousy, success, release, life itself—all that is out of your hands. There is not a single thing, apart from your defeat.

I love you both,
Fareed

At five thirty a.m., the city trash removers arrived. The garbage truck stopped noisily outside the house, but the inhabitants kept sleeping. The house was still dark. Two workers in green uniforms hopped off the truck. They entered the courtyard, dragged out bags of garbage, and tossed them into the truck's belly. Then they went back into the house. The front door was open, and one went into the kitchen for a drink of water. The other followed him. It wasn't easy to see them in the dark, although the first light was emerging and beginning to touch the rooftops, the solar water tanks, the top-floor windows, the curtains. But the sun's rays did not yet hit the ground. The earth was dark and slightly damp from dew.

The two workers stood in the kitchen, drinking tea and nibbling leftover wafer cookies from a packet on the table. One of them walked down the hallway, into a room, and soon returned to his friend in the kitchen. A moment later they left the house with a third worker, also dressed in the green uniform. They all hopped on the back of the truck and held on as the truck drove away.

As the garbage truck barreled down the streets of Jaffa, one of them shouted to the others, "I feel like we're liberating the Sabena plane in Beirut!" They all laughed. The truck drove on through the silent streets. Lights were appearing in a few of the houses. On the left they could glimpse the sea dancing in the first sunlight. The smell of the sea mingled with the stench of trash that came from the back of the truck, and the three temporary workers, unaccustomed to this job, turned their faces away in disgust.

———

When the garbage truck crossed Jaffa–Tel Aviv Road and carried us toward Clock Tower Square, I looked at Fareed. He was saying goodbye to Yafa with his eyes. Honi watched Fareed, then they both looked at my own flushed, impervious face. I thought about how we would get to Honi's apartment soon, where we would shower off the stench of garbage and lie down together to sleep.

I BEGAN WRITING *THE DIAMOND SETTER* IN 2008, shortly after starting work as an apprentice in my father's jewelry shop, not far from Plonit Alley in Tel Aviv. For three years I sat every day at a small workbench and learned the art of jewelry making. One day the shopkeepers in the building learned that it was to be converted into a boutique hotel. My father refused to get upset. He'd spent more than four decades in the shop that had been opened by his father, Moshe Sakal, who came to Tel Aviv from Damascus, and he firmly believed that no financial calculations or real estate deals could uproot his little business. But sometimes the winds of change are stronger than willpower, and as fate would have it, on the day I wrote the very last line of the novel—in January 2014—my father relocated the family business to a new, more spacious spot in a nearby street.

During my days as a jeweler's apprentice, I immersed myself in books about diamonds and precious stones. Their tales seemed like human adventures, and I followed my curiosity to track down the histories of these treasures, which had surfaced in India or South Africa and made their way through a succession of owners—both royalty and commoners—whose fates they either blessed or cursed. I also researched the intertwined histories of Tel Aviv and Jaffa throughout the twentieth century, and the stories of immigrants from Syria and Egypt, in which I often found a fascinating blend of East and West. In the summer of 2011, while I studied places that no longer exist and contemplated people long gone, the social protest movement began simmering in Israel. Ironically, the movement was inspired by the popular uprisings in neighboring countries that Israelis had turned their backs on for generations.

While on hiatus from *The Diamond Setter*, I wrote another novel, *Yolanda*, which is largely based on the life of my grandmother, a native of Cairo. The book depicts a group of Egyptian-born Levantines who have lived in Israel for six decades or more and yet still feel exiled there. They exist in a sort of double diaspora, having lived as Francophones in Cairo and been overcome with nostalgia for Cairo once they came to Israel.

In *The Diamond Setter*, unlike in *Yolanda*, there is no ignoring the characters' immediate geographic sphere. My Syrian grandparents' family had always talked about the days of open borders, when the people who dwelled in this region— at least those who belonged to a certain class—could move freely from one country to another, traveling from Jaffa to Cairo, from Beirut to Haifa, from Hebron to Damascus. Anyone who lived in Palestine before the State of Israel was established in 1948 had tales of brave relationships that survived even the bloodiest of times, love affairs and friendships between Jews and Arabs, and cooperation—economic and otherwise—even as the two nationalist movements hardened their stances and stepped up their acts of hostility.

One day when I was about ten, I walked past a house on Sha'arei Nikanor Street, in Jaffa, with my father. I remember him pointing and saying, "This is where Grandfather's best friend lived." That memory, as well as the story of Hassan Hijazi, a young Syrian teacher who managed to get into Israel in 2011 and make his way to Jaffa, where he explored his family's roots, were both inspirations for my writing. I was fascinated not only by Hijazi's courage but also by the symbolism of his act, and his story sparked my imagination, leading the way to a plot that integrates multiple facets of this country and its surroundings. Syria has changed course since then and is now mired in a bloody civil war whose end, as I write these words, is nowhere in sight. I often think about Damascus, my grandfather's beloved city, and about his dream of traveling there with me—a dream that will never come true.

While writing *The Diamond Setter* I also finally learned Arabic, from a Jaffoite named Ali al-Azhari. I was amazed by all the raised eyebrows when people heard how I was spending my summer ("Arabic? What for?"), even when I explained that it was my father's native tongue, the language of our neighbors, a rich and beautiful language.

Another source of inspiration was Yehuda Burla's book *Meranenet*, a historical novel about the young female singers and musicians who performed in Damascus during the latter days of the Ottoman Empire. These performers, whose stories Burla recounts without any reproof or moralizing, were Jewish-Arab geishas of a sort, conducting relationships with eminent Arab men. The Jewish community disparaged and condemned them, yet there was also a measure of esteem and gratitude, since these young women were able to give their community significant aid in times of economic hardship and political challenges.

My grandfather, Moshe Sakal, was born in Damascus near the end of the First World War, and as a young man he taught French at the Alliance Française and worked at the stock exchange. He also wrote fiction, in Arabic, some of which was published in the Syrian press. The word "coexistence" does not begin to describe the way my family lived in Damascus. They were, quite simply, locals. When they came to Israel, they were fortunate enough not to be sent to one of the *ma'abarot* (Israel's notoriously harsh "transition camps" for new immigrants in the 1950s), as they had the means to purchase a small apartment in Tel Aviv. Were they subjected to socioeconomic discrimination? No. Did my father, who grew up in the heart of urban Tel Aviv, suffer from racism? Not at all. And yet something was missing. And that thing, which in recent years I have begun to acknowledge as having left a void in my family, was the bond with Arabic culture and language, the affinity between the old and new homes. Some might view this loss as the inevitable collateral damage of immigration. Be that as it may, my writing is informed by my awareness of the hollowed roots in my family, and by memories of my grandfather, who stopped writing on the day he came to Israel.

*The Diamond Setter* is not a historical novel, nor does it purport to be one, although it is based on extensive research. The plot is an amalgamation of historical facts, family stories, and the fruits of my imagination. I learned a lot about Syrian Jewry from issues of the journal *Peamim* and from the book *Syria*, edited by Yaron Harel. *Jaffa: A Historical-Literary Reader*, edited by Yosef Aricha, and *Around the Clock Square* by Yaakov Yinon taught me a lot about life in Jaffa from the Jewish perspective. I made extensive use of descriptions of the market that was destroyed in the First World War, as documented by Haim Hissin and Benjamin Brenner, from the latter book, which allowed me to see the period in living color.

I wove together some of the details of Fareed's arrival in Jaffa and his residency in the "People's House"—though perhaps in a reversal of sorts—inspired by the protagonist's stay in Jaffa in S. Y. Agnon's *Only Yesterday*, and certain lines in the book allude to that novel. I also made use of *City of Oranges* by Adam LeBor, *Jaffa* by Yadin Roman, *Jaffa, Bride of the Sea* by Dan Yahav, and essays by Tzur Shezaf on his blog. All these tell a story that interweaves the histories of various residents of this complicated, fascinating city. I was further enlightened by *Dionysus at the Center* by Tamar Berger; *The Birth of the Palestinian Refugee Problem* by Benny Morris; *Returning to Haifa* by Ghassan Khanfani; *The Pessoptimist* by Emile Habibi, in Anton Shammas's Hebrew translation; and issues of *Sedek*, a journal published by the NGO Zochrot (Remembering). I learned about the life of the Turkish sultan Abdul Hamid II and his palace from his daughter's memoirs, in a French book kindly given to me by Benny Ziffer. I learned the stories of Palestine during the British Mandate, interwoven with the history of mysterious diamonds, from *The Adventures of a Blue Donkey* by Nachum Gutman, and also made use of *Intrigue and Revolution: Chief Rabbis in Aleppo, Baghdad, and Damascus, 1774– 1914* by Yaron Harel.

A grant from the Fulbright Foundation (America-Israel Education Fund) enabled my participation in the International Writing Program at the University of Iowa, and allowed me to conduct research on Palestinian refugees throughout the Arab world, from 1948 to the present. I was greatly assisted in this research by Dr. Edward Miner at the University of Iowa. During my time at the IWP, alongside writers from thirty different countries, I had long talks with the poet and filmmaker Hind Shoufani, daughter of the historian and former PLO member Professor Elias Shoufani, who later died in Damascus.

The excerpts quoted from *The Book of the Thousand Nights and a Night* are from Richard Burton's translation. The quotes about housing in Tel Aviv from *Haaretz* are taken from the book *Tel Aviv—Half Jubilee*, edited by Maoz Azaryahu, Arnon Golan, and Aminadav Dykman (published by Carmel). The Baudelaire excerpt is from *Intimate Journals*, translated by Christopher Isherwood. The quote from the newspaper *Falastin* appears in "Jaffa and Tel Aviv Through the Double Prism of the Arab Press" by Rachel Hart in the magazine *Kesher* (Bronfman Institute for the Study of Jewish Press and

Communications, Tel Aviv University, vol. 39, 2009). The poem by Israel Najara was quoted in an article by Professor Haviva Pedaya on the website Piyut. The story about the slave suspected of grave robbery is based on a text in the book *Not a Thousand and Not a Night* by Joseph Sadan. Furthermore, in one of the conversations between Ramadan and Fareed, I rely on answers Emile Habibi gave in an interview with Yaakov Agmon on the radio program *Personal Questions*, on Galei Zahal.

I am grateful to the many people who contributed their experience, advice, and knowledge: David Grossman, who read the book and urged me to have faith that it should be published in other languages and reach readers around the world; Jessica Cohen, who accompanied the book with dedication and professionalism, and whose translation is wonderfully in sync with the characters' heartbeats; my agent, Ellen Geiger of Frances Goldin Literary Agency, who believed in the power of these words to touch people far away from where the story occurs, and Matt McGowan, also of Frances Goldin; Judith Gurewich, who brainstormed with me over countless transatlantic phone calls, and Alexandra Poreda, who gave excellent comments, and everyone else at Other Press.

I would also like to thank my friend Sharon Bar-Kochva, for many years of a close and eye-opening friendship along the Paris–Tel Aviv route; my friend Aviad Eliya, for his good advice and illuminating comments; Sivan Beskin, Eran Shuali, Azi and Nitza Manor, Ali al-Azhari, Matan Hermoni, Lilach Netanel, Nitza Ben-Ari, Fadi Daeem, Iris Mor, Tzvika Bavnik, Alma Igra, Nadav Linial, Omer Waldman, and Ruti Grossman.

Thanks to the staff of the IWP at the University of Iowa, and to the staff of the writers' house in Manosque, France. Thank you to my editor, Dror Mishani, to Einat Niv, and everyone at Keter.

Thanks to my beloved family: my father and mother, Meir and Nitza Sakal, my sister and brothers and their families, and all my friends.

Thank you to Dory Manor, with whom I share my life wherever I may be, who read the book in all its drafts and infused it with his wisdom, and to Yair Dovrat. Over the years of working on this book, they both taught me a great deal about literature and about life.

It took six long years to write *The Diamond Setter*, during which time I repeatedly made the short trip from Tel Aviv to Jaffa and back. The distance between the "first Hebrew city" and the "Bride of the Sea" is very short geographically, but extremely long in every other way. I wandered the streets of Jaffa for days on end, always returning to my apartment in a Tel Aviv neighborhood. But two months after *The Diamond Setter* was published in Hebrew, I decided to come full circle: My partner and I moved to Jaffa, right to the heart of the area where the protagonists of this book led their lives. In those days in 2014, the country was once again mired in turmoil and bloodshed. And then came the death of my grandmother, Ora (Sobhiya) Sakal, after a long life that began in Syria and ended in Israel. Her voice was silenced, but her story of life in Damascus, Beirut, and Aley—as I heard it from her, and as I imagined it myself—remains. And for that I am grateful.